CHANTRESS
ALCHEMY

ALSO BY
AMY BUTLER GREENFIELD

Chantress

Chantress Fury

A Perfect Red

Virginia Bound

CHANTRESS ALCHEMY

A **CHANTRESS** NOVEL

AMY BUTLER GREENFIELD

MARGARET K. McELDERRY BOOKS
NEW YORK LONDON
TORONTO SYDNEY NEW DELHI

MARGARET K. McELDERRY BOOKS † An imprint of Simon & Schuster Children's Publishing Division † 1230 Avenue of the Americas, New York, New York 10020 † This book is a work of fiction. Any references to historical events, real people, or real places are used fictitiously. Other names, characters, places, and events are products of the author's imagination, and any resemblance to actual events or places or persons, living or dead, is entirely coincidental. † Text copyright © 2014 by Amy Butler Greenfield † Cover photograph copyright © 2015 by Marie Hochhaus † All rights reserved, including the right of reproduction in whole or in part in any form. † MARGARET K. McELDERRY BOOKS is a trademark of Simon & Schuster, Inc. † For information about special discounts for bulk purchases, please contact Simon & Schuster Special Sales at 1-866-506-1949 or business@simonandschuster.com. † The Simon & Schuster Speakers Bureau can bring authors to your live event. For more information or to book an event, contact the Simon & Schuster Speakers Bureau at 1-866-248-3049 or visit our website at www.simonspeakers.com. † Also available in a Margaret K. McElderry Books hardcover edition † The text for this book is set in Granjon LT. † Manufactured in the United States of America † First Margaret K. McElderry Books paperback edition May 2015 † 10 9 8 7 6 5 4 3 2 1 † The Library of Congress has cataloged the hardcover edition as follows: Greenfield, Amy Butler, 1968– † Chantress alchemy / Amy Butler Greenfield.—First edition. † p. cm † Summary: "Lucy, a chantress who works magic by singing, is called to court to find a lost instrument of Alchemy. But her magic isn't working properly"—Provided by publisher. † ISBN 978-1-4424-5707-2 (hardcover) — ISBN 978-1-4424-5710-2 (ebook) † [1. Supernatural—Fiction. 2. Magic—Fiction. 3. Singing—Fiction. 4. Great Britain—History—Stuarts, 1603–1714—Fiction.] I. Title. † PZ7.G8445Chd 2014 † [Fic]—dc23 † 2013021193 † ISBN 978-1-4424-5708-9 (pbk)

FOR MY PARENTS,
CRISPIN AND BARBARA,
WHO RAISED ME WITH
MUSIC, BOOKS,
AND LOVE

"You are an alchemist; make gold of that."

—William Shakespeare (1564–1616)

✝   ✝   ✝

"Bad men need nothing more to compass their ends, than that good men should look on and do nothing."

—John Stuart Mill (1806–1873)

CHANTRESS
ALCHEMY

CHAPTER ONE
A SONG FROM THE SEA

One more spell, that's all I meant to sing. One more song-spell, and then I'd go home.

I blew on my icy fingers and faced the wintery sea. I'd been out for hours, honing my magic, and the sun had long since vanished behind sullen clouds. My boots were damp from the froth of the ocean, my cheeks wet with its salty spray. The wind sawed along my very bones. I thought with longing of the snug cottage I shared with Norrie and the soup that would no doubt be simmering on the fire.

Something easy to finish on, I promised myself. *Something that won't go wrong.*

Clutching my woolen cape, I tilted my ear toward the ocean and its tangle of watery music. A simple song-spell, that's all I needed. . . .

But what was that sound? That distant humming?

Forgetting my frozen hands and feet, I listened, perplexed.

1

No one knew better than I that the ocean could sing a thousand songs: music to cradle me, music to drown me, music to call up waves and tides and storms. I was a Chantress, after all. Yet this wasn't a tune I had heard before. Indeed, its faint thrum was quite unlike any melody I knew. That alone was disturbing.

"Lucy!"

A woolen bundle clumped toward me: Norrie in her winter wraps. The wind snatched at her hood and cap, and her silver hair stood out like dandelion fluff around her wrinkled face.

"You've been out here too long," she called. "You'll catch your death of cold."

I was about to reply when I heard it again: a disquieting drone in the midst of the sea's other songs.

Norrie marched up to my side, her gait uneven. "Lucy, are you listening to me?"

"Yes," I said quickly. "Of course I am." But I was listening to the humming, too. If I concentrated hard enough, I usually could make out at least the gist of the sea's songs. Of all elements, water was the easiest for me to understand. Yet these notes held fast to their secrets.

"There's no *of course* about it." Norrie scrutinized my face. "Is something wrong?"

"No." Norrie might be my guardian, but I hated to worry her, especially when I had no clear idea what the trouble was. She wouldn't be able to hear the song anyway; only a Chantress could do that. "You shouldn't be out here, Norrie. Not on such a bitter day."

"Maybe not, but what else can I do when you won't come home?" Norrie said.

The elusive drone was fading now. I swung back toward the sea, trying to catch its last echoes.

Norrie kept after me. "You've been out here since dawn, Lucy. You need to come home now."

The drone was gone. What did it mean? "Just one more song, Norrie—"

"That's what you always say. And then you stay out, working till all hours, in all weathers—"

"But that's why we're here," I reminded her. "So I can work."

Nine months ago, I had freed England from a terrible enchantment, and as a reward King Henry the Ninth had offered me any gift in his possession. To my alarm, he'd talked of building me a palace. What I'd asked for instead was a secret refuge by the sea.

The King, bless him, had abandoned his palace scheme. Norrie and I now lived on a remote part of his estates in Norfolk, in a cottage just big enough for two. Almost no one in the kingdom knew where we were, and the King made sure we were left alone. Although his gamekeepers patrolled the outer limits of the estate, we never saw them. Every month we had supplies of food and fuel delivered to us, and occasionally the King's messenger came by. But that was all.

"Working's one thing. Toiling till you're skin and bone is another." The wind chafed Norrie's cheeks, turning them red. "You're seventeen and nearly grown, so I've tried to bite my tongue. But you're getting worse and worse, Lucy. We came here so you could rest, too. You've forgotten that part."

"I can't rest yet. Not until I've learned more magic."

"But you already know so much," Norrie protested.

"I know hardly anything."

"You knew enough to put an end to Scargrave and those horrible Shadowgrims," Norrie countered.

"At a cost. Don't you remember how bad it was when we came here? I had nothing. Not one single song." My hand went to my heart, where a bloodred stone nestled underneath my woolen scarves. The stone had once allowed me to work the safe song-spells of Proven Magic, but in battling against Scargrave and the Shadowgrims I had shattered its powers. Now the only enchantments open to me were the dangerous ones of Wild Magic.

A fraught path—and I had no one to teach me the way. Among Chantresses, Wild Magic was almost a lost art. Even before Scargrave had worked to destroy my kind, very few could have instructed me in it. Now there was no one. I was the only Chantress still living.

To guide me, I had only a letter my mother had written before her death years ago. Although it was replete with wise advice, it was not nearly as long or as detailed as I needed. Most of the time, I had to rely on my own instincts.

"Yes, that was a bad time," Norrie agreed. "But look at all you've learned since then. You can make the waves come when you call. You can sing water up from the ground. Heavens, child, you can even make it rain when you want to."

"Only for a minute or two, and only—"

Norrie rolled on, ignoring me. "That's more magic than most of us can dream of."

"It's not enough."

Norrie looked unconvinced.

How could I explain matters more clearly? My magic made Norrie nervous, so we rarely talked about it, but I could see I'd have to spell things out now.

"I'm good with water, yes—but not with anything else. I can kindle a flame, but I can't keep it burning. I almost never hear music from stones or earth or wind. I'm no good at making plants grow. Even the sea's songs don't always make sense to me. And when they don't make sense, they're dangerous. If I sing them, I could do harm to others. I could harm myself."

My cape snapped in the wind, and I stopped.

Norrie laid a mittened hand on mine. "Child, I know there are dangers, and of course I'm concerned about you. But I'm not sure you make yourself any safer by practicing till you're worn to a thread." She gripped my fingers through the wool. "Scargrave's gone now, Lucy. You've won the war. Yet you're still driving yourself as hard as you did when he was alive. Why not take things a bit easier?"

"And what if I have to defend myself? What do I do then?"

"Why should you need to defend yourself?" Norrie said. "The King would have the head of anyone who hurt you."

It was true: King Henry had sworn that the old days of Chantress-hunting were over. Nevertheless, I lived in terror that those days would begin again—and that I would not be ready. Night after night I dreamed hunters were coming after me, only to wake up alone in the dark loft, heart shuddering.

I was pushing myself too hard, that's what Norrie would say. But she was wrong. My nightmares didn't come from working too hard, but from the terrible truth of my situation. *The Chantress line is almost dead. We are hunted; we are prey.* So my godmother Lady Helaine had warned me before her own untimely end. To be a Chantress was to face enemies, for the world feared women with power.

"I'm glad the King wants to protect me," I told Norrie, "but I need to know I can protect myself. And my magic is too weak for that. It has too many holes. So I need to keep working. I need to make myself strong."

Norrie looked at me with a compassion that tightened my throat. "Oh, Lucy. You're strong already. Much stronger than you think. Can't you see?"

"But—"

She waved me away. "Let's not argue about it now. You're turning blue, and I'm not much better. Come home, and we'll talk about it in front of the fire."

I'm not cold, I wanted to say. But it wasn't true. And Norrie's lips were pinched as if she were in pain. *She's been out here too long*, I thought with concern. Her back and hips had been bothering her lately, especially on cold, damp days like this one.

"All right." I pulled up my hood. "We'll go home."

We had only just started trudging up the shore when a sharp

gust of wind swirled around us. It blew my hood back, and I heard the ocean humming again in its troubling new way. Had it been quiet all this time? Or had I just been too wrapped up in my wrangle with Norrie to hear it?

Hoping she wouldn't notice, I trained my attention on the drone, trying to understand it. With patience, I could usually unravel the basic meaning of a song, even if I couldn't fathom all its subtleties.

This time, though, the tune wouldn't yield. *More*, I pleaded.

As if to deny me, the strange song twisted in on itself and coiled into nothingness. But just before it vanished, I heard the meaning at the heart of it:

Danger.

The word slipped into my head as if the song itself had placed it there. I felt my unease grow.

"Wait here," I said to Norrie. "I'm just going up to the bluff to have a look about."

Before she could object, I ran up the steep bank that rose directly behind us. Reaching the crest, I looked up and down the coast, then out to the watery horizon. I saw no warships, no fishing boats, no vessels of any kind. Nothing met my eye but the endless wind-churned waves of the sea.

I turned my head in the other direction, to the rolling hills that sheltered our cottage, and the stretch of the King's wood beyond them. All was well.

And then, out by the wood, something moved.

A deer? No. A rider. And more behind him.

I sank behind the bluff's waving grasses and watched them emerge from the wood, one after the other. Half a regiment of mounted men, clad in armor and bearing spears.

Armed men, coming here in such great company?

Holding my breath, I shielded my eyes with a rigid hand as I looked out. They were riding straight for our cottage, the tips of their spears sharp against the gray sky.

Danger, the sea had said. Was this what it meant?

I skidded back down the bluff. "Norrie, quick! We need to run."

CHAPTER TWO
HUNTED

"Run?" Hunched against the wind, Norrie turned startled eyes on me. "Why?"

"Armed men," I gasped. "Coming after us."

Her hand flew to her heart. "Are you sure?"

"Yes. And I've had another warning, too . . . a song from the sea. . . ." There was no quick way to explain. Instead, I grabbed her hand. "Come. We'd better run."

"Where?"

"To the high cliffs." They were only a little way down the shore, and their tumbled rocks and shallow clefts would shield us from view. "I may need to work some magic, too. But I want us hidden before I start."

Accepting this, Norrie followed my lead, but her run soon slowed to a hobble. We were nowhere near the cliffs when the sea shrieked at my back. Turning, I saw two riders and their mounts picking their way down the track that led to the shore—and to us.

We needed to take cover. I pulled Norrie with me behind the only shelter available: a mass of spars and driftwood, not yet swept out by the tides.

Too late. They had seen us. One soldier sounded his horn, another raised his spear.

My mouth went dry. *Chantress-hunters*.

"Lucy," Norrie quavered, "should we try to get to the caves?"

"No." Even the closest caves were too far away. "We'll make our stand here."

Only my magic could save us now. But to work it, I knew I must quiet my terror. Magic might be in my Chantress blood, but casting a song-spell required all my attention. It couldn't be accomplished through rote recitation, for Wild Magic, like nature itself, was never quite the same twice. The time of day, the weather, the direction of the wind, even the emotions inside me: all of these subtly affected the song I needed to sing. And if I missed those subtleties—whether through carelessness or panic—the magic could go terribly wrong.

I bent my ears to the sea's songs. Yet the more I told myself to keep calm, the more fear barraged me. I had schooled myself for a moment such as this, but practice was one thing, a real battle another. And even in practice, it was easy to make mistakes.

The horn blasted again, distracting me. More and more riders were gathering on the shore. Were they about to charge?

Listen, I told myself. *Forget everything else and listen.*

Despite the blood pounding in my ears, I could hear songs shimmering in the sea. The most insistent one promised a great wave to knock them down. Tempting music indeed. But could

I control such a potent song? Did I have enough experience?

Doubting my strength, I fell back on a tune I'd sung before, one that often lingered along these coasts, a blurred melody of mist and fog. It was a weaker magic than the song for calling up waves, but I was sure—almost sure—it was in my grasp.

As the men galloped toward us, hooves thudding on sand, I started to sing. The salty air thickened between us.

A shout went up from the riders, and they checked their horses.

Pressing my advantage, I let the song swell in my throat and grow stronger. What Norrie made of this as she shivered beside me, I don't know. *Eerie* was a word she'd once used about my singing. *Unearthly. Fair gives me the chills.*

Yet if my singing was unearthly, the sea mist I conjured up was real. Wet and gray as sodden wool, it was impossible to see through. By the time the last phrases poured out of me, it covered the riders completely.

Inside the clammy cloud, armor clanged and horses whinnied. Men shouted in blind panic.

"Help!"

"Halt!"

"Chantress magic! God save us!"

It was a strong spell; I could tell that much. With luck, we could get well away before it faded.

But in my triumph, I hung on too long to the final note of the song. The fog kept billowing out, and though I stopped the moment I realized what was happening, an instant later it swamped Norrie and me. I almost choked in dismay. We were as blinded as the soldiers were now—which was no rescue at all.

"Lucy?" Norrie's voice was soft and afraid.

"Here." I groped for her hand.

Before I could find it, however, a voice shouted out from the fog. "Chantress, put an end to this magic! We come in peace, in the King's name."

I was not at all reassured. Who knew if the man was speaking the truth?

"My lady Chantress, I beg of you: listen." Another man spoke this time, and his voice sounded familiar. Was it Rowan Knollys, head of the King's guard?

I bit my lip. If it really was Knollys, then perhaps we were safe after all.

"King Henry sent us here." Yes, it was unmistakably Knollys who spoke. "I promise on my sacred honor: no harm will come to you. We carry his ring as a sign."

I let out my breath. The ring was a token the King and I had devised beforehand, so that I would know whom to trust. Perhaps it was time to sing the mist down.

Remembering those spears, however, I decided to take precautions.

"Put down your weapons," I called out.

A slight pause.

"Must we, sir?" a shaky voice asked.

"Yes," Knollys ordered. "Drop them to the ground, men. Spears and swords both."

Through the fog, I heard swords sliding from scabbards and armaments thudding on the sand.

12

"There, Chantress," said Knollys. "We've done as you asked. Now sing us out of this blasted fog of yours, before every last bit of our armor rusts."

I stifled a laugh. That was Knollys, all right.

"Give me a moment," I called back. I breathed in the mist, letting its music circle around me until I was certain I had the song I needed. Closing my eyes, I sang it out loud.

It was a complex song, one that drew on the water's own longing to return to the sea, but I could tell I had chosen the right strain. The foggy air thinned and streamed into the ocean. I saw Norrie first, and moved to her side so that I could protect her if need be. Then, in the swirling gloom, more faces: Knollys foremost among them, his battle-scarred cheeks rough and red under his helmet, his chestnut mustache bristling. Behind him, his men sat in disarray on their horses, regarding me with a mix of wonder and terror.

One look at their awed faces told me I had the upper hand here. I could afford to let the mist go completely. I sang one last phrase to finish my work, careful this time not to linger at the end. The air cleared.

"Thank you, my lady." Knollys dismounted his bay charger and came toward me, bearing the ring. "I must say, we hoped for a better reception."

"You would have done better to come without so many men and arms, then." I nodded at the spears and swords scattered on the sand. "All that, for me?"

He shook his head. "Say, rather, for your safety and ours. It is a dangerous time."

"You were aiming those spears at *me*."

"I am sorry, my lady. The King is anxious for your welfare, and we had orders not only to find you, but to capture anyone we found here who was behaving in a suspicious manner." The red of his cheeks deepened. "I'm afraid we did not recognize you until you started singing."

Knollys's embarrassed gaze made me flush too. The last time he and his men had seen me, I'd been at court, attired in silken robes fit for a queen, with my hair elegantly coiffed. Now I was wearing my oldest clothes, water-stained at the hem and darned where they'd snagged on driftwood—and my hair had sprung free from its coil, its black tangles whipping on the wind.

No wonder they'd failed to recognize me.

But really, what did it matter? I was here to work, not to be a figure of fashion. Given the choice between a new song-spell and new skirts, I'd pick the song-spell any day.

"The ring, my lady." Knollys offered the gold circle to me.

Forgetting about my appearance, I held the ring up to the light, the better to see the rose etched in its amethyst stone. No doubt about it: this was the King's ring. I showed it to Norrie, who was still looking askance at the scattered horses and the men dismounting to collect their swords and spears.

"I still don't understand why you're here," I said to Knollys.

"I am here because the King wishes to see you," Knollys said. "Pack your belongings as quickly as you can. We must leave within the hour."

CHAPTER THREE
THE KING'S COMMAND

I felt the blood drain from my face. "You intend to take us to London?"

"To Greenwich Palace, rather," Knollys said. "The King has held court there since Christmas."

I knew nothing about Greenwich Palace except that it was a few miles outside London, but if the Court was gathered there, then it was the last place I wanted to be. After Scargrave's downfall last year, I had spent a few weeks at the King's side, and I had been shocked by the naked ambition of his courtiers. Half of them seemed to hate me—and most of the others had been desperate for me to do magic for them. To make matters worse, my magic had been at its lowest ebb then. To be so powerless, and to have to hide it, had been the stuff of nightmares.

Since then, I'd heard that there had been changes at Court, that some of the King's old advisers had been cast off, and that new men had risen in their place. But still . . .

I can't face them. Not yet. Not now. Not until I'm certain I have the power to deal with them.

"I regret that I must refuse," I said to Knollys. "Please tell the King I appreciate his invitation, but I shall remain here."

Knollys's stance changed, and I saw why he was regarded as a fearsome leader of men. "My lady Chantress, you misunderstand. This is not a request. It is a direct command from your King." His flinty voice brooked no dissent. "I am to bring you back with me, and you will attend His Majesty at Greenwich."

So much for thinking I was safe with Knollys! I would have summoned up another mist then, if only I could have been sure of it. I was tired, though, and cold to my marrow, and I was not certain I could pull off such a song twice. And if I lost myself in the fog again, what then?

Perhaps the wish showed in my face, however, for Knollys's next words were more conciliatory. "My lady, the King does not act for idle reasons. He wishes you to come in part so that he may safeguard you. As I have said, these are dangerous times. Enemies are working against King Henry, and they may target you as well."

Norrie and I exchanged glances of surprise and alarm. I remembered the sea's song of danger. Was this what it meant? Not Knollys and his men . . . but something even more daunting?

"Who are these enemies?" I asked.

When Knollys didn't immediately answer, Norrie said, "Have there been more riots?"

Riots? This was news to me. "Who's rioting?"

"Didn't you hear what the King's men said when they last delivered our supplies?" Norrie asked me. "Bread's more than twice the price it was last year, and wheat's in short supply everywhere. There've been riots in some places."

I vaguely remembered the delivery, but not the conversation. My mind had been on my magic the whole time they'd been talking. "Is that why you're here?" I asked Knollys.

"I'm not at liberty to say," Knollys said. "The King himself will explain when he sees you."

Behind him the men were regrouping.

"We must leave right away," Knollys urged. "If we hurry, we can reach the King's hunting lodge at Letheringham by nightfall. After that, I judge it will take us four days to reach Greenwich."

I glanced over my shoulder at the gray curve of the sea beyond the bluff. Whatever Knollys said, this place felt safe to me. It was the world beyond—including the Court at Greenwich—that felt dangerous.

But perhaps that was just an illusion.

Certainly Norrie seemed to think it was. Close at my side, she murmured, "Lucy, I know you don't want to go. But I really think we must. We'll be safer with the King."

I bit my lip. How could I stay if it meant exposing Norrie to attack?

And there was the King to consider too. It was through his grace and favor that I had been granted this refuge. When it came down to it, I could ill afford to displease him. And I genuinely wanted to help him if I could. Henry was only a couple of years older than I was, and in the brief time I'd known him, he'd struck me as determined and brave, with a keen sense of honor. Saddled with the task of setting the kingdom to rights, he was intent on doing his duty. If he was in danger, I ought to help him, both for his sake and the country's.

Next to that, how much did it matter that the very notion of Greenwich Palace filled me with dread?

I turned to Knollys, the frozen wind thrashing at my cape. "Will I be able to return here?"

"As soon as the danger is over," Knollys assured me. "The King gives you his word."

That was something. And I supposed it was something, too, that I'd managed to sing up the sea mist under pressure and disarm the King's men.

You're stronger than you think, Norrie had said. Perhaps I was more prepared to face the world of court intrigue than I'd feared.

"My lady," Knollys said. "We await your answer."

"Very well," I said. "We will go with you to the King."

† † †

Three-quarters of an hour to pack, that was all Knollys allowed us. "And less would be better."

"We'll have to move fast," Norrie huffed as we heaved ourselves up to the loft. "You'll need your court clothes, of course—the ones you wore last year. I'm not sure they'll fit any better than what you've got on now, but at least they're not patched and stained like your work clothes are." She opened the trunk at the foot of my bed. "Put on the blue wool, and I'll pack the mulberry silk. Quickly now!"

Shivering, I changed out of my water-stained skirts and dived into the sea-blue wool. The soft fabric warmed my skin, but even when I tightened my stays, the bodice strained to hold me. The skirts, too, were slightly too short, and the fabric pulled across my hips. It was only with difficulty that I managed to slide the precious letter from my mother into the secret pocket. I couldn't leave that behind.

Norrie paced a circle around me. "I suppose it will do for the trip," she said doubtfully. "But thank goodness there will be seamstresses aplenty in Greenwich Palace. You can have a whole new wardrobe made." The thought seemed to cheer her. "No cloud without a silver lining, is there? I've been wanting to do something about your clothes for a while. Maybe it's just as well we've been called to Court. Nothing like a change to do a body good."

Surprised, I stopped twisting back my tangled hair. "But you were glad to leave Court behind. You said so last summer, when we came here."

"I did say that, yes," Norrie admitted. "I think we both wanted a life more like the one we'd been used to, back on the island."

I nodded. We would never see the island again—it was an enchanted place, lost to us now—but we'd lived there in peace and safety for seven years. At the time, I'd longed for a way to leave it, but now I often dreamed about its grassy bluffs and golden shores.

"Trouble is, I forgot what a lonely life we had there," Norrie said. "And this place is almost as bad."

I looked at her, dismayed. "You don't like it here?"

"I like having a house of my own, and a garden. But a garden's not much use in winter, is it? And the cottage—well, it's darker than I expected, and quieter, especially with you always out practicing your magic." She gave me a crooked smile. "I suppose I got used to seeing people last year. It was nice having someone to talk to of an afternoon."

My heart smote me. "I'm sorry, Norrie. I didn't know. I thought you were happy here."

"I was at first, child. It's the winter that's been hard. But never mind. Everything's about to change now."

Norrie turned back to the packing. "Now, let me see . . . what else do we need to bring?" She dived into the trunk and came up with two stacks of linen shifts. A bundle of papers fell out of them. Face flaming, I snatched it from the floor.

Norrie smiled. "Nat's letters?"

I couldn't lie, though part of me wanted to. "Yes."

I should have burned them.

Burning, however, had been more than I'd been ready for. That's why I'd buried Nat's letters in the trunk instead. Putting them out of sight had helped, but now that I held them in my hands again, the wrenching pain came roaring back.

Nat and I had never had an easy relationship, but there was a spark between us that I'd never felt with anyone else. And last summer, once we'd won the battle against Scargrave, we'd become closer than ever. We'd laughed together, and spent lazy days in the sun together, and shared kisses that made my heart sing. But now . . .

"Such a shame he couldn't come to us for Christmas," Norrie said, refolding the shirts. Nat was a favorite with her. "Still, I can't blame him. It's like that boy to put his country before himself. 'The kingdom has to come first.' Wasn't that what he said in his letter?" Her lips quirked. "Well, the bit you read out to me, anyway."

I winced. I hadn't had the heart to show the full letter to Norrie. It had been disappointment enough to her that he wasn't coming, and I . . . well, I'd been too humiliated to tell her the truth.

Even now, I could remember all too clearly the rainy November afternoon when I'd returned to the cottage, wet and weary, to find the letter waiting. Merely seeing Nat's strong handwriting had filled me with joy—until I'd read what he'd had to say.

Such a thin excuse for a letter, it had been. Stilted and half-hearted, with none of his usual affection. It had taken me only a minute to read the brief lines saying that he couldn't come as expected, that the King needed him at Court. He'd finished with a formal phrase or two. And he'd signed the letter with his full name.

Since then I'd not heard one word from him.

I thrust the letters back into the trunk.

"You don't want to take them?" Norrie said.

I stuffed my shifts into a bag. "There's no need."

"I suppose not," Norrie agreed. "Letters can't hold a candle to seeing somebody in the flesh. And once we're at Court, you'll be seeing Nat all the time."

I kept quiet, but Norrie wouldn't let the subject drop.

"Like as not, he'll be there to greet us. And I must admit it will be a comfort to have him at our side." Her eyes crinkled with sudden merriment. "Indeed, if it's anything like last summer, we'll have a job prying him away from you."

My cheeks burned. "It won't be like that."

The words shot out of me. I couldn't call them back.

Scenting trouble, Norrie stopped packing. "Won't be like what?"

Maybe it was time to tell her. After all, there would be no hiding the truth once we reached Court.

"He hasn't visited, Norrie. And he's stopped writing. You must have noticed: I haven't had a letter in three months." It was an effort to keep my voice even. "I don't think he wants to see me."

Norrie blinked. "Why, of course he does, child. He's been busy, that's all."

"Too busy to write?" I said.

"It happens."

"Maybe. Or maybe he's met someone else." I tried to hide how the idea ate away at me. "That happens too."

"Someone else? Oh, child." Norrie set down the slippers she was trying to cram into the bag. "Letters or no letters, Nat's a young man who knows his own mind. He won't have changed toward you, you mark my words."

She sounded so sure that she half convinced me—and goodness knows, I wanted to believe her. Yet how could I, after that awful letter in November, and the silence ever since?

Boots thumped below.

"What do you want done with your chickens?" a deep voice called out.

"Oh, goodness." Norrie hastened for the stairs. "I completely forgot. Maybe we can put them in baskets and bring them to Letheringham? I expect the cook there will be glad of the extra eggs. You finish up with the packing, Lucy, and I'll go down and see to it."

Left to myself, I filled the bags and tied them shut. More boots tramped downstairs. *Be quick*, I told myself.

When I went to close the trunk, however, I glimpsed Nat's letters again and paused. For a moment, I was tempted to bring them after all.

But no. Whatever Norrie might say, I wasn't going to do that to myself. I flipped the lid down.

A quarter hour later, we set off for Greenwich.

CHAPTER FOUR
THE RABBLE

By the time we reached the hunting lodge, it was twilight, and I was hungry. But food had to wait. After hours of riding pillion behind one of the King's men, Norrie's back pained her so much that she could neither sit nor stand. Waving away her supper, she collapsed onto the pallets that had been laid out for us.

I wished that I knew a song-spell for soothing pain, but that was not where my gifts lay; my magic was more elemental. Instead, I prevailed upon the lodge cooks to brew some willow bark tea, and I made Norrie drink it all.

"And you ought to eat something too," I said.

"I've no appetite, child." Her face contorted as she shifted on the bed.

"Oh, Norrie." I knelt by her side in distress. "What can I do?"

"Nothing, child. It's just that dratted pillion. Thanks be I shan't have to ride it again on this trip."

I nodded. Knollys had already told us that from this point

onward, Norrie and I would travel by carriage. I hadn't been best pleased by the choice—carriages, in my experience, were a stuffy and bone-rattling way to travel—but Knollys had said that we would need to travel all day and most of the night, and that we would find it impossible to keep up with his hand-picked riders on horseback. Despite my protests, he'd insisted on the point, and now I was glad. Norrie could never have ridden all the way to Greenwich.

"A sound night's sleep, that's what I need," Norrie said, grimacing as I tucked the blankets around her. "I'll be right as rain tomorrow."

"Let's hope so." I hated having to go to Greenwich at all, but seeing Norrie in such terrible pain made it harder.

† † †

That night, just as I was about to slip into bed, I heard the strange droning again. This time it was difficult to locate the source: perhaps the river nearby? It was so faint that I could make no sense of it at all, but I feared it still meant danger. I checked on Norrie, but she was sleeping peacefully. When I crept out to the hall, I saw only Rowan Knollys and his men standing guard.

There was nothing more I could do.

When I finally did fall asleep, however, I was restless. Toward morning I dreamed I was in the Tower of London, running through its maze of rooms in panic. I heard a scream behind me. *Lady Helaine . . .*

I woke, my heart hammering at my ribs. Above me was the low-beamed ceiling of the hunting lodge.

It was just a dream, I told myself. But then I heard the yelp again.

It was Norrie.

"I can't move," she groaned, still flat in bed. "I'm so sorry, child, but I can't get up."

An hour later, after the application of salves and plasters and heat, she still had not managed to stand. The only medicine that helped was poppy syrup, and it merely took the edge off the pain while making her very sleepy. Any attempt to lift her made the pain come roaring back.

"She's in no condition to travel," I told Knollys, who was watching from the door. "We'll have to wait."

"We can't wait," Knollys said. "My orders are to bring you to Greenwich without delay. The King requires your presence immediately."

"But a carriage ride would be torture to her right now," I said.

"To her, perhaps, but not to you. And you're the one the King needs to see." He went over to Norrie and leaned down to her, speaking loudly and clearly. "Miss Northam, I need to take the Lady Chantress to Greenwich. When you're better, there will be another carriage at your disposal, and you can follow her in easy stages, if you like. Unless, that is, she has already returned to you, which is what we all hope for."

I resented the way he was making all the decisions. But the suggestion that I might be back so soon was a welcome one. If that were the case, better I should go right away, and spare Norrie the rigors of the trip entirely.

"Lucy?" Norrie searched me out with sleep-fogged eyes. "You can't . . . go alone. I will . . ."

I took her hand. "I'll be fine, Norrie. It's you I'm worried about. You must stay here and get well. I wish I could stay—"

"No, no. Must go. King needs . . ." Her eyes were closing. Succumbing to the poppy syrup, she fell fast asleep.

"Come," Knollys said. "We can't delay any longer."

I bent and kissed Norrie's cheek, soft as worn chamois. "Will she be safe here?" I asked Knollys.

"With the King's household to look after her and the King's gamekeepers to guard her? Absolutely." As he guided me out of the room, he added, "There will be more peril on the road, truth be told."

I stopped in the doorway. "What kind of peril are you expecting?"

"Nothing you need worry about, my lady." Knollys looked uncomfortable. "It's time we were off."

And although I pressed him again, that was all he would say.

† † †

Two weary days later, I was still in the dark about the perils Knollys had hinted at. But I had ceased to care. Instead, I sat hunched in the King's carriage, bracing myself against its interminable bounce and jiggle. My one comfort was that I couldn't hear the strange drone anymore—though that might have been because I was too sick to my stomach to hear anything. Listening for Wild Magic required patience and concentration, and right now I had neither.

We were lucky, Knollys told me, that the weather had remained so cold, and the ground was frozen. Otherwise, we'd have been mired in mud, for the roads from Norfolk to London were a mess of ruts and holes.

As we jounced along, however, I did not feel in the least lucky. Nor could I take any pleasure in the luxurious trappings of velvet and gilt in the carriage itself. Every mile seemed endless. My only comfort was that Norrie was not having to suffer the journey along with me.

This particular stretch of road was one of the worst yet. Trying not to retch, I clenched the padded arm of my seat. My head jerked this way and that. Not for the first time, I wished I knew a song-spell that would allow me to fly.

I'm opening a window, I decided at last. *I don't care what Knollys says. I need some fresh air.*

It was Knollys who had ordered the windows shut and the curtains drawn. When I'd protested that the weather wasn't as bad as all that, he had shaken his head. "It's for your own safety that we do this. No need for all and sundry to know that the Lady Chantress is passing by." Only when we were rumbling through lonely countryside did he allow me to open the windows, and only for the briefest of intervals.

We were not in the countryside now. Above the jostle of the carriage, I could hear the clatter of cobbles, the cries of children, and the barking of dogs. When I pushed back the curtain, my eyes confirmed it: We were in a town. Not a very considerable one, but a town nonetheless, with its own pump and market cross.

"My lady!" The carriage slowed, and Knollys cantered his horse to the window. "You must not be seen."

"I have to have air," I said, "or I'll be sick—" I broke off as I caught sight of the people pressing forward to line our path. "Dear heaven, look at them. So thin you can almost see their bones."

"Never mind, my lady," Knollys said. "It is your safety that concerns me."

The carriage juddered to a halt. I leaned out the window and saw why: a rabble of scrawny children had darted out in front. They ran toward me, hands outstretched. "Please, mistress. Please, my lady."

"Away with you!" Knollys drew his sword.

"No!" I cried out. "Let them come."

Knollys gave me a furious look, but he stayed his sword. "My lady, you must leave this to me."

"What is it they want?"

"Food, of course. Like everyone else."

"Everyone else?"

Knollys's voice hardened. "England's a hungry place these days. But hungry or not, this rabble can't be allowed to block our way, not with so much at stake." He called out to his men. "Prepare to advance."

"No," I said again. "Not yet. Surely we can give them something."

"We have only our own rations. And yours."

The men's rations were not mine to give. But the King's servants at the hunting lodge had laden me down with rich provisions—far more than I could eat by myself, even if my appetite hadn't deserted me.

"Give them my food," I told Knollys.

"You cannot be serious."

"I am."

In the end, he did as I asked—in part, I suspected, because it was the quickest way to get the children out of the way of the carriage. As two of our men hauled the provision baskets over to the market cross, Knollys ordered the company forward.

"Close that window," he commanded, looking at me. This time I reluctantly followed orders.

The last thing I saw before the curtain fell were children leaping into the air for grapes and biscuits.

"Boudicca blesses you, lady!" The cry came as the curtain sealed out the light.

The syllables rang out plainly: *Boo-di-kah*. But all the same, I was sure I'd misheard. The only Boudicca I knew of was the warrior queen who tried to drive the Romans out of Britain. Lady Helaine had told me the story, for female power was something she had prized, and Boudicca, though not a Chantress, had been a woman to be reckoned with.

Why would anyone now be talking of Boudicca, dead these thousand years and more? And talking of her here and now, in this stricken town? Surely there was some mistake. The only concern here was hunger.

Putting the words out of my mind, I sank back against the cushions. The carriage lurched forward, and I was trapped in my velvet prison once more.

Still, there were worse fates. . . .

Bread more than twice the price that it was last year, and wheat in short supply everywhere. That's what the King's men had told Norrie. And I hadn't bothered to listen, let alone think about what it might mean for ordinary people.

Perhaps it was just as well I'd been dragged out of my safe haven.

CHAPTER FIVE
LABYRINTH

The next day the weather warmed up, and the carriage wheels had to plow through mud. Encased in the nauseating confines of the carriage, I was unable to see the outside world. I only guessed we were drawing close to Greenwich Palace when we made several wrenching stops, each accompanied by creaking gates and guards shouting for passwords.

I braced myself as the carriage swerved once again and slowed to a halt. From somewhere outside, Knollys shouted, "We've arrived, my lady!"

Apprehensive, I reached for the curtain. Before I could tug it back, the carriage door swung open, revealing a footman in bright red livery, who offered me his gloved and spotless hand. Behind him a riot of men, horses, and dogs gamboled in a courtyard bounded by high brick walls.

"You're a day late, Knollys," a young man called out. His tawny hair and striking good looks set him apart from the crowd, and he wore his high boots with a swagger.

"We made the best time we could, Lord Gabriel," Knollys said with dignity. "And we had to take great care, given who was with us."

"The Chantress?" Lord Gabriel's dark eyes gleamed. "She's in there?"

My throat tightened. Already it was beginning: the curiosity, the whispers, the calculations. And I had only just arrived.

But there was no going back now. Squaring my shoulders, I took the hand the footman had offered me and stepped out of the carriage.

"My lady Chantress." Lord Gabriel swept a deep bow and approached me with a devastating smile. He was perhaps a year or two older than I was, and even more handsome up close. "May I escort you inside?"

"I will escort her inside myself," Knollys said curtly. "My lady, if you will follow?"

I let him lead the way, but out of the corner of my eye I saw Lord Gabriel sauntering behind.

When we entered the palace, more footmen came rushing up to us. "The King commands that the Lady Chantress be brought to her rooms, where she may rest for a short while before joining him in the Crimson Chamber," one announced to Knollys.

"If that is what the King wishes, then so be it," said Knollys.

After he left me, I followed two of the footmen up a grand staircase. At the top, Lord Gabriel caught up with me.

"You must be tired from your journey." He matched my pace with easy grace.

"Not very." I didn't want to admit to a stranger how exhausted I was, or how the horrible lurching in my stomach still hadn't quite gone away, but my feet betrayed me: I tripped.

He caught my arm. "You are perhaps more tired than you think. But never fear. I'll see you safely to your room."

Righting myself, I pulled back from him. "I thought that's what the footmen were for."

He gave me a lazy grin. "Ah, but will they look after you as I can? I think not."

He spoke in the witty tones that courtiers used when flirting with grand ladies. I felt out of my element, and yet flattered as well. Nat might have no time for me, but it seemed others did.

"Besides, you can never have too many guides in Greenwich Palace," Lord Gabriel continued as we followed the footmen through a room bedecked with portraits and silk-fringed furniture, on a carpet so thick and soft it was like walking on sand. "It's a calendar house, you know."

"A calendar house?"

"Twelve courtyards, fifty-two staircases, three hundred and sixty-five rooms." He waved a careless hand as we passed through another grand salon. "Well, more or less, anyway. The place wasn't so big in Plantagenet times, I'm told, but the Tudors and Stuarts more than doubled it. And now here we are, in a palace like a labyrinth."

"With a monster in the middle?" Wasn't that how the story of the labyrinth went?

His eyes met mine, suddenly watchful. "Indeed." He bowed

once more as we reached the door leading to my rooms. "I will leave you here, my lady. If I can be of any help to you, you have only to call on me: Charles, Lord Gabriel, at your service."

As he walked away, the footmen opened the door. Both this and the inner door had golden lions on them, with glorious manes. After I murmured my thanks, the footmen withdrew.

Alone, I surveyed my new quarters. The room I stood in was as large as the entire cottage I shared with Norrie in Norfolk. Despite its size it was surprisingly warm, owing to a great fire blazing in the marble hearth and tapestries that lined every wall, sealing out the cold. Cozy, however, the room was not. The tapestries, enormous and dramatic, depicted a royal hunt in merciless pursuit of a unicorn. In the corner stood a bed as big as a boat, an extravagant affair of red and gold with hangings that reached nearly to the ceiling. Even the ceiling itself was decorated: an elaborate cloverleaf pattern twined across it, high above my head.

Glancing through an open doorway, I saw another room adjoining mine: smaller and less showy, with a much more modest bed. While it, too, was hung with tapestries, they looked from here to be much plainer, and the room overall was much darker, having merely one tiny window.

Still chilled from the journey, I retreated to the fire. Only after I'd let the heat soak into me did I walk over to the window, large and cantilevered, with a seat carved in the bay beneath it. I'd hoped for a view of the Thames, which Knollys had told me ran right past the palace. Instead, I saw the gardens, the clipped hedges like a stark maze in the low February light.

Behind me, I heard the door open. I turned, and my breath left my body.

Nat was standing in the doorway.

We stared at each other without moving, and for an instant I could have sworn that I saw longing in his eyes. But then he advanced into the room, shoving the door shut behind him, and all I could see was a desperate fury.

"What are you doing here?" His voice was raw. "Why couldn't you stay away?"

I'd thought I was prepared for rejection. In that moment, I discovered I was not.

I tried to contain my shock and hurt. "It's the King who called me here. It's nothing to do with you."

"It's everything to do with me." His eyes were as fierce as I'd ever seen them. "You shouldn't have come."

My hurt turned to anger. "And who are you to speak so? You never came at Christmas. You haven't written since November. If you think I'm going to listen—"

"Lucy."

It was all he said, my name alone. But the pained confusion in his face stopped me cold.

"They wouldn't let me go to you for Christmas," he said. "But they said if I agreed to that, I could still write. I wrote to you all through November and December and January. Did my letters not reach you?"

"No." A sharp joy blossomed inside me: He *had* written. He *had*.

"You didn't get them? Any of them?" He drew closer, and I saw that what anger remained in him was not directed at me. "Lucy, is that why you stopped writing to me?"

"I—I thought you had stopped writing to *me*."

"No. Never." He took my hand.

Such a small thing, holding hands. A very long way from the kisses we had shared last summer. Yet as his fingers gripped mine, my heart beat faster.

"I'm sorry," he said. "I shouldn't have greeted you like that. I should have guessed you didn't know—"

"It doesn't matter," I said, and it was true. It didn't. Not now. "But I don't understand. Who said you couldn't visit me?"

"The King's Council," he said.

"But you're *on* the Council." Nat was only a little older than I was, but he had been a key figure in the Invisible College—an alliance of mathematicians, engineers, and natural philosophers that had led the resistance against Scargrave. He had also helped the King cope with the immediate aftermath of Scargrave's fall. All this had led to his appointment.

"In name only, these days," Nat said. "I've been away most of the autumn and winter, and even when I'm here, I'm hardly ever called to meetings anymore. It's the Inner Council—the men at the top—who are running things now."

I tried to picture Sir Barnaby Gadding, the dapper aristocrat who headed the Council, forbidding Nat to see me. "But why would Sir Barnaby do such a thing?"

"He wouldn't," Nat said bleakly. "But he's not on the Council anymore."

"He isn't?" I was surprised—and worried.

"The last time I saw Sir Barnaby was in early September, when he sent me out to investigate the wheat blight. I didn't get back to Court till late October, and by then he'd already stepped down. He'd started having fits, I was told; it made him too ill to do business. So new men had to take his place."

"But why would they stop you from visiting me?" I persisted.

Nat's hand tensed around mine. "It's complicated. Tell me, what was the last letter you had from me?"

"Your note in early November, saying you couldn't come for Christmas as we'd planned."

"The one they dictated to me?" His voice was bitter.

"Dictated?" I stared at him, hardly able to believe it. "Nat, what's been going on here?"

"I'll tell you—"

The outer door handle rattled. Releasing my hand, Nat sprang back, touching a finger to his lips. "Don't let on that I'm here," he whispered.

I reached the door just as a footman opened it. "The King has called a meeting of the full Council in the Crimson Chamber, my lady, and he wishes you to attend. If you will come with me?"

"Of course I will. But first let me have a moment to collect myself," I replied. While he waited beyond the outer door for me, I went and found Nat in the adjoining room.

"It's a meeting of the full Council," I said, keeping my voice down. "And I'm invited. Believe me, I'll have some fine words to say when I get there."

"No," Nat said, low but firm. "You must not say anything. And you must not let them know that you've seen me. That will only cause more trouble."

"But why—?"

"I'll find you later and explain," he promised, his lips close to my ear. "But in the meantime, don't worry if I'm quiet when in Council. In fact, don't think of me at all. Just guard yourself well. The entire Court has gone mad, and this place grows more dangerous by the day. I wish for your sake that you were anywhere but here."

CHAPTER SIX
FRIENDS AND ENEMIES

My second walk through the palace proved as bewildering as my first. Lord Gabriel was right: the place was a labyrinth. As I followed the footman through a multitude of opulent rooms and halls, I lost any sense of direction. Instead, my mind whirled with what Nat had told me.

"The Crimson Chamber, my lady." The footman pointed to the grandest set of doors yet, spangled with gold stars and crescent moons. Before them, two stone-faced men with sharp halberds stood guard.

The footman backed away, but I did not move forward. How could I meet with the Council and pretend that nothing was wrong? How could I ignore what they had done to Nat—and to me?

"Lucy?"

Dr. Cornelius Penebrygg came toward me, his silver beard streaming over his loose coat, his velvet cap askew. "My dear girl, how wonderful to see you again." His eyes twinkled above his drooping spectacles as he folded my hands in his.

I smiled back at him. As a member of the Invisible College, Penebrygg had been a key ally in the fight against Scargrave. But more than that, he'd been my good friend. "I'm very glad to see you, too. How is your head?" The last time I'd seen him, he'd still been recovering from a blow Scargrave's men had dealt him.

Penebrygg dismissed the injury with a wave of his hand. "Oh, that's been healed for many months now. I'm fit as a fiddle."

"That's what Nat said in his letters." The few letters, that is, that had reached me before they'd been cut off.

Penebrygg took my arm and ushered me toward a quiet corner, well away from the doors and the guards. "My dear, you seem upset. Is something wrong?"

"I—I just saw Nat." I lowered my voice to a whisper. Penebrygg was as close as family to Nat, so surely it was all right to confide in him, but I didn't want anyone else to overhear. "We didn't have long to talk, but he said certain things . . ."

Penebrygg adjusted his velvet cap. "I see."

"He warned me to be on my guard. He said the entire court had gone mad."

"Did he?" Penebrygg shook his head.

"You don't agree?"

"He's a good lad," Penebrygg said. "But no, I don't."

"But they wouldn't let him visit me—"

"Yes, that was a bad business," Penebrygg said. "A very bad business indeed. And you should know that I argued against it, and so did several others on the Council. Do not fret, however: they cannot possibly hold to such a ridiculous policy, not in the long run." He pushed his spectacles into place and regarded me owlishly through them. "But, my dear, that isn't why he considers us mad."

"Us?" I echoed in surprise. "You mean he includes you?"

Penebrygg nodded.

Nat thought *Penebrygg* was mad? The mentor who'd rescued and raised him? I took a sharp breath. Perhaps I'd been too quick to accept Nat's views as the truth. Perhaps there was another side to the story.

Whatever it was, I had no chance to hear it, for a pair of footmen started shepherding us into the Crimson Chamber.

"Come, my dear." Penebrygg offered me his arm. "We must take our seats."

We were not the last to enter. Through another set of doors, more councillors were hurrying into the room, which was as crimson as its name. Against the bloodred walls, gilt frames and sconces gleamed. Scores of candles lighted the room, and a fire burned bright in the onyx fireplace. In the center of the room, on a thick rush mat, stood a heavily carved table that looked as though it had hulked there since Plantagenet times.

Penebrygg walked up to it and pulled out a chair. "Here, my dear."

The seat he offered me was at the right hand of what was obviously—from its size and position—the King's own chair.

"I shouldn't be sitting here," I said.

"I think you will find that the King wishes it. He has been eagerly awaiting your arrival."

After helping me into my chair, Penebrygg rushed away to his own seat farther down the table. Nat entered and sat beside him, his face set and grim. He did not so much as glance in my direction.

In my worry about him, I only half took in what was happening around me, so I was startled when another old friend from the Invisible College, Samuel Deeps, greeted me.

"My lady Chantress, how delightful to meet with you again." A dandy by nature, he fingered the ruff of lace at his throat as he sat down on my right.

"How are you, Mr. Deeps?" I said, my mind still half on Nat.

He beamed. "Actually, it's Sir Samuel now."

That got my full attention.

Still beaming, he explained, "Quite a number of us on the Council were knighted this autumn." He nodded at the long-nosed, long-chinned man sitting across the table from him. "Including Sir Isaac."

Isaac Oldville gravely inclined his head in greeting to me. He looked abstracted, as if he were doing calculations in the back of his mind—a great improvement, I thought, on the irritable expression he'd so often worn when we were fighting Scargrave.

Of madness, I saw not a single sign, either in him or in Sir Samuel. Again my doubts stirred about Nat and his account of the Court.

But I had other questions too.

"Why wasn't Nat knighted?" I asked Sir Samuel. "Or Penebrygg?" They were both on the Council—and no one else in the Invisible College had done more to help me defeat Scargrave.

Sir Samuel's face clouded. "Well, that was rather awkward. They were offered the honor, you know. But they turned it down."

Why? I wanted to ask. But the question caught in my throat as I glimpsed a sandy-haired man coming into the room.

He was an unmistakable figure, built like a Viking warrior, with vast shoulders and eyes the cold, pale blue of a winter sky. I wanted to dive for the floor. It was the Earl of Wrexham: Marcher Lord, guardian of the borderlands—and Scargrave's chief Chantress-hunter.

The King had long since forgiven him. Having been deeply in thrall to Scargrave himself, no one believed more in the possibility of reformation and repentance than the King. Fruitless to point out that when Scargrave had first come to power nine years ago, the King had been a small boy, while Wrexham had been twenty-three years old. In those dark days, people much older and wiser had found themselves powerless to resist Scargrave's fearsome magic—and Scargrave had brought great pressure to bear on Wrexham, holder of one of the oldest titles in the land.

If Wrexham had aided Scargrave more than most, he had also rejoiced when Scargrave was deposed. He was Henry's man now, one of the very first to swear an oath of fealty. The King had told me I had nothing to fear from him.

Nevertheless, there was something about Wrexham that made

my blood run cold. Even the beautiful symmetry of his face—so compelling to others—was unnerving to me, perhaps because I feared what lay behind it. During those brief weeks at Court last year, I'd felt those pale eyes stalking me as they'd once stalked other Chantresses. Even worse, I'd overheard him telling other courtiers that I was poisoning the King's mind, using my magic and my wiles to my own wicked ends. I'd been relieved to leave him far behind when I went to Norfolk.

"What's Wrexham doing here?" I murmured to Sir Samuel.

"Why, he's head of the Council," Sir Samuel said.

My stomach lurched. Head of the Council? No wonder Nat's visits and letters to me had been curtailed. "I—I didn't know."

I watched Wrexham cross the room, speaking first to this man, and then to that one, while others waited their turn. It was as if he were holding his own small court within a court. For sheer presence, no one in the room could match him. Arrayed like royalty in cloth-of-silver and jeweled trimmings, he stood nearly a head taller than the others, and his massive hands were studded with glittering rings.

"He was the obvious choice after Sir Barnaby fell ill." In a very low voice, Sir Samuel added, "Not that some of us didn't suggest other candidates, of course. But Sir Isaac was about to leave for France, and Sir Christopher Linnet had just agreed to serve as ambassador to Spain. So when Wrexham came back to Court, fresh from his victory against the rebellion, it was clear to us all who Sir Barnaby's successor would be."

"The rebellion?" What had I missed?

"You don't know about that, either?" Sir Samuel looked a little surprised. "It happened at the beginning of October. It was that old troublemaker the Earl of Berwick who led it. He was one of the last to swear fealty to the King, you know. I suppose we shouldn't have been so surprised when he tried to break away from England."

"Was it because of the famine?"

"In a way. The blight didn't hit as hard up there, and Berwick thought he'd take advantage of our trouble and make his move while we were weak. He wanted to set up his own kingdom up there in the North, would you believe, and ally himself with the Scots. And he might well have done it too, if Wrexham hadn't raised an army on the spot. Together, Wrexham and the King rode into battle against Berwick and won. So naturally Wrexham's leader of the Council now."

Naturally. My stomach flipped again.

"It doesn't hurt, either, that he's second cousin to the King," Sir Samuel added. "They say he saved the King's life on the battlefield, too—he and his men. " And then he said no more, for Wrexham was striding toward us, his hair as gold as a coronet, his neck as thick as a tree.

He halted before me. Only the table—not nearly wide enough—separated us. I braced myself for insults.

What happened instead was even more shocking: he smiled at me, his teeth gleaming like a wolf's.

"My lady Chantress." His faded blue eyes gazed unblinking into mine. "How good to have you with us."

I couldn't look away, but neither could I smile back. *You have nothing to fear from him*, the King had said. But my heart was pounding.

Wrexham slammed himself down into the chair opposite me.

"The King!" the footmen cried out.

We all rose as King Henry himself strode in, his red-gold hair shining above the somber black of his clothes. He wasn't much older than I was, but he had lost his old diffidence. Although he couldn't match Wrexham for stature, he nevertheless carried himself with the assurance of a true king. He looked like a man who had done battle and won, not only on the field but off it. Yet I saw a glimpse of the old anxiety in his eyes as he sat down.

Was it Wrexham he was worried about? No, that was *my* worry. Doubtless Henry had other matters on his mind—including whatever threat had caused him to summon me here.

Motioning for us all to be seated, he turned to me with grave politeness. "Well met, my lady Chantress. I am sorry I could not welcome you on your arrival, but I trust you were properly received?"

"Yes, Your Majesty." I gave the expected answer. I had no intention of explaining that the most important welcome had come from Nat.

"Very good." As the guards bolted the doors shut, the King raised his voice to address everyone. "Greetings, my lords and gentlemen. I have called you all here because matters are at a critical point. But at least one in our number"—he nodded at me—"knows nothing of what has transpired in this place. My lord Wrexham, perhaps you would summarize for her?"

Summarize Wrexham did, in words as blunt as his broad, bejeweled hands. "It comes down to this, Chantress. Some devil's run off with the Golden Crucible. And you'd better get it back for us, or else."

CHAPTER SEVEN
THE GOLDEN CRUCIBLE

There was a chill in Wrexham's eyes that unnerved me, but mostly I was confused. Had the King called me all the way down to Greenwich to solve a simple robbery?

"I must say, I had thought to break the news a trifle more gently," King Henry said, turning to me. "But the gist of what Wrexham says is true. We have suffered a great loss, and we very much need your help."

"If I can help, I will," I said, trying to avoid Wrexham's gaze. "But I don't understand. If it's a matter of ordinary thievery, why do you need me?"

"Because nothing else has worked," the King said. "And because the entire future of the realm depends on it."

"On a . . . crucible?" I tried to keep the incredulity out of my voice.

"Yes," the King said. "If we're ever to fill the royal coffers, we must have it back."

I still did not understand.

"Perhaps I might explain matters more fully, Your Majesty?" Isaac Oldville—Sir Isaac—no longer looked so abstracted.

"By all means." The King waved his hand. "After all, you know more about the business than anyone else."

What business? I was still in the dark.

Sir Isaac leaned forward to enlighten me. "As you doubtless know, the kingdom has suffered greatly over the past six months. Blighted wheat has led to a ruined harvest, a ruined harvest to hunger, and hunger to great unrest everywhere."

"Unrest?" Wrexham snorted. "Call it what it is, man. Mobs. Riots."

Sir Isaac ignored the interruption. "Some people are questioning the King's rule," he told me. "They say that under Scargrave they never went hungry. Rebels preach sedition, and the poor are listening. Indeed, some parts of the country have become almost lawless. Much of Suffolk, for instance—"

"I wouldn't call Suffolk lawless," Penebrygg interrupted from his place far down the table. "Boudicca is actually keeping the peace quite well."

"Boudicca?" I remembered the benediction from the road: *Boudicca blesses you.* "Who is she?"

"No one's quite certain," Sir Samuel told me. "Which is unsettling in itself. Her real name's Goody Boot, some say, but Boudicca's the name she's adopted. They say she takes from the rich and gives to the poor. And she has a fanatic core of followers."

"Some of the rich have given willingly, I hear," Penebrygg said.

"It's little enough to them. And they say the woman Boudicca puts it all toward feeding the hungry."

"They're a rabble of cursed Levellers." Lips twisting in distaste, Wrexham extended a hand to the King. "There will be no order in the kingdom until we crush them. If you would only see reason, Your Majesty, and let me lead an expedition against them—"

"A valiant offer," the King said, "but first let us see how Boudicca explains herself when she comes before us. She professes loyalty to the Crown, after all, and she made no objection to my summons. Indeed, she is making good speed toward Greenwich, by all accounts."

"With a host of followers," Wrexham pointed out. "Five hundred at last count. What does she need five hundred men for, if not to foment rebellion?"

"They're not just men," the King countered. "The report says there are women and children in that number too. Which suggests it's not exactly an army she's bringing. For all we know, they're following her for reasons of their own. Hunger makes men—and women—do strange things."

"All the more reason to put a stop to the fool woman now," Wrexham said. "Cut her down before she can do any real damage. If we don't make an example of her and her followers, we'll soon see open rebellion again. And after that, who knows? Spain and France might well take advantage of our weakness."

There was a murmur of agreement from many at the table.

"It is true these are dangerous times," the King conceded. "But we've discussed this before, and I stand by my opinion: if we attack Boudicca before we've even attempted to meet with her, we could provoke exactly the kind of rebellion that we dread."

Anger sparked in Wrexham's pale eyes, but the King did not seem to see it. He was speaking to me. "What we need to do instead is find ways of remedying the real problem: the famine. Once we get hold of more food, all these troubles will pass. Fortunately, the Continent wasn't touched by the blight, and they're willing to sell us grain."

"Which would be good news," Sir Isaac said wryly, "if only we had the money to buy it."

Anger still burned in Wrexham's eyes. "The reparations have beggared us, just as I warned they would."

"Yes, but we had to make them." The King was resolute. "So much of what Scargrave took, he took wrongfully. That money shouldn't have been in our coffers to begin with."

"It's a principle we could ill afford," Wrexham said. "Giving back the money has made us weak. We've run the Treasury dry."

"Not quite dry," Penebrygg put in. "But with your program of fortification draining what's left, Lord Wrexham—"

"Defense must come first," Wrexham growled. "That is the first duty of a sovereign lord: to protect his people. Everyone knows that."

"I would put food first myself."

"That's because you've never put down a rebellion." Wrexham gazed at Penebrygg in disdain. "You philosophers know nothing about how to run a country."

"We know something about it," Penebrygg said, adjusting his spectacles. "At any rate, we have seen how one can be mismanaged."

"What are you saying?" Wrexham snarled.

"Enough." The King cut through the exchange. "I have need of both warriors and philosophers at my table. And I would prefer that they not attack each other."

The argument ceased, but the tension at the table did not.

"I don't yet understand where the crucible comes in," I said.

"It's simple," Sir Isaac said. "We need money. That's why we've turned to alchemy."

I sat back in my chair. Alchemy? Could this be the madness that Nat meant?

I stole a quick look at him, but his face seemed calm enough—so calm, in fact, that I wondered if perhaps he was thinking of something else. In any case, it seemed unlikely that alchemy would bother him, now that I thought about it. Last year, he'd mentioned lightheartedly enough that Sir Barnaby had once dabbled in the art.

There was nothing lighthearted, however, about Sir Isaac's remarks now. He sounded as serious as I'd ever heard him—which was very serious indeed. "Are you at all acquainted with the principles of alchemy?" he asked me.

"I know almost nothing." Alchemy was said to be an arcane discipline, difficult for a novice to understand. I knew better than to pretend to knowledge I didn't have.

"Let us begin with the fundamentals, then," Sir Isaac said. "Our intent is to create the Philosopher's Stone—"

"Which isn't actually a stone," King Henry interrupted. "It's a red powder. Or sometimes a liquid."

Already I was feeling confused. A stone that was a liquid? "I thought alchemists wanted to make gold."

"And that's exactly what the Stone does," Sir Isaac said. "It transmutes base metals into pure and dazzling gold, the king of the elements."

"Some say the Stone can also heal the sick," the King added. "A few believe it may even confer immortality."

Sir Isaac shook his head. "With all due respect, Your Majesty, we need not concern ourselves with immortality. As I have said, Flamel's papers are quite explicit on that point. A long, healthy life, yes. Immortality, no. Such dreams are the stuff of fairy tales, not science. And it is science we are concerned with here."

"You have papers to guide you?" I asked.

"Yes," Sir Isaac said. "From Nicholas Flamel—a French alchemist who discovered how to create the Stone three centuries ago. He kept his secrets well hidden, however." His eyes gleamed above his beaky nose. "Until I came along."

"You found them?"

"I did indeed. When I was in France last autumn on the King's business, I took the chance to follow up on a reference in Paracelsus—"

"Another alchemist chap," Sir Samuel whispered to me. "Wrote books."

"—and after many twists and turns, it led me to Flamel's papers about the Stone." A touch of the old restless energy came back into Sir Isaac's eyes as he talked. "A mere seven pages, but they contained the critical information from which the remaining mysteries could be elucidated."

"Took him a month to work it out," Sir Samuel murmured in my ear. "He didn't eat or sleep."

"So you truly think you can do it?" I asked Sir Isaac. "You can make the Philosopher's Stone? You can make gold?"

"Under the right conditions, yes. Without question."

From some, the statement would have been an empty boast, but Sir Isaac was the most gifted member of the Invisible College. Indeed, some said he had the greatest mind in the history of England. He accepted nothing without proof.

"But this is wonderful!" I thought of those hungry children I had seen on the road. If brass could be turned into gold, we would be able to feed them all—and thousands upon thousands more. We could save England from starvation and ruin.

"Wonderful, indeed," Sir Isaac agreed. "But we cannot succeed without the right equipment. And the most crucial piece has been stolen."

I was piecing things together. "The Golden Crucible?"

"The very same. It was the instrument Flamel himself used for the work—a rare vessel said to have been created in Egypt over four thousand years ago by the great Hermes Trismegistus, the founder of our alchemical art. Flamel's missing papers allowed me to locate it, and I brought it back to England. And now it has disappeared, just as our efforts were about to come to fruition."

"You mean you were about to make the Stone?" I asked.

"In a manner of speaking," Sir Isaac said. "All was in readiness, but we cannot commence the Great Work—that is, the actual creation of the Stone—until the heavenly bodies are correctly aligned."

"And when will that be?"

Sir Isaac took out his pocket watch. "Sixty-two hours and thirty-five minutes from now, at dawn on the sixteenth of February. Judging from Flamel's papers and my own calculations, that is the only time in which the Stone can be made. Another chance will not come again this century. So it is vital that we find the Golden Crucible before then."

"So soon?" I was taken aback. That was less than three days from now. "And you have no idea who stole it?"

"None." King Henry took up the tale. "Since our arrival in Greenwich in December, the crucible was kept in the palace Treasury. It has an armed guard and walls six feet thick, so we thought it the safest place. And every night Sir Isaac and I went to check on it."

"When was it taken?"

"In the small hours of the twenty-ninth of January, sometime between two and a quarter to three. Just before two, one of the Treasury guards saw smoke coming down the corridor. Fearing a fire, he went to investigate. The smoke thickened, but he saw no flames—and then someone grabbed him from behind and smothered him with a foul-smelling cloth. When he revived, the Golden Crucible was gone, and his fellow guard was lying dead in a pool of blood outside the Treasury door."

Dead? "So there was murder done as well as theft?" I said.

"Yes," said the King. "We hunted for the villain straightaway, of course. The guards in the outer ward swore that no one had passed through the gates or climbed over the walls, so it seemed certain we would corner him."

"I called out the hounds." Wrexham's fists tightened at the memory. "Together we searched every inch of the place. And every being and beast."

The thrill of the chase lingered in his voice. I tried not to flinch. After all, he hadn't been hunting Chantresses this time, but a murderer. . . .

"Fortunately, I had the able help of Lord Roxburgh." Wrexham acknowledged the man immediately to his right, a weasel-faced aristocrat in willow-green brocade.

Roxburgh trained his beady eyes on me. "We dragged them from their beds, every last man of them."

"Lord Ffoulkes was of great assistance as well," Wrexham said, nodding at a beefy nobleman with florid cheeks sitting farther down the table.

"Rather a lot of us were offended at first," Sir Samuel confessed. "It was most distressing to be rousted out from one's bed and questioned like that. But of course it was a most desperate matter. And alas, few of us had alibis."

"Which is why we have called upon you," the King said to me. "Our own efforts to locate the crucible have failed. But we hope that with your magic, you will succeed—and find the culprit as well."

If he'd demanded that I call up a mist, I could have done it.

But find the crucible? He was asking for something beyond my powers. I hated to say so, however, when Wrexham was sitting right across from me.

I chose my words with care. "Your Majesty, I'm not sure this is a case where my magic is terribly useful. If I could have some time, perhaps, to consider matters?"

"My lady Chantress," the King said with a trace of impatience, "you are too modest. I have discussed matters with my most trusted councillors, and it has been brought to my attention that you have just the magic we need."

The King stopped short, as if he were reluctant to say more. I remembered what Nat had said about danger, and my fears began to grow. What did the Council know about my magic? Very little, I would have said. But more to the point, what had they promised Henry I would do?

I broke the silence. "What is it you expect from me, Your Majesty?"

The King regarded me with a wary look in his wide, blue eyes. "I am told that you can read minds."

CHAPTER EIGHT
MOONBRIAR MADNESS

I stared at the King in dismay. Here was madness indeed.

"We have some moonbriar seeds here," the King said to me. "You hear a song inside them, do you not? And once you sing it, you can read minds. So I am told."

"Yes, that's how it worked when she did it for the Invisible College," Sir Samuel said with enthusiasm. "I was there, and I'll never forget it. Amazing trick, what?"

"Amazing indeed," the King said. "And rather disturbing as well, when it is your own mind she enters—without permission."

So he'd heard how I'd gone into his thoughts, back in the days of Scargrave's rule. That explained the wariness in his eyes. Had Sir Isaac mentioned the incident, or had Sir Samuel? Truly, it could have been anyone from the Invisible College. They all knew.

"It was a long while ago, Your Majesty," I began, "and it happened by accident—"

"We will overlook it," he said, "as long as you use your skill at my command now."

"*No.*"

At first I thought it was I who had spoken, for heaven knew it was what I wanted to say. But it was Nat who was rising from his chair, Nat who was refusing the King, Nat who stood before us all, eyes blazing. "You cannot ask her to do this."

The words were hardly out before Wrexham was shouting him down. "You don't say *cannot* to a king, boy. The Chantress will do the King's bidding, and that's that."

Ignoring him, Nat focused only on King Henry. "Your Majesty, mind-reading is a danger to her. Perhaps they didn't tell you that, but it's true."

The King looked at me. "Is it?"

I hated admitting to any weakness at Court, and especially in front of Wrexham. But Nat, with the best possible intentions, had made it difficult for me to do anything else. "Yes, Your Majesty. It is."

"I can attest to that." Penebrygg's manner was much calmer than Nat's, but he was just as firm. He touched Nat's sleeve and murmured something, and Nat sat back down in his chair.

"Can you explain in more detail?" the King asked me.

I fumbled for words. Since I did not wish to reveal the workings of my magic in too much detail before men like Wrexham, I found it hard to argue my case. But a case I most certainly had, and a strong one. Yet did I dare tell them how easy it was for me to get lost inside another person? Or how dire the consequences could be, if that person were an enemy? Of those assembled here, only Nat and Penebrygg had witnessed firsthand how close I'd come to dying that way.

As if sensing my fears and doubts, the King took a gentler tack. "My lady Chantress, I see that we unknowingly have placed you in an awkward position. You must, of course, make your own decision."

I looked at him with relief, then tensed again as he added, "I do find it troubling, however, that you will not even tell me what these purported dangers are."

"You don't understand what you're asking," Nat said stubbornly.

Penebrygg touched Nat's arm again, as if to caution him. Wrexham wasn't the only one glaring at Nat now. Whispers went up and down the table.

"That lad's a troublemaker," Lord Roxburgh said audibly, beady eyes bright.

"And what about *her*?" Ffoulkes muttered, looking straight at me.

Any response would be better than nothing, I realized, provided it showed good intentions. I turned to the King. "It is quite true that mind-reading is dangerous, Your Majesty, in more ways than I can easily describe to you here. But I should also warn you that the dangers are not all on my side."

The King looked disconcerted. "What do you mean?"

"I mean that perhaps not everyone at Court would wish me to know their true thoughts. *All* their thoughts . . . for that is how the magic works sometimes."

That hit home, to judge from some of the faces around me. Perhaps I could win this argument after all.

Wrexham banged his fist on the table. "Don't muddy the waters, Chantress! There should be no secrets from the Council or the King. If a man is true, he will have nothing to fear, but let traitors beware. All those without alibis will be tested. You may ransack every last corner of their heads, as long as you find the thief."

"I'm not sure it's that simple—" I began.

"Chantress, it *is* that simple." Wrexham leaned across the table toward me, his face ominous. "I lead men in battle who brave terrible dangers for their country's sake. With your power, why should you be different?"

I stared at him, my cheeks flaming. Was the man saying I was a coward?

"My lady Chantress, we all know you have the heart of a lion." The King spoke with exquisite politeness, but he did not rebuke Wrexham, and there was frustration in his gaze now as well as respect. "That is why we find your refusal so hard to accept. Can you truly see no way to help us? By *us*, of course, I do not mean merely me or the Council. I speak as well for all those in this kingdom who will go hungry today, for the children starving in the streets, for every soul in this kingdom who needs what the crucible can bestow, if only it can be found."

His words made me feel ashamed. It was true: I had been thinking only of myself. And it was possible I had an exaggerated sense of the perils involved. After all, I had read many minds before I had gotten lost in one—and since then I had learned much more about magic and about myself. If I sensed danger, surely I'd have a good chance of turning back before harm could befall me. In any case, who was I to exempt myself from danger when so many were suffering?

"I ask one last time," the King said. "Will you use the moon-briar song for us?"

I hesitated. Was there any other way forward? Any other magic I could use? None that I could see. "I will do as you ask, Your Majesty."

Nat flinched. "You can't!" This time he spoke directly to me.

Much as I appreciated his instinct to protect me, I could not yield to it. Not for his sake, and not for mine. This was my battle to fight, my risk to take. "I can," I said. "And I must."

It hurt to see his dismay. We stared at each other a moment more. Then, with an expression of pain, he bowed his head. It seemed I had won the argument. But at what cost?

It can all be sorted out later, I told myself. *As long as we come through this.*

I pushed back my chair and stood. "You said you had the seeds, Your Majesty?"

"They will be brought here now," the King said.

Sir Isaac and Wrexham rose from the table and left the room. When they returned, they were carrying a locked, gold-studded coffer, which they set before the King. Each man then produced a key—brass for Sir Isaac, silver for Wrexham, and gold for the King—and inserted it into the matching lock. Three clicks, and the coffer opened.

The King took hold of the stoppered glass vial inside it. "Here they are." He raised the vial to the light, illuminating the tiny seeds within it. "The sole store of moonbriar left in the world. The rest has been destroyed, as I'm sure you know."

I nodded. I had heard that the Council had taken this decision, and I approved of it. Moonbriar seed was one of the last things in the world that I wanted to see distributed widely.

For a fascinated moment, the King stared at the seeds. Then he lowered the vial and asked me, "Are you ready?"

"You have not told me which minds I am to read."

"Why, the minds of those without alibis," the King said. "I thought that was clear."

"Yes, but where am I to start?"

"Here." Wrexham did not hesitate. "With the Council. If there are any vipers here, we'll roust them out now."

"I find it hard to believe that anyone here would betray us, but I suppose it is well to be sure," the King said. "Who among you shall go first? Wrexham has an alibi, but most of the rest of you do not."

The question was met by unhappy silence. Everyone except Wrexham kept his head down.

Nat stood up. "Let it be me."

I gaped at him. He'd been completely against using the moonbriar seeds, and I knew for a fact that he loathed having his mind read. Why on earth was he volunteering for this? Was it a bluff?

It was only when he came toward me, and I saw the desperate concern in his eyes, that I realized the truth: there was no bluff here, no subterfuge. Nat was simply trying to protect me in the only way he knew how, the only way he had left. *If you have to walk into someone's mind, let it be mine*, his eyes said. *You know I would never harm you.*

I couldn't reach out to him; I couldn't thank him. Too many people were watching us. Afraid they would read my emotions in my face, I looked down at the floor.

"Well, well," said Wrexham. "You surprise me, young Walbrook. And it seems you have surprised the Chantress as well."

"Well done," the King said to Nat. "Now tell us, Chantress, what do we do next?"

"We prepare ourselves." I pushed back my chair and turned to Nat, still not daring to touch him, or even to look straight at him. I backed away from the table and motioned to a spot an arm's length away. "Could you stand here?"

To the King, I explained, "Once I have sung, I must touch the person whose mind I wish to read. Or, at the very least, touch something that belongs to him. But having the person close by is especially helpful."

The other Council members came away from the table and assembled around us. The King handed the vial of moonbriar seeds to me. "You will sing now?"

"Yes." I tried not to let my hands tremble on the smooth glass. Moonbriar, like all magic things, had music that was especially potent—and sometimes especially deceptive as well. Where would it take me this time? Would I be its master? Or would it overmaster me?

I eased the stopper a fraction upward, listening for the first faint strains of moonbriar song. The only music I heard was a muted strain from the Thames—and even that was surprisingly soft, given how close the river was. The walls here must be very thick.

Ignoring the Thames, I pulled the stopper all the way out. This time an acrid smell and a soft melody twined up to meet me.

I brought the open vial closer. Yes, there was a song here— but was it the right one? I didn't recall it twisting and turning this way.

"There's something odd about the music," I told the Council.

"If it sounds wrong, then don't sing it," Nat said.

The King, however, simply gave me a long, hard glance. "Are you saying you can't proceed?"

"I'm saying it might be risky, Your Majesty."

Wrexham growled. "We all have to take chances, Chantress."

Reluctant as I was to admit it, there was something in what he said. And in truth, I couldn't be sure there really was anything wrong with the song. Memory wasn't all that reliable where song-spells were concerned. That was one reason why I'd needed the seeds themselves to do this work. And these seeds were older and drier than the ones I'd used before. That alone might account for the difference in the songs. I just wished the melody were clearer and simpler, so that I could understand its subtleties more clearly.

Well, perhaps I'd understand it better once I started to sing it. It worked that way sometimes. I bent over the vial of moonbriar seeds and let the song spin into me.

Nat didn't try to stop me. Perhaps he sensed that it would be hard to turn back now.

Catching hold of the tangled tune, I gave voice to the first trill. The sinuous lines looped around and around, and as I sang them, I relaxed, lulled by their smooth sound. I'd been wrong to worry: the song was still a mystery to me, but nothing bad had happened so far—

The seeds sizzled.

I stopped in alarm.

The vial erupted into flame.

CHAPTER NINE
ACCUSATIONS

Fiery tendrils shot out of the glass, thickening and swirling like a burning vine. Shocked, I dropped the vial, but the matting cushioned its fall, and the vine only grew faster. A monstrous plant took shape before us: a moonbriar bush made of flame. Flowers bloomed on its branches, scorching my face and dress.

The King drew back. Councillors bellowed and shouted.

"Look out!" Nat leaped toward the heart of the fire and flung his leather coat over the vial. Smothered, the flames went out. Only a ghastly smoke remained, smelling of rotten moonbriar fruit. Through it, the King and Council peered at me, aghast.

"What in heaven's name was that?" The King's light freckles stood out like copper constellations against his white face.

"I—I don't know," I said. "It's never happened before."

"You *made* it happen," Wrexham accused. His hand was on the jeweled hilt of his dagger, I was alarmed to see.

"I never meant to," I said. "I swear I didn't."

Sir Isaac, Sir Samuel, and Nat were kneeling over the half-charred coat and the vial underneath it.

"The seeds are gone," Sir Samuel cried out. "The fire's consumed them!"

As cries of consternation filled the room, Wrexham's hand slammed into the table. "God's blood, Chantress! Are you playing with us?"

My hands tensed into fists. "Of course not, Lord Wrexham."

"So you say. But you were against mind-reading from the first . . . and now, suddenly, the moonbriar seeds are gone. How fortunate for you."

The room had gone quiet again. Everyone was waiting for my answer. I glanced at the King, who looked back at me with troubled eyes. Why was he allowing Wrexham to hector me like this? Did he, too, think I was guilty?

"I told you the song sounded wrong," I reminded him. "I told you at the start."

The King acknowledged this with a thoughtful nod. "It's true: you did warn us that something wasn't right." He looked more sure of me now. "Tell me, Chantress: Is it possible someone tampered with the seeds somehow—by magic or other means? Would that change their song?"

"I suppose so." I didn't have much experience in such matters, but something had clearly altered the moonbriar song.

Sir Isaac wrapped a handkerchief around the vial and set it on the table. The glass was cracked and misshapen by the heat.

"Did you notice anything else that wasn't right about the seeds, Chantress? Their appearance? Their scent?"

"They had a strange smell," I remembered. "A bit like vinegar, only more bitter."

"Ah!" Sir Isaac seemed intrigued. "Most unusual. So perhaps someone did tamper with them, then. It remains to be seen, however, whether the change was effected by chemical or magical means."

"Who would do such a thing?" Wrexham demanded, swinging closer to me.

"I have no idea," I said. Without thinking, I looked at Nat—not to accuse him, but out of a foolish instinct to seek his help when I was in trouble.

The others in the room followed my gaze.

"I see," said the King. "He has never been happy about the existence of moonbriar, has he? And he would do almost anything to protect you." He spoke with distress, as if the idea pained him, but also with growing conviction.

"He didn't do it," I said quickly, raising my voice as I saw how many others were leaping to the same conclusion. "He wouldn't. He's not like that."

"Of course I wouldn't," Nat said hotly. "I'm not sorry the confounded seeds are gone. But I wouldn't go behind everyone's backs that way."

I wished he'd left out the bit about not being sorry. But that was Nat all over: he was forthright to a fault. It was hard for him to follow his own advice to keep quiet, to be discreet.

Not that I found it easy to follow, either. I couldn't help defending him. "He objected to my using the moonbriar seeds," I pointed out to the Council. "Why would he have bothered to do that if he'd known the seeds were going to burn up?"

"The Chantress speaks sense." Penebrygg's voice was calm, but he was stroking his beard in a way he only did when very worried.

Lord Roxburgh shrugged. "Maybe Walbrook wanted to throw us off the scent."

"But how could I have done anything to the moonbriar seeds?" Nat countered. "I don't have a single one of the three keys, and you need them all to open the coffer."

"We do," Wrexham said. "But a thief wouldn't."

Nat's eyes flared. "I'm not a thief."

"You stole things from Scargrave, did you not?" Wrexham said.

"To help defeat him, yes. But that doesn't mean I'm a thief."

The other members of the Invisible College and I backed him up.

"He was a spy," I said. "That's entirely different."

"Quite correct," Sir Isaac confirmed. "Nat did steal on occasion, but only at the direction of the Invisible College, and only to aid the resistance."

"A more honorable lad would be hard to find," Penebrygg said.

"Couldn't have succeeded without him," Sir Samuel agreed.

Wrexham ignored us. "Once a thief, always a thief," he said, and the meeting dissolved into shouts.

"Order," the King cried. "Order!" When the room quieted, he said wearily, "And you wonder why it is that I do not call a full

Council more often. Please let us return to our seats and try to conduct our business without breaking into a brawl."

The Council members went back to their chairs, Nat more slowly than the rest. I sat too. Once we were settled, the King gestured across the table. "Sir Isaac, you wish to say something?"

"Only that the coffer possesses a most unusual and intricate set of locks," Sir Isaac said. "Even if Nat could force them—and however great his skill, I'm not sure he could—the attempt would have left scratches and damaged the mechanism. And the locks show no such signs. So that, by itself, should defend him against idle accusations."

Wrexham looked set to interrupt again, but Sir Isaac wasn't finished. "Not only that, but Nat had no way of reaching the coffer. Aside from this meeting, it has been kept in the Treasury at all times, under guard."

"With the crucible?" I asked.

"Yes." The King looked at Sir Isaac. "Are you suggesting—"

"I am." Sir Isaac tapped his fingertips together. "Whoever stole the crucible may have tampered with the moonbriar seeds too, in hopes of forestalling our efforts to find him."

"But the keys," the King said. "He wouldn't have had the keys."

"There aren't any copies?" I asked.

"No," the King said.

"There might be," Sir Isaac said more slowly. "The one person who would know for certain is the man who had the coffer made: Sir Barnaby Gadding."

The King looked alarmed. "Then we must send someone to him at once."

"It won't be that easy," Sir Isaac warned. "You will remember, Your Majesty, that after Sir Barnaby was taken ill last autumn, he retreated to his estate in Devon, in the hopes of improving his health. Sadly, I had a letter less than a fortnight ago from Lady Gadding, who tells me Sir Barnaby's condition has worsened. He lives, it seems, but he cannot speak, or even understand most questions."

"We shall send someone to him regardless," the King said. "If he cannot help us, perhaps Lady Gadding can, or one of his servants."

"It sounds like a wild goose chase to me, Your Majesty," Wrexham griped. "The guilty party is certain to be here, not in Devon. We would do better to take action here and now."

"We cannot act without evidence." The King, I was glad to see, was not in Wrexham's pocket, even if he did allow him more latitude than I would have liked. "All we can do is what we've done so far: allow no one to leave the palace until the crucible is found and the mystery is solved." He turned to me. "Chantress, you must remain here for now."

"I understand," I said, but it was a blow. I had hoped for a speedy return to Norrie and Norfolk. Instead, I had to contend with a theft, a murderer, and a Council that mistrusted me.

"The moonbriar magic has failed," the King said, "but you must have other enchantments that can help us. I understand, for instance, that you can sing yourself invisible?"

I had once had that power, yes. But it had come to me through Proven Magic, not Wild Magic, and so it had vanished when my ruby had cracked. I was loath to explain as much, however. After my failure with the moonbriar, it would make me look very weak indeed. "That would not be the best way forward, Your Majesty," I temporized. "You have set me a difficult problem, and I will need some time to consider how to approach it."

The King frowned. "Very well. We shall speak more of this when you are rested from your journey. If you think of a way to aid us, come find me at once, no matter what the hour." He cleared his throat. "And there are other matters, too, that we must speak of."

There was a flutter of anticipation in the room.

"But that can wait," the King said. "My lords and gentlemen, my lady Chantress—I thank you for your counsel. For now, our business is done."

† † †

It was not quite done, however. Not as far as Wrexham was concerned. I was one of the last to leave the Crimson Chamber, and when I did, he cornered me in the hall. "Don't think you can run away so easily, Chantress."

"I'm not running away." I tried to duck around him. "I'm going to my rooms."

But I wasn't going anywhere, not while he was in the way. The man was built like a mountain, and he was armed. It was impossible to step around him.

I didn't like being trapped—and my discomfort pleased him, I could see it. He almost smiled as he stood there blocking my way. It was only when his eyes caught the light that I saw the anger in them.

"A word of warning, Chantress."

Tired out by the journey and by all I'd been forced to confront since my arrival, I tried to preempt him. "Look, I know you don't want me here—"

"Oh, but that's where you're wrong, Chantress. I do want you here. I want you where I can watch you. Not out gallivanting on a Norfolk beach, far from sight. Not that I haven't found ways to watch you even there. But Greenwich is decidedly more convenient."

"You've been watching me?" The mere idea made my skin prickle.

"I've had you watched, yes. Ever since you defeated Scargrave. And I've learned a great deal."

I would not let him intimidate me. "Such as?"

"I know, for instance, that the ruby you have tucked in your bodice is cracked . . . and I know what that means."

I forced myself to stay very still, as one does with a wild animal about to strike. If Wrexham knew about my closely guarded ruby, what other secrets had he unlocked?

Wrexham's pale eyes never left my face. "I know this, too: You still have power—enormous power. You can call up mist; you can make it rain. By God, you held off the King's own guard by yourself." His mouth twisted in fury. "How dare you tell the King you cannot help him right now? How dare you tell him he must wait?"

I recoiled.

"Confess," he hissed. "You are lying. You are shielding the thief: Walbrook."

"No," I said. "No, I—" How to explain myself, without getting lost again in a wrangle about Nat's innocence, or revealing even more than Wrexham already knew about my magic? "I am not trying to shield anyone. It is just that finding the crucible isn't as simple as you think. I need the right song, for a start. And I don't yet have it."

"Then find it!" He swung even closer to me, cutting off most of the light. "We need that crucible, Chantress. So find your song and sing it." His hand flexed on the hilt of his dagger, rings bulging like carbuncles. "And don't think you can use your magic against me. I have ways of protecting myself, believe me. I've dealt with your kind before, remember."

How could I forget? I forced myself to stand straight. I must not let him see how he frightened me. I must not. I must not.

"And remember this, too." His voice was low and full of menace. "If I had eyes and ears in Norfolk, I have even more here at Court. I am watching you every minute, every hour, every day. So do not cross me."

CHAPTER TEN
THE SECRET ROOM

Having made his threats, Wrexham left, still fingering his dagger.

I sagged against the wall. I burned to show him that I could not be crossed either. Yet if I used magic against him, what would that lead to? Wrexham was the King's man, and it would not be wise to displease the King. And any enchantment I worked would surely be traced back to me. It was best if I did nothing—for now.

Still, there was comfort in remembering that I had real power here, even if I didn't choose to use it.

But what was it Wrexham had said about protecting himself? I tried to remember his exact words. I'd never heard of a way to guard against Chantress magic—unless it was by killing a Chantress or preventing her from singing, as Scargrave had done. Was that what Wrexham had meant?

Maybe. But there was so much about Chantress magic that I did not know, so much knowledge that had been lost or stolen.

After his many years of Chantress-hunting, Wrexham might well know more about my kind than I did myself.

Perhaps Wrexham really could protect himself against my magic. I would have to assume, for now, that it was possible.

And assume, too, that wherever I went, he was watching me.

† † †

After the bruising encounter with Wrexham, I intended to go straight to my room, but his threats had thrown me off balance, and I took one wrong turn after another. Before I knew it, I was lost in a part of the palace I hadn't seen before.

Going around a corner, I found myself in a frigid chamber with massive stone pillars, dimly lit by two flickering candelabras. When a hand touched my arm, I jolted around in fright.

"Sorry!" Nat whispered, releasing me. "I didn't mean to scare you."

Right then and there, I almost spilled out what Wrexham had said to me. But then I thought about how hotheaded Nat had been in the Council meeting, and how his impulsiveness had led to trouble. If I told Nat about Wrexham's threats, would he rush off to confront the man? That would only antagonize Wrexham—and make matters worse for both Nat and me. I decided I'd better keep the Marcher Lord's threats to myself, at least for now.

"I've been looking for you," Nat said. "I couldn't come close after the meeting. Everyone was watching."

"I know." I'd kept away from him for the same reason. "I saw Penebrygg pushing you out the door."

"He wanted to say a few words to me about caution and moderation. Which I suppose were warranted," Nat admitted. "A fine show I gave the Council, after all my advice to keep quiet. But moonbriar, of all things! I wasn't expecting that."

"Nor I."

"And then the fire . . ." He cast a wary glance around the echoing room. "Look, it's not really safe to talk here, but I know a place nearby that's better. Will you come?"

"Of course."

He grabbed a taper from a candelabra and guided me past the pillars into a maze of rooms. Though substantial, these rooms were not airy and graceful like some of the others I'd glimpsed in my wanderings. Lower and squatter, they had dark paneled walls and arched doorways and figures carved in stone: a hound, a hare, a woman's face covered in leaves.

In the last of these rooms, Nat stopped short, listening. All was quiet. It felt as if we'd reached the ancient heart of the palace, the core of the labyrinth.

At last Nat walked up to a panel and fiddled with the decoration. With a muffled thump, the panel swung inward, revealing a small, hidden chamber.

"How did you find it?" I marveled. In truth I hardly needed an answer. The first time I'd ever laid eyes on Nat, he'd been coming out of a secret door. The same curiosity that made him a born scientist also had made him a born spy.

"Oh, this place is full of hideaways," Nat said. "And I've had some time on my hands since we got shut up here."

His hand touched the small of my back as he ushered me in. Even after he turned away and tugged the door shut, my whole spine tingled.

"We'll still need to keep our voices down," he warned me. "The walls are quite thick, and not many people come by, but there's always a chance someone might be listening."

I nodded and looked around in the light of the lone taper, which he'd wedged into a battered candlestick. Tiny and windowless, the secret room was almost bare, boasting only a three-legged stool and a small, iron-banded chest.

"What's in there?" I pointed to the chest.

"Nothing much." Nat flipped the lid open. "Another candlestick and a flint. They were here when I found the place."

When I leaned forward to look, my sleeve brushed his. I glanced at him, and his wide hazel eyes held mine. He was so close I could feel his sweet breath on my cheek.

Just as I was sure he was about to kiss me, he turned away and banged the chest shut. "How are we going to get you out of this?"

I was bewildered by his sudden change of mood. "Out of this?"

"Away from this court and its dangers. That fire could have killed you." He gave me a sharp look. "Unless maybe you sang it up on purpose? To destroy the seeds?"

"No," I said. "It was as much of a surprise to me as to you.

Something really was wrong with those seeds. I just wish I knew who tampered with them—and how, and why."

"I wish I knew too. But the fire's only part of it. It's not safe for you to be here, not when the Court's in the grip of this alchemy madness."

I looked at him in surprise. "You think it's madness?"

"Of course!"

"You didn't say so at the meeting."

"Only because I've said it too many times before." Frustration darkened his eyes. "The Inner Council voted to throw me out if I brought it up again, so now I have to keep quiet. But not by choice."

"You don't have to keep quiet with me."

He smiled then, though his body stayed tense. "There is that, I guess. The one silver lining to this disaster." He let out a deep breath. "I've missed you, Lucy."

It helped to hear that, but I noticed he didn't come any closer. Was it shyness keeping him away? Well, that I could understand. I felt shy too. Although it was thrilling to be so close after our months apart, it was also unnerving. Maybe talking would help.

I sat down on the stool. "So tell me: What's wrong with the alchemy plan? Don't you think it will work?"

Nat shrugged. "Who's to say? Isaac Oldville's a genius, and he's convinced he has the answers. But that doesn't mean he's right." Keeping his voice down, he perched himself on the curved top of the chest. "People have been trying to make the Philosopher's Stone for thousands of years, and as far as I can see, there's no clear evidence that anyone ever has."

"Not even—oh, what was his name? Flamel?"

"All we have is Flamel's own word for it. And legends. And stories. But that's not proof, no matter what Sir Isaac thinks. In the end, alchemy's a gamble—and yet it's all the King and Council are willing to spend money on." He paused. "Well, that and Wrexham's castles."

"You mean the fortifications that Penebrygg was talking about?"

"Yes. Wrexham says these are perilous times, and we need to shore up the old strongholds against rebellion. Shore up his own holdings, more like," Nat said in disgust. "Almost all the money so far has gone to his own lands. Which grow more extensive all the time."

"And the King allows this?" I asked.

"Some say he's rewarding Wrexham for putting down the Berwick rebellion," Nat said. "And for saving his life."

"So Wrexham really did save him?"

"Yes. He's a fearless warrior, I'll give him that. When the King's saddle twisted beneath him in the battle, Wrexham and his men held back the attackers and dragged him to safety."

"So the King gives him whatever he wants, in gratitude?"

"That might be why, yes," Nat said. "But maybe the King feels he can't afford to say no. Wrexham's holdings extend from the Welsh borderlands up through the North of England; no other lord controls so much land. He has the power to split England in two."

I hadn't understood before quite how powerful Wrexham was. It was sobering news.

"Anyway, there you have it." Nat ran a hand through his dark hair. "We're spending every last coin in the Treasury on Wrexham's forts and Sir Isaac's alchemy, and there's not a penny left for anything else."

"Alchemy costs a lot?"

"I'll say. Flamel's ingredients cost the earth. We've also had to build an entirely new laboratory and an astronomical observatory, all to Sir Isaac's demanding specifications. And, of course, we've had to pay for extra soldiers and guards to protect the whole place."

"What would you spend the money on instead?" I asked.

"Real things. Practical things."

"Like . . ." I prompted.

"Potatoes."

I blinked at the unexpected response. I'd heard of potatoes—a new food from America—but I'd never actually eaten them. "Why on earth . . . ?"

"The blight," Nat explained. "We need new crops that can resist it. When I was over in Holland, I found some European wheat varieties that might work, but I discovered that potatoes are even better—easier to plant, and a much better yield. But everyone at Court is too obsessed with alchemy to think the idea is worth pursuing. Wait till we can make gold, they keep saying."

"Even Penebrygg?"

"When we talk about it, he agrees there's some sense in what I say. But alchemy has him dazzled. I don't see much of him these days. He's always in Sir Isaac's laboratory." Nat looked discouraged. "Like the rest of them, he thinks the Stone will be the end of all our troubles."

It was hard to know what to tell him. Perhaps his skepticism in alchemy was justified. But could he really be completely right, and everyone else completely wrong?

I shifted on my stool. "Maybe it won't turn out as badly as you fear," I said. "Sir Isaac could be right, you know. If we find that crucible, maybe he'll make so much gold we can buy whatever we want. Including your potatoes."

Nat put his head in his hands. "Don't you start too."

"I'm not trying to take sides, Nat. But I think we have to hope, for everyone's sake, that Sir Isaac's alchemy works. Even if you planted potatoes now, you'd have to wait months to harvest them. And people are hungry now."

"Yes, they are," Nat said, lifting his head. "And a fortnight ago, when I was still in Holland, I found some merchants who can ship us potatoes right away. Not just seed potatoes, but potatoes to eat as well—tons of them, all much cheaper than wheat. I'm talking about real food, Lucy. Not wish-on-a-star alchemy. But we have to pay for it, and the King and Council say they don't have a penny to spare."

"You need the money now?"

"As soon as possible." Nat's jaw sharpened. "If we don't buy them, someone else will. And it's our best chance to save people from starving."

Money. I was so used to not having any that it took me a moment to remember my circumstances had changed. Along with my refuge in Norfolk, the King had granted me the estate that had belonged to my godmother before Scargrave had stolen it. It was a substantial inheritance. "Why don't you borrow some money from me?"

Nat shook his head. "The sum I need is probably more than you've got, and I doubt the Council would let you give it away, anyhow. They're holding the money in trust for you, or so I've heard. Besides, there are others who can afford it more."

"Who?"

"King Henry, for one. He has far more palaces than he can visit in a year, and half of them are filled with treasures he never looks at."

"And he won't give any of them up?"

"Left to himself, I think he might. But Wrexham's always at his ear, saying it would look like weakness, that it would set a bad example. And of course it *would* be a bad example—for Wrexham. He collects estates and jewels the way some people collect skipping stones, and he doesn't want to have to yield up a single one. But if he and his friends all gave a little, we'd have enough."

"You make it sound as if there's no need for alchemy," I said.

"There isn't." Nat was emphatic. "Even if it does work—and I doubt it will—it'll just create more problems."

"What kind of problems?"

"To start with, no one knows for sure what the powers of such a Stone would be."

"Sir Isaac says—"

"He thinks he knows," Nat said. "But how can he? Everything about the Stone is shrouded in mystery. If it turns out it really can make men immortal, what do we do then? Who will we give it to? Who will control it?"

"The King?" I ventured.

"Perhaps at first. But how long would that last? Even if all the Stone can do is make gold, every man in Europe will be after it, and probably half the rest of the world, too. And the moment the Stone falls into bad hands, where will we be?" He shook his head. "It may look like a solution, but we're better off without it."

Gently, I said, "I think maybe you're worrying too far ahead."

"Someone has to."

"But why you?"

A slightly rueful note entered his voice. "Because I'm built that way."

Too true. Nat never just accepted an idea. Instead, he thought it through from every angle, and he had a skeptic's talent for asking awkward questions. To ask him to be different would be to ask him not to be *Nat*. Yet in this case, I feared he was just borrowing trouble—for himself, most of all.

"I'm worried half out of my mind about you as well," he went on. "This alchemy obsession keeps the Council from thinking straight. How could they ask you to sing the moonbriar song like that, as if there were no consequences? And what will they ask you to do next?"

"I'm worried about that too," I confessed.

He leaned forward on his makeshift seat, every line in his

body tense. "I swear I'll do everything in my power to keep you safe, Lucy."

His fierce concern made me catch my breath. Yet when I leaned toward him, he stood up without a word, fists clenched.

"Nat?" I rose too, but I misjudged the small space. My shoulder bumped against his, and he put out a hand to steady me. I had a moment to wonder what was in his eyes, and then his arms were around me, and we were kissing as if we could not bear to stop.

Oh, those kisses! So heady and bittersweet. In them I tasted each day we'd spent apart and each letter gone astray.

But he was here now, I reminded myself. Here with his deft hands tangled in my hair. Here with his warm lips on mine. My heart raced as our kisses deepened.

Yet when I reached to pull him closer, he broke away. "I . . . can't," he said, sounding dazed. "I shouldn't. Not when—"

Still dazed myself, I waited for him to finish, but he didn't.

"Not when *what*?" I asked.

"We have to get you back." He sounded shaken but determined. "You'll be missed."

"But we—"

"I'll show you the way." Pulling back from me, he peeked through a spy hole in the panel, then opened the door and slipped out.

There was nothing I could do but follow him.

CHAPTER ELEVEN
SYBIL

Within minutes we were skirting past the massive pillars again and threading our way through a doorway I hadn't seen before. As we padded down quiet staircases and echoing galleries, I was reminded of the many expeditions we had taken through Gadding House when he was training me in spycraft last year. Then, too, he had kept a certain distance between us.

But why was he keeping his distance now? The question ate away at me.

At last we halted in the shadows of a quiet room that I vaguely recognized as being near my own.

"I should leave you here," Nat whispered. "It's still unwise for us to be seen together. More so than ever, I imagine, given how the Council session went. Can you find your way back?"

"I think so. But Nat—"

"What?"

Why did you stop kissing me? It was too bald a question; I couldn't ask it when his eyes were so remote. Instead, I said, "You never told me: Why wouldn't the Council let you visit me?"

"Tomorrow," he said softly. "I promise I'll explain everything tomorrow."

I thought for a second that he would reach for me, but instead, he moved away.

"But where will I find you?"

"I'll find *you*. It's safest that way." By now he was moving out of whispering distance, but I could see his lips shape the words. "Take care. Watch your back."

"And you."

I kept up a brave face, but as he disappeared from sight, my fears about Wrexham and his spies rushed in on me. What if they had seen Nat escorting me back here?

Knock on wood they haven't, I told myself. *And if they come across me now, at least I can make sure they don't see me staring after him.*

Mustering up all my resolution, I walked toward my rooms. I was nearly there when I heard someone behind me.

"Lucy? Is that you?" The voice, young and sweetly tuneful, was the most beautiful I'd ever heard.

Startled, I turned to find a tall girl about my own age coming up to me. Rosy and dimpled, with golden-blonde hair knotted in artful curls, she had a face as lovely as her voice.

"Oh, Lucy! It *is* you." Her rich soprano was full of joy. "You do remember me, don't you?"

Remember her? As I stared, she smiled. "Oh dear, I see you don't. I'm Sybil Dashwood. You stayed with me for a whole summer when we were seven, at Dashwood Hall. All of you came to visit: you and your mother and Norrie."

I had no recollection of her at all. But that didn't mean much. To protect me, my mother had once sung a song-spell of forgetfulness. It had worked only too well, destroying many of my childhood memories, especially the ones that involved my mother herself in some way.

But was it really possible that an entire summer of my life had been wiped away? Maybe this beautiful girl was lying to me. I would have to tread carefully.

"Oh, I am sorry," I said. "I didn't recognize you. It was a long time ago, I'm afraid. And, er . . . you've grown."

"So have you," she said, laughter in her voice.

"Not as much as you, I think." Although I told myself that appearances didn't matter, I felt a twinge of envy. Tall and radiant, Sybil was wearing a rose-and-gold gown that fit her curvy figure beautifully.

"Fine feathers, that's all." She dismissed her silken flounces with a grin. "Underneath, I'm still the same girl you knew. Cross my heart, three times."

The silly saying had the ring of a childhood vow. Had it been ours? I smiled at her in case it was. "You know, I don't remember why we came to visit you—"

"Chantress business, I suspect," Sybil said calmly.

I looked at her in astonishment. "Are you a Chantress too?"

The words burst out of me before I had time to think them through. Maybe this was something I ought to have known already, something Sybil would expect me to remember. But fortunately, she didn't seem taken aback by my question.

"Oh no." Sybil shook her head so vigorously that it set her golden ringlets bouncing. "I know they had hopes for me, back when I last saw you, but the magic died out with my grandmother, I'm afraid."

"So your grandmother was a Chantress . . . and yet you aren't?"

Sybil nodded. "Grandmama was very wise, but she wasn't a very powerful Chantress, by all accounts. And not a single one of her daughters inherited the gift. Mama hoped I would be a throwback, but I haven't a bit of magic in me."

She smiled, but beneath the charm I saw a certain sadness.

"I'm sorry," I said.

"Oh, heavens, don't think it's a worry to me! Quite the opposite, in fact. Magic's a terrible responsibility. All things considered, I've had a lucky escape." She put a hand to her mouth. "Oh dear. I shouldn't have said that, should I? To you of all people."

She looked so horrified that I couldn't help it—I started to laugh. With an air of relief, she joined in.

"It's still my besetting sin," she confessed. "I'm forever putting my foot in my mouth."

It was hard to believe someone so frank could be lying to me. "Never mind," I said. "It's true: magic *is* a terrible responsibility."

"But it's one you've handled well." Her heart-shaped face was full of honest admiration. "If it had been up to me to defeat Scargrave, I'd still be cowering in a corner somewhere. Or, more likely, vanished into that Raven Pit of his." She shrugged in self-deprecation.

"I suppose it's just as well Mama and I moved to France before he ever came to power. Having a Chantress grandmother was as good as a death warrant during his reign. And he didn't care overmuch whether there was any magic left in the family or not."

"But you found safe haven in France?"

"Well, to a point. Scargrave had a long reach. Even in France, it was necessary for us to be discreet about our origins. And you can imagine just how hard that was for me." Her lips quirked, but again I saw the sadness in her eyes. "I had a habit of saying the wrong thing to the wrong people, and then we would have to move again. Mama was so frustrated with me."

"Is your mother here with you now?" I asked.

The sadness in Lady Sybil's eyes deepened. "I'm afraid Mama died last spring, in Paris."

It was my turn to feel as if I'd said the wrong thing. I knew all too well how terrible it was to lose a mother. "I'm sorry," I said awkwardly.

Sybil acknowledged my words with a gentle nod. "You're very kind. She'd been ill for some time, so it wasn't unexpected, but I miss her a great deal. And, of course, it's been rather difficult moving back here."

"You're living with your father?"

"No. He died just before Mama and I left for France. But his sister has taken me in. And her husband, of course—but it's Aunt Goring who made the decision. She was quite a bit older than my father, and her children are all grown up." With an openness that would have surprised me in anyone else, Sybil added, "I think she's hoping I'll make an advantageous match, and be of use to the family. In fact, that's why I'm here at Greenwich. Aunt Goring wished me to be presented at Court. We only meant to be here for a few days, but then the crucible was stolen, and we were all commanded to stay. I've been here ever since. And by now, of course, I'm out of my mind with boredom."

Her face was so comic I couldn't help laughing again—and oh, how good it felt to do that, after all the fearful events of the day.

I said impulsively, "Why don't you come to my rooms, and we'll have some supper together?"

"Oh no. That wouldn't be right. Why, anyone can see you're half wilting from exhaustion. And no wonder, after your long journey. Besides, Aunt Goring will be wondering where I am."

"Well, then come and see me tomorrow."

"I will," Sybil said. "With the greatest of pleasure. But for now, get some rest." She grinned. "And remember to put some bay leaves on your pillow for Valentine's Day."

"Valentine's Day?"

"It's tomorrow. They say if you pin the leaves onto your pillow, then you'll dream of your true love tonight."

I'd never heard of this, but then I knew barely anything about Valentine's Day. "And if I don't have any bay leaves?"

"Oh, I wouldn't worry," Sybil said, laughing. "It's just an old tale, you know. They also say the first man you meet on Valentine's Day will be your sweetheart—and goodness knows that's hardly ever true." Quick as a bird, she kissed me on the cheek. "Sleep well, dear Lucy! I'm so glad we've met again."

Only after she left, and I was out of the orbit of her charm, did I wonder if I'd been right to be so friendly with her. After all, Wrexham had told me point-blank that he had spies everywhere. Maybe Sybil was one of them.

Or was I just seeing spies everywhere?

I need rest . . . and food.

Rounding the corner, I was relieved to see the gilded lions that marked the entrance to my rooms. I was disconcerted, however, to learn quite how accessible those rooms were. The first door bristled with an assortment of locks, but none of them appeared to be in use. At any rate, I'd received no keys for them, and they had all been left open. I halted for a moment in the tiny antechamber to examine the second door. This had no locks at all.

I opened it and stopped dead. There was someone in the room.

Caught between panic and anger, I sized her up: a girl all in gray, perhaps a couple of years older than I was. Although she was short, you could see the strength in her wiry body, and in her well-muscled forearms and wrists. Her face, cold as the North Sea, gave nothing away.

"Who are you?" I demanded.

For a moment, I feared she might attack. But then, sweeping her dull skirts back, she curtsied low before me. "I am Margery, my lady. Your new maidservant."

"A maidservant?" I repeated, startled. And then, suspicious: "Who sent you here?"

Her eyes met mine, and I saw something defiant in them.

"The Earl of Wrexham, my lady."

CHAPTER TWELVE
LISTENING

The state of my room gave evidence that Margery was—at least in part—exactly what she claimed to be: a maidservant, and a very capable one at that. The hearth had been swept; the fire was burning brightly; my clothes had been rescued from their bags. She even had supper ready for me: a tureen of oyster soup and a basket of soft, snowy rolls.

The buttery smell made my mouth water, yet I couldn't do more than nibble. Maidservant or not, Margery had been sent here by Wrexham. It was almost certain she was one of his spies.

Toying with my food, I questioned Margery. She busied herself about the room and gave me the barest answers she could. She had started working for Wrexham's family as a child. Of late she had served as maidservant to his wife, the Countess, until that lady's death a short while ago. It was Wrexham who had recommended her to the King's Master of the Household as a maidservant for me.

"He didn't need to do that," I said. "I don't require a maidservant. I can look after myself."

"A fine lady like you, doing her own work? The Master of the Household would never permit it, and neither would my lord Wrexham."

No, I supposed Wrexham wouldn't. Not now that he had one of his spies in my very own room.

"Besides, there's enough work here for two people, just getting your wardrobe in order." Margery cast a cool eye on my skirts and bodice. "Those barely fit you, my lady. And you've brought hardly anything else with you, I see. We must send for a seamstress first thing tomorrow."

"I don't plan to be here long," I said.

"First thing tomorrow," she repeated, fingering the mulberry silk.

It unsettled me to see Wrexham's creature handling my clothes. Would she expect to help me dress? Would she watch me sleep?

Oh, how I wished it were Norrie who was here with me instead! Even better, that I'd never had to leave Norfolk.

But since that wasn't to be, I hoped Norrie would come soon. If her recovery had been swift—and for both our sakes, I prayed it was—she might only be a day or two away from Greenwich by now.

Cheered by the thought, I considered the situation anew. Wrexham might have his spies, but I was hardly powerless, not when I had my magic. Tired though I was, I ought to take stock now of what I could do.

One point in Margery's favor: she was quiet. As she silently tweaked the draperies and turned down the bedcovers, I let myself sink into the music in the room. During the journey, I'd been too seasick and weary to have any concentration for this kind of listening; the most I'd heard was a snatch or two of Wild Magic before falling asleep. But going so long without song-spells had made me feel out of kilter. It was time to center myself, to return to the heart of what made me a Chantress.

As I stood before the fire, I heard only the ordinary sounds of the room at first: the cheerful ticking of a clock, the pop of coals in the hearth, the airy breathing of the fire itself. But that's how it always was at the beginning. Beneath these—woven in and around them—I knew I would find the music of Wild Magic. It was simply a matter of breathing slowly, staying calm, and letting it come to me.

This time, however, no music came.

The minutes ticked by. At last I heard a smattering of faint notes from the River Thames, but nothing more.

Of course, it had been much the same in the Crimson Chamber, I remembered now. I had thought then that it must be the walls that were getting in the way. After all, bricks and mortar had never had much of anything to say to me. Indeed, as I'd struggled to master Wild Magic, I often found they had a dampening effect.

Nevertheless, alarm stirred. I went to the window.

"You're not going to open that, my lady?" Margery said.

"I am." I pulled on the latch. "It's too stuffy in here."

"But it's freezing out there, my lady."

"I don't mind." And I didn't, not if opening the window meant hearing the river's songs properly.

Swinging open the casement, I leaned out into the night. Below me were the winter bones of the palace gardens; above me, the stars. Icy air flowed around me. I closed my eyes, listening.

An instant later, my eyes were bolt open. All I could hear of the Thames—the mighty Thames, running past the palace walls—was a faint snarl of bizarre melodies, flitting in and out on the breeze.

Something was terribly wrong.

Forcing myself to stay calm, I leaned a little farther out the window. For a moment, one line resolved into something that resembled a song-spell, but before I could even guess at its meaning, it blurred into discord again.

My hand went to the necklace my mother had given me. Once upon a time, the ruby-red stone had blocked the sound of Wild Magic—but by silencing the music, not distorting it. Besides, the power in the cracked stone had long since fled. Nevertheless, I pulled it off, just to be sure.

Still no song-spells. Nothing but the strange snarled notes, and even they were fading now.

My chest tightened, and I pulled back from the window. First the moonbriar song, and now this. *Something's wrong with my magic.*

"I did warn you, my lady," said a colorless voice behind me.

I whirled around to find Margery watching me. "Warn me? About what?"

"Why, about opening the window, my lady. It's far too cold at night." Margery reached past me and swung the casement shut, then turned her sharp eyes back on me. "What did you think I meant?"

"I—I wasn't quite sure." My hand tightened around my necklace as she continued to study me. *How can I defend myself if I can't sing magic?*

"Are you quite well, my lady?"

"I'm fine."

Margery kept studying me. "You look very white, my lady. Very peaky."

"I'm tired, that's all." I turned away from her searching gaze. "I think I'll go to bed now."

And so I did.

But sleep eluded me.

CHAPTER THIRTEEN
THE SNOWDROP

For many hours, I lay awake, listening for music and hearing none. Even my mother's letter, which I'd managed to hide from Margery, failed me. I could hear only the ghost of its soft, sweet voice. What was worse, however, was that I knew—having long since learned my mother's words by heart—that there wasn't anything in her letter that explained what was happening to me. I felt utterly alone.

At long last, exhaustion overwhelmed me, and I slipped into a restless sleep. When I woke again, I heard the click of a door closing in the darkness.

I lay in stillness for some moments, fearful that some intruder had entered the room. But as my eyes adjusted to the dim light of the half-banked fire, it occurred to me that perhaps the click had marked not someone coming in, but someone going out: Margery.

Sliding out from the covers, I pushed away the bed curtains and crept to the smaller room attached to my own, where Margery slept. She wasn't there. Did she have duties to attend to elsewhere? Or was this perhaps the hour she was expected to report to her spymaster?

Taking advantage of her absence, I raced to the window and pulled back the draperies. Along the eastern rim of the sky, the night was thinning out, but everywhere else it was still blue-black. No one was in sight. I flung the casement open and put my head out.

As the cold morning air rushed past my ears, the only sound I heard was the distant chirp of a stalwart robin, heralding the winter dawn. That and the merest hint of a discordant tune coming from the Thames.

It was even worse than yesterday. What on earth was happening?

Heart thudding, I told myself to be sensible. *I'll go down to the river. Perhaps if I stand right by it, I'll hear it properly.*

Knowing I had to slip away before Margery returned, or else face questions, I grabbed the first clothes I could find: the mulberry silk that Norrie had packed for me and that Margery herself had pressed yesterday. As with the blue wool, the skirts were a tad too short, the bodice a strain to put on. But it was ready to hand, and that was all I asked.

After fastening the last button, I let myself out. Only as the door clicked shut did I realize I should have had the foresight to bring a candle with me. It was so dark out here I could barely see my own hand on the doorknob.

"Lucy?"

I whirled around, heart racing. "Nat?"

I saw only a movement in the darkness, a shadow among

shadows. But a hand reached out to clasp mine—indisputably Nat's.

"So it *is* you." I let out a sharp breath. "What are you doing here?"

"I could ask the same of you."

I kept my voice below a whisper, afraid Wrexham or his spies might overhear. "I need to get down to the river."

"The river?" He sounded surprised. "They've cut off our access to it. They don't want anyone escaping that way."

"A window, then, as close to it as possible."

"Come with me."

His grip was warm and reassuring, but the palace seemed more of a maze than ever. At last we halted in a long room, dark except for a sliver of pale, gray light between two draperies. When Nat twitched them back, I saw the Thames.

But only saw. I heard no music.

My heart thudded again.

"We should be safe enough here for a while," Nat said.

"Can we open the window?" I asked.

"I think so. But why?"

I hated to say it out loud, but it had to be done. "Something's wrong with my magic." Swiftly I went over what had happened last night.

In the faint light from the windows, I saw his jaw tense. Before I was done speaking, he was pushing back the latch. "Try that."

I leaned out. Fifteen feet away, the wide River Thames rolled past, dark and deep and mysterious in the sullen not-quite-sunrise.

I closed my eyes and listened to the murky waves, lapping and gurgling against the brick palace walls.

This close, the river's music ought to have overwhelmed me. Strain as I might, however, I couldn't hear more than a few muted, dissonant notes.

"It's no use," I said at last—and then a faint melody, high and tremulous, emerged from the discord.

I went still. The song did not peter out, but instead swelled louder, spilling itself out before me: Wild Magic, a true song-spell. And not only that, but a song-spell I could understand, one for calling up mist. It reminded me of the song-spell I'd sung when the King's men had come, though of course there were differences. This was the Thames, after all, not an ocean; the songs couldn't be exactly the same.

"Do you hear something?" Nat whispered behind me.

"A song for mist. Shh . . ." I barely breathed the words, so afraid was I of losing the music.

Closing my eyes to concentrate, I gathered the song to me. Then I let it spin out again, my lips and tongue relishing every blessed note.

Even without opening my eyes, I knew the magic was working. The very air was changing; I could feel it thickening around me. Soon mist clung to my bare hands and face; it dampened my hair. Elated, I kept singing, following the line of the song even as it slid into odd cadences and strange rhythms. Half dreaming, I felt as if I were rising up into the mist myself, becoming part of the river, part of the air . . .

"Lucy!" Nat jerked me back from the window.

Furious that he'd broken my beautiful song, I opened my eyes. A second later I was staring at myself, horrified.

The air around me had not changed. All that was different was me: I was half-dissolved, more wraith than girl. When I tried to touch my hands together, they passed through each other like vapor.

Don't panic. Don't panic.

I put my hands to my cheeks and felt nothing.

Nat slammed the window shut, cutting off the music.

"My face." Even my voice sounded thin and far away. "Is it gone?"

"*You* were almost gone." Nat was beside himself. "One moment you were there, and the next you were thinning out into nothing. If I hadn't grabbed you when I did—"

"My face?" I asked again. "Nat, do I have a face?"

Nat made a visible effort to get hold of himself. "Yes," he said. "You have a face. Very ghostlike, but it's there. And the color's coming back to it."

Maybe it wasn't a permanent magic, then? I glanced down at my wispy hands again. They looked more substantial this time; they had the right shape. I touched my fingers together. This time they steepled properly; I felt the pads pressing against each other.

"That's better." My voice was almost normal now. I hoped the rest of me was too.

"What exactly did you think you were singing?" Nat said.

"A song to bring mist up from the river." I looked through the glass at the murky water below. What in heaven's name was happening to me? Was the world going mad? Or was I?

My face must have recovered enough to reveal my frantic thoughts, because Nat led me away from the window and sat me down in a low chair. I saw then that we were in a library. The walls were filled with books. It was too dark to read the titles, though, or even to guess how many volumes there were.

"All right," Nat said, kneeling beside me. "Let's think this through." Calmly, deliberately, he ticked off everything that had gone wrong with my magic. The moonbriar song. The strange, muffled music last night. The river song I'd just sung. "There may be one simple explanation behind all of it."

I made an effort to sound as rational as he did. "It might just be tiredness. Or illness. Sometimes they weaken me."

"As much as this?"

"After I defeated Scargrave, I was so exhausted that it took me weeks to hear magic again. Don't you remember?"

"Of course. But back then the problem was that you couldn't hear any magic, not that you heard the wrong magic. Besides, you haven't been fighting great battles lately. And you haven't been ill—or have you?" He searched my face with concern.

"No."

"So why?" Nat asked again. "Why has your magic gone wrong?"

"*I don't know.*" In distress, I went back to the window.

As I looked down on the dark river below, Nat came up

behind me, close enough that I could feel his warmth through the silk of my dress.

"Lucy, could someone be using magic against you?"

"I should think I'd be able to smell it, if someone were."

"Maybe you can't smell magic-making anymore," Nat said. "Just as you can't sing Proven Magic."

It was an awful possibility. I thought of Wrexham and his threats—his confidence that he knew how to deal with Chantresses—and again I almost told Nat about what he'd said to me. But I was too afraid of what Nat might do.

"I've never heard of a way of stopping Chantress magic," I said instead, arguing the thing out for myself. "If there were, wouldn't Scargrave have used it?"

"I reckon he would have," Nat admitted. "He used everything else."

"So maybe there isn't any magic at work here. Maybe the problem lies with me instead. Maybe there's something I've done, something I've sung, something I've eaten or drunk—*something* that's done this to me."

There was a definite note of panic in my voice now. Even I could hear it.

Nat laid his strong hands on my shoulders and gently turned me to face him. "Whatever's happened, it's not your fault."

I put my hands over his, trying to draw strength from them. It didn't work; I felt small and cold.

"We don't know that," I said. "And in the meantime, I'm trapped. They expect me to work magic here—and how can I do that when I can't trust what I hear?" I shut my eyes. *Wild Magic will betray you when you least expect it*, my godmother had warned me. Perhaps this was what she meant. It felt as if my world had turned upside down. "Oh, I wish I'd never left Norfolk!"

"I wish so too," said Nat. "But we'll get to the bottom of this, I promise."

"And in the meantime?"

"In the meantime, we'll put it about that you're not feeling well, and you'll keep safe in your rooms."

My rooms weren't safe with Margery there. But I couldn't explain that to Nat without telling him about Wrexham. . . .

"Only let in people you know," Nat was saying. "And if you have to go out, guard against strangers especially. This court is full of people who have no alibis, and who I wouldn't trust with tuppence."

"Such as?"

"Lord Gabriel, for one. He spent the Scargrave years in Sweden, studying alchemy, and somehow he's wangled his way into Sir Isaac's good graces. And then there's Sybil Dashwood. Her father was Lord Wycombe, but she and her mother lived on the Continent during the Scargrave years, and she's only just moved back. Nobody knows much about her."

"I met her last night," I told him. "Well, not *met*, exactly. Apparently we knew each other when we were children."

"Apparently?"

"Well, I don't remember her. But then I don't remember lots of things, you know. She says I spent a whole summer with her when I was seven."

"And you have no way of knowing if you really did?" Nat shook his head. "That's not good."

"It could be true, I guess. She said she comes from a Chantress family. I guess that's why my mother brought me there. But they don't have magic anymore."

"That's what she says, yes. But who knows what the truth is." Nat's anxiety for me was plain in his eyes. "Think about it, Lucy: she could know more about Chantress magic than anyone else here, barring you. Maybe she knows enough to interfere with it in some way. Don't let yourself be fooled by her—or by anyone else. Keep to yourself, if you can. I won't be able to visit you in the day, but at night I'll try and watch over your door."

I thought about how he'd been standing there in the darkness outside my room this morning. "Were you keeping watch last night?"

He looked abashed. "I couldn't sleep, so I came down," he admitted. "And there was this, too."

It was growing light now, light enough that I could clearly see the snowdrop he held out to me, fluttering like a tiny white dove on a slender green branch. "For you," he said. "For Valentine's Day."

I forgot my fears in a rush of surprised delight. *The first man you meet on Valentine's Day will be your sweetheart,* Sybil had said, but I hadn't remembered it till now. "Oh, Nat. It's beautiful."

I reached to take it from his hand, then stopped. There was something wrong in his expression, something painful. He had the eyes of a man who wants what he cannot have.

"Nat?"

He wrapped my fingers around the snowdrop. "The letters. The visit. I said I would explain."

What could the explanation be, to make him look like that? My hand tightened around the flower.

"It started after you left last summer," Nat said. "Wrexham and his cronies on the Council wanted to know where you'd gone. At first the King wouldn't say, but eventually they convinced him that your whereabouts were a state matter, and he agreed they should have a voice in any decisions he made about you. It was about then that Sir Barnaby became ill and had to resign. I was away at the time—I'd been out in the countryside for weeks, learning as much as I could about the blight—but when I got back, I found myself up in front of Wrexham and his handpicked committee, being questioned about my letters to you and my visit to Norfolk and . . . other things." His face reddened.

"They had no right." I was angry on his behalf. Angry on mine.

"But that's just it," Nat said. "The King has decided they do have the right. The right to decide who gets to visit you, who can send letters to you, who can communicate with you in any way. And more than that—"

"There's *more?*"

"Much more." The flush on his cheeks deepened till it looked like a burn. "Lucy, they get to decide who you marry."

CHAPTER FOURTEEN
HEARTS AND FLOWERS

I was so shocked, I nearly lost hold of the snowdrop. I was seventeen, it was true, but I had imagined that marriage was still some years away for me. And I had always assumed that when the time came, I could marry whomsoever I chose.

Nat wouldn't meet my eyes. "It's a matter of state, they say. And Lucy—they've told me quite plainly that I'm not on the list of candidates."

I stared at him, dumbfounded. Had Nat told the Council he wanted to marry me? Or had they interrogated him simply because of his letters? I didn't have the heart to ask. If there was to be talk of marriage between us, this was not how I wanted the conversation to run.

Nat's cheeks were still an angry red. "I don't have the necessary standing, they say. They don't want me anywhere near you. At first I thought it was because I turned down the knighthood the King offered me last year, back when we defeated Scargrave."

He glanced at me now, as if asking forgiveness. "I'm afraid I just couldn't see my way to it—all that bowing and scraping, and being called 'Sir.' I'm an engineer and a scientist, not a courtier."

"I understand." His independent spirit was part of what had drawn me to him. I'd be a hypocrite to want anything else from him now.

"But it turns out that the key issue isn't my lack of a title. According to the Council, it's that I know nothing about my family, my lineage."

I mentally cursed Court snobbery. Nat had been orphaned young and sold into servitude; he had no real memory of his parents. He'd needed courage and strength to survive such a childhood, but some people looked down on him because he'd once been a servant. "What does that matter? You are you, and there's an end to it. Your worth has nothing to do with your bloodline."

"That's not . . ." He strode to the window. "Oh, Hades. This is damnably hard to talk about."

"Nat, whatever it is, tell me." What piece was I still missing?

"It's a matter of breeding."

I didn't follow at first. "Breeding?"

He wouldn't look at me. "If you are to produce more Chantresses, you must be married to a man who is of Chantress lineage himself."

"This is about *children*?"

"Yes."

I tried to pull myself together. "But it makes no sense. Why should the Council care if I marry a man of Chantress lineage? Men can't inherit Chantress powers."

"Not in any detectable way, no." Nat's voice was even, but I could hear the strain in it. "It seems, however, that the sons of Chantresses carry something of their mother's blood inside them, all the same. If they or their issue marry a Chantress, their bloodline strengthens the magic in the family. If a Chantress marries an outsider, she weakens her blood, and over time the magic in the family is lost."

My body went cold, then hot. "And why should this concern the Council? Do they expect me to produce a line of Chantresses for their own benefit?"

He turned from the window, and I saw my own anger and frustration mirrored in his face.

"The Council is undecided." He clipped the words tight. "Most wish you to marry a man of Chantress lineage, in order to produce more Chantresses. But others wish you to marry a man without such lineage, since they mistrust Chantress power." Quietly, he added, "Either way, I have no standing, for I do not know what my bloodline is."

I could not bear this. I *would* not bear this.

"I shall go to the King." Still clutching the snowdrop, I turned toward the door. "I shall go to him straightaway and tell him this must be stopped."

"He won't listen, Lucy."

"He must. It's my business who I marry, and when. Not the Council's."

"And you think he'll agree with that?" Nat's eyes were bleak. "King Henry—whose own marriage is a matter of state scheming? The Council is brokering an alliance for him now, and let me tell you, there's no room for sentiment there."

This stopped me in my tracks. "And he accepts this?"

"As a matter of duty, yes. And he will take it very badly if you do not do the same."

My hand crushed the fresh green stem of the snowdrop. "So you think that's what I should do, then? Take the first suitor the Council appoints for me?" I tried to keep my voice from shaking.

"No!" He crossed the few steps between us. "That's not what I think at all."

"What, then?"

Before he could respond, distant voices broke the silence. I started in alarm. The household was waking.

"I have an idea." Nat spoke low and fast. "But it's going to take some time to work out."

"Can I help?"

"It's better if you don't. For now, just keep out of sight. The Council is still arguing over who you should marry, and I doubt they'll be able to settle on anyone soon. It's possible that they'll even let the matter drop for a while—especially if you aren't ever seen with me."

I cast an anxious glance at the door behind me. The voices were coming closer. "If we're not careful, they're going to see us together right now."

He nodded toward a door on the other side of the room. "Not if I head out that way. Will you be all right here?"

I nodded. "Go, before they catch you! And be safe."

Quick as the wind, he kissed my cheek and sprinted for the door. A moment after it closed behind him, the door on the other side of the room opened.

"Perhaps she's in here," said a laughing voice, and a young man strode into the room. As the light caught him fully in the face, I saw it was Lord Gabriel.

"Ah, my lady Chantress!" He swept a bow.

Behind him, Sir Samuel Deeps barreled in, his lace cravat askew under his puffy cheeks. "My dear lady!"

Another man piled in behind them. "Lady Chantress—"

"Oh no, you don't." Elbowing them both away, Lord Gabriel offered me a frilly bunch of rosebuds with a flourish. "For you, Chantress."

I looked at the bouquet as if it were a nest of snakes. Was he *courting* me?

"I am the first, am I not?" Lord Gabriel said, bringing the flowers closer. When I still didn't answer, he clarified, "The first man to see you this morning. Your valentine."

I couldn't give Nat away. My hand closed around his snow-drop, keeping it from sight as I slipped it into the linen ruffles of my sleeve. I accepted the roses. "How kind of you."

The others had valentine offerings for me too. As they bestowed them upon me, more courtiers piled in, bearing still more flowers and sweets. For some, perhaps, it was merely a game, but their avid expressions confused and repelled me. Were they angling for marriage—and perhaps the chance to control small Chantresses of their own?

Receiving their attentions was a miserable business. They expected me to flirt with them, but banter didn't come easily to my lips. When at last I escaped to my room, pleading fatigue, I dropped every one of their bouquets on the floor.

Although the room had been straightened and a breakfast tray had been laid, Margery evidently had gone off again. A quick scout of the room assured me that I was all alone. Carefully I retrieved Nat's snowdrop from my sleeve, only to find that it had snapped off its stem and lay crushed against my palm.

At the sight, something inside me snapped too. I tucked the snowdrop into my bodice and went back out into the hall.

I don't care what Nat says. I'm going to the King. This marriage business has to stop.

CHAPTER FIFTEEN
AN AUDIENCE WITH THE KING

It was not quite as easy to see the King as I had imagined. To be admitted to his presence, I had to pass through a host of guards, stewards, and secretaries. At last, however, I was invited into an antechamber outside his staterooms.

"Wait here," a steward told me. "The King is meeting with the Inner Council, but I will let him know you wish to see him."

He slipped through a high, arched door into the next room. The door didn't quite catch. Through the crack I glimpsed a small group of councillors seated around a table, and I could hear some of what they were saying.

"It's time we dealt with Boudicca." Wrexham was speaking, and he sounded angry. "My scouts say the wretched woman has upward of a thousand followers now, all moving toward London."

"Do her followers still include women and children?" the King asked.

"Yes, Your Majesty." I recognized Rowan Knollys's voice. Was he one of the scouts? "Perhaps as many as half are women and children. But some of the men—and even a few of the women— are armed."

"Has she responded to our emissaries?" was the King's next question.

"Yes, Your Majesty," Knollys said. "She says she did not order these people to come with her, but she cannot prevent them from following her if they choose. She will not drive them off when they have nothing. She still maintains that she is coming to Greenwich merely to obey your summons, Your Majesty. When we suggested she come alone, she refused. She said we must have misunderstood your instructions, for the King would never fear his own people."

"Shades of Wat Tyler," Lord Roxburgh said.

"Surely not," Sir Samuel protested. "That was three hundred years ago."

"What does that matter?" Wrexham growled. "His name lives on, and so do the stories: how Wat Tyler took over London with his thieving peasant followers, how they murdered and pillaged as they went. We need to stop Boudicca before she does the same."

"I'm not convinced—" The King broke off, and I heard nothing but murmurs. Then the King spoke again. "My lords and gentlemen, the Chantress wishes to speak with me. I must leave you for a short while. You will, of course, make no decisions while I am gone."

Moments later, the King and his steward came through the

door. At a word from the King, the steward rushed away, and the King came toward me. "My lady Chantress. How good to see you!"

"And you, Your Majesty." Although it had taken me a while to reach him, now I was glad I'd persisted. Up close, the King looked strained—he had shadows under his eyes, and stubble along his pale jaw—but he seemed genuinely glad to see me.

"What news do you bring?" He guided me through another door, this one leading into what appeared to be a small study. Set against its elaborately carved walls was a vast desk inlaid with mother-of-pearl.

"News?"

"About the crucible." He gazed at me eagerly. "That's why you've come, isn't it? You've thought of a magic to find it?"

I shook my head. "No, Your Majesty." I didn't dare tell him that my magic was dangerously broken. I wasn't sure he'd believe me, and even if he did, he might react badly. "The trail is cold," I said instead. "I have thought and thought about it, but at this point I see nothing that can be done."

The King's face fell. "You cannot help us?"

"I would if I could, Your Majesty. I am sorry."

The King crossed his arms over his chest. "You have no hope to offer? Nothing else to say?"

This was going to be a more difficult interview than I'd thought. But there was no point waiting to put my case to him. He had interrupted a meeting for me, and he was not an easy man to see. "Yes, I do have something to say, Your Majesty. Not about the crucible, but about another important matter: this business of marriage."

"Yes?" He was still listening, but his face was now set in stern lines.

"You cannot do it," I said. "You cannot let your Council marry me off."

"*Cannot*, Chantress?"

Despite the warning in his voice, I couldn't contain myself. "Surely I have a right to decide for myself—"

"No," the King said.

His flat denial floored me. "No?"

"Legally speaking, you have no such right," the King said. "With all due respect, you are a female, under the age of majority—"

"I'm a *Chantress*. That makes a difference."

The King frowned. "Yes: it makes it all the more vital that the Council take a hand in determining your future."

I couldn't believe quite how much he had changed. "When I was last at Court, you cared as much about my opinion as that of the Council's."

The King didn't blink. "Your opinion still matters to me, of course."

"But not as much as the Council's?"

"Should it, when you chose to leave me, and they stayed by my side?"

I stared at him. Was that how he saw me? As a deserter?

"You had your reasons, I am sure," he said without rancor. "But still, that is the truth of it. Since you left, the country has had to weather many crises, and I have needed to lean heavily on my Council to get through them. Whatever their individual failings, I could not keep the kingdom together without them."

I remembered what Nat had said: *Wrexham has the power to split England in two.*

"To rule is to make hard choices," the King said. "I have to think always of the country as a whole. And that means I must ask everyone to compromise.

"But let us try to find common ground," he went on. "You are loyal to me, I know; you swore your fealty. And I know, too, that you love your country. So this should not be so difficult. All I ask is that you serve your country as best you can. Your magic must strengthen us, not weaken us."

"I agree." He had spoken of compromise, so perhaps there was room for hope. "What I don't understand is why that means the Council should choose my husband."

"No? Think what would happen if you were to fall in love with a scoundrel or a schemer, Chantress. Don't you see that the whole country could be put at risk? That's why we need to find a man who can look after you properly, a man who has the good of the country at heart."

A man to look after me? "You don't think it's enough that *I* have the good of the country at heart? I am the one who restored your kingdom to you, after all."

I had gone too far.

The King looked at me, his gaze hard as steel. "You did, yes. And I am grateful. But that is exactly why we must be so careful.

You have a great deal of power, and it must be managed wisely."

The world fears women with power. . . .

"I really don't see—" I began, but the King cut me off.

"Enough. I ask no more of you than I ask of myself. My own marriage is a matter of state as well. My wife will be determined by the deliberations of the Council. That is a burden that those of us with great power must bear." His eyes looked more shadowed than ever. "I regret any pain it causes you, but truly, our lives are not our own."

I started to speak, but he was already halfway over the threshold. "The next time you come to me, Chantress, I hope you bring better news."

As he slipped back into his meeting, the steward appeared at my side. Although his offer to show me the way out was couched politely, I knew I had been dismissed.

Unwilling to be treated this way, I turned to the door that the King had walked through, then froze as I heard Wrexham shouting behind it.

"The Chantress refused to help? How dare she!" A thump and a scrape like a chair being pushed back. "Is she still out there?"

The King started to say something, but I didn't wait to hear more. Racing after the steward, I left the state apartments as fast as I dared.

CHAPTER SIXTEEN

BOXED IN

After escaping the King's apartments, I wanted to barricade myself alone in my rooms. But I knew Margery would be waiting for me there, so instead, I wandered in whatever direction seemed quietest. I felt sunk in defeat. Nat was right: the King was not going to listen to me. Not when he saw the Council as the true power in the kingdom. Not when Wrexham was his right-hand man.

What was I to do?

Up ahead, a clutch of young men crowded together. Fearing they might be more suitors, I darted away through a narrow doorway—and bumped into Penebrygg.

"My dear!" He fumbled for his hat, which had slipped down to meet his spectacles. "I'm afraid I walked right into you." And then, after straightening his spectacles, "My dear Lucy, are you quite all right?"

It was quiet around us; no one was there to overhear. "No," I said. "No, I'm not." And I told him about the audience with the King.

Dear old Penebrygg! His brow furrowed in sympathy as I spoke.

". . . and so there's no hope," I finished.

"I would not go quite so far as that, my dear. It is not a good situation, I agree. But of course there is hope. As of yet, the Council cannot agree who is to be your husband. As you can imagine, it is a contentious subject. The Earl of Wrexham, for instance, has suggested it should be his son—"

"His son!"

"You might not want to speak quite so loudly, my dear." Penebrygg looked cautiously about. Seeing no one, he continued in a low voice, "Really, it shouldn't surprise you: Wrexham craves power, after all, and he would like to commandeer yours for his family. Yet there are obstacles. For one, his son is not yet fifteen, which is rather young for marriage."

"And rather young for me," I put in.

"Yes. And it's said he takes after his mother and is rather frail. Wrexham denies it, of course, but we all notice he has yet to bring the boy to Court."

It sounded as if a match with Wrexham's son was not so likely after all. My spirits rose a notch.

"And, of course," said Penebrygg, "others on the Council wish to advance candidates of their own—sometimes even themselves."

"So I've gathered." And I had a mountain of bouquets to prove it.

"Indeed, there are so many rival candidates that the Council has been deadlocked. I expect it will be some months before any decision can be reached. And perhaps before then you will be able to put an end to the discussion altogether."

"How can I do that when the King won't even listen to me?"

Penebrygg pushed back his velvet cap. "He would listen to you, my dear, if you found the crucible for him."

It was true: if I could find the crucible, the King would almost certainly grant me a hearing—and possibly much more than that. I remembered how eager he'd been to reward me the last time I'd helped him.

"But I don't know any song-spells for finding it," I told Penebrygg.

Indeed, the situation was a hundred times worse than that, though I didn't tell Penebrygg so. He was a good friend, but the fewer people who knew how weak I was, the better.

"Well, that's a pity," Penebrygg said. "But I wouldn't assume all is lost. Something may come to you. And you might be able to set us on the right trail without magic. Singing isn't your only gift. You have a good head on your shoulders too. Perhaps you will see something the rest of us have missed."

"After all this time?"

"Time is often the friend of truth," he said. "And of course I will help you in any way I can." He pushed his spectacles down his nose. "It might be useful, for instance, if you knew a bit more about alchemy—and about the crucible as well. Sir Isaac gave a good summary yesterday, but there's more to learn if you care to hear it."

As ever, there was something cheering in Penebrygg's commonsense approach to even the most deplorable circumstances. If nothing else, he made me realize that I was accepting defeat too easily.

"All right, then," I said. "I'd like to hear more about the crucible. And about alchemy, too." Whatever Nat thought of the Philosopher's Stone, it was clear Penebrygg was staking everything on it. And when it came down to it, he had far more experience than Nat had—and so, of course, did Sir Isaac. I ought to learn as much as I could from them. Perhaps it would help me to see the situation more clearly.

Penebrygg's eyes gleamed. "It's a fascinating subject, my dear—"

He broke off as a footman came racing up to us.

"Doctor Penebrygg!" The footman bowed, panting for breath. "The Inner Council calls you to the Crimson Chamber. They have questions about the alchemical furnace. You're to bring the calculations on fuel."

"Ah." Straightening his floppy cap, Penebrygg gave me an apologetic smile. "I'm afraid the Inner Council waits for no man, my dear, especially on a matter concerning alchemy. I must go. But shall we talk again soon?"

"Please," I said.

After he followed the footman out, I walked on, feeling encouraged for the first time since my magic had gone. Penebrygg was right: I might not have magic, but that didn't mean finding the crucible was impossible. I could keep my eyes and ears open—and while I was at it, I might also discover some clue to why my magic had gone.

Long odds, perhaps, but it seemed a better prospect than huddling in my room with Margery.

I could start, perhaps, by visiting the Treasury and talking to the guards. Or by going to the alchemy laboratory myself—

Slippers tapped behind me. I whirled around.

"There you are!" Sybil bounced toward me, her carnation skirts swaying like petals in a storm, her hair charmingly topsy-turvy. "You must come and visit me. I've been looking for you everywhere."

"Have you?" I made myself smile, but it was difficult. A visit with Sybil wasn't part of my plan.

"Oh yes. Your maid is quite upset with you for vanishing, you know. But never mind." Sybil laced her arm through mine. "I've found you first, so I shall claim you. Come see my rooms."

She tugged my arm, but I remembered Nat's warning and slipped free. "I'm not sure I can. I need to"—it seemed unwise to tell her the truth—"to see the seamstresses."

"Oh, that's all settled. I heard your maid say that you're to visit them this afternoon. But that's not for a few hours, so you've plenty of time to stop by my rooms. They're just around the corner." She looked closely at my face. "My dear, are you sure you're quite well? Perhaps I should call Margery after all."

So she knew my maid's name. Hardly sinister, I supposed, but it threw me. Surely they weren't allies?

"No," I said quickly. "No, I'm fine. I didn't have breakfast, but—"

"No breakfast? Then you really must come to my room." Sybil took my arm again. "I've loads to eat." When I still hesitated, she teased, "If you don't come, I'll tell Margery you're on the verge of collapse. And then your life won't be your own."

Her voice was merry and kind, but she'd boxed me in. Seeing no way out, I agreed to go with her.

With a squeal of delight, Sybil whisked me off, and I wondered what was in store for me.

CHAPTER SEVENTEEN
PROSPECTS

Sybil's rooms, unlike mine, were locked. A slender key sufficed to open them, and she led me in. The main chamber was smaller than mine, but it was hung with equally fine tapestries—of the moon goddess Diana—and it had an equally warm fire.

It also held a great many nosegays.

Sybil caught me looking at them. "So many flowers!" She bent down to smell some violets, then glanced at me, eyes laughing. "Though not half as many as you received yourself, I hear."

I was still taking in all her own tributes—a comforting sight, especially since many were an exact match of mine. Perhaps I had not been singled out after all. Or at least not as much as I'd feared.

"It seems you had plenty of visitors too," I said. "And what's more, yours were clever enough to bring vases."

"Oh, *they* didn't think of vases. My maid Joan did." Sybil's rich voice rang out like a bell. "Joan?"

Wizened as a dried crabapple, a head popped out from behind a small connecting door.

"Ah, there you are." Sybil threw her arm around the tiny woman. "Come and meet the Lady Chantress, if you please. Do you remember when she came to visit us, years ago? Or no—you were with Aunt Goring that summer, weren't you?"

So Joan couldn't prove or disprove Sybil's story. How frustrating. I wished yet again that Norrie were here; she would have known the truth of the matter. After all, Sybil had claimed she had come on the visit too.

Which, come to think of it, was a great point in Sybil's favor. Why make such a claim if Norrie could disprove it once she arrived? I felt myself relax a little.

"A pleasure to meet you, my lady." Wrinkles deepening as she drew closer, Joan bobbed a curtsy.

I flushed. I'd had people curtsy to me at Court last year, after Scargrave's defeat, but I still wasn't used to it. I turned to Sybil, feeling clumsy and out of my element—and badly dressed as well. In bright midday light, it was all too obvious that I had outgrown my mulberry silk. Sybil, in her billowing curves of satin, looked far more elegant.

Sybil gave no sign that she noticed any difference between us. "Come and have something to eat," she urged me. "I've biscuits here and currant buns, and a basket of fruit. Do you like grapes? Peaches?"

Her side table, overflowing with delicious tidbits, would have tempted even someone far less hungry than I.

"Is that a pineapple?" The fruit was so rare that I'd only tasted it once before, when I'd been King Henry's guest last year.

"Yes." Sybil's cheeks turned rosy as she laughed. "King Henry sent it—I think as a way of making amends for our prolonged stay here. I haven't a knife big enough to cut it, though. Not here. Perhaps you'd prefer an apple instead?" She held one out to me, bloodred and perfect.

It looked almost too good to be real—and despite Sybil's warmth, I couldn't entirely forget Nat's warning. I needed to be on my guard.

"I'll have this orange instead." Still in its peel, plucked from the bowl at random, it seemed a safer bet than a hand-picked apple.

But it seemed my fears had been overblown, for Sybil accepted my choice with cheerful good grace. "Please, take whatever you like." She handed me a plate and turned to Joan. "I'm so sorry, but I'm afraid Aunt Goring's run out of red silk for her embroidery. She wants you to run some more down to her."

Joan rummaged through a sewing basket. "I told her she'd need more." With another small bob to me, she left.

I took a bun from the basket—Sybil had already eaten several, to judge from the crumbs—and added it to my plate. Seating myself in an embroidered chair, I smiled at Sybil. While I was here, I might as well try and learn as much about her as possible.

"I don't think I've met your aunt," I said.

"She has the adjoining room to mine. But she's out now. Working on her everlasting embroidery and drumming up a match for me while she's at it, no doubt." For the first time, Sybil's laugh sounded strained.

"You don't care for the prospects she has in mind?"

"It's not that I don't care for them, exactly. It's just that it's hard to have her hawking me about like a prize cow." Sybil deepened her voice to an auctioneer's patter: *"Finest cow in three counties, of excellent breeding and fortune, comes with her own golden bridle . . ."*

She caught my eye and grinned. "Well, I suspect Aunt Goring doesn't put it quite like that. . . . Still, it's a humiliation to know that she's flogging my charms to anyone who will listen." She shook her head. "But what am I doing, complaining to you? At least I don't have the entire Council talking about me as if I were a brood mare."

My hands stilled on the half-peeled orange.

Sybil touched her hand to her lips. "Oh dear. That came out all wrong. And now I've offended you."

"I'm not offended." I started peeling the orange again. After all, what she'd said was no more than the truth. "I'm just . . . surprised. I didn't know the Council's plans for me were common knowledge."

"I'm afraid it's the talk of the Court." Brightly, she added, "But I don't believe it's reached most of London yet. Or so Aunt Goring says. And she should know, as she's the worst gossip of them all."

I winced. It had not even occurred to me that the affair would be discussed in London.

"Don't take it to heart," Sybil said. "In the end, it's just talk, you know."

"*Just* talk?"

Sybil nodded. "We're lucky, you know. Most girls have their husbands chosen for them. But you're like me—you don't have to marry if you don't want to."

It wasn't as simple as that, I thought, but all I said was, "You don't?"

"No. I've some money from Mama, you see, and a larger inheritance that comes to me when I turn twenty-one, according to Father's will. I needn't rush to marry anyone."

So Sybil was rich. I ought to have guessed that from her beautiful clothes and her confident manner. "And yet your aunt is trying to find you a husband?"

"Oh, Aunt Goring is a born meddler. She and Uncle want me to marry well and give luster to the family name." Sybil rolled her eyes. "It drives me mad, the way she goes on about it. But what can I do? I'm only seventeen. If I went about on my own, it would be a scandal. And when you come down to it, Aunt Goring's bark is worse than her bite. She fancies herself a matchmaker, it's true, but she's not actually tried to make me marry anybody. And she doesn't watch me closely; she's too much of a gadabout for that. If I ever wanted to, I expect I could elope without too much trouble."

I stopped eating my orange. "And do you? Want to elope, I mean?"

"Heavens, no! I'm not attached to anyone that way." Sybil blushed. "The men who flock around me are mostly fortune-hunters. I'd rather have my independence." She cast me an inquiring glance. "Though I hear it's different with you?"

I carefully freed another section of orange. "Is that part of the gossip too?"

"There's something between you and Nat Walbrook, isn't there? Is he as dangerous as he looks?"

"Dangerous?"

"So still and watchful, and yet so sure when he moves. And then there are those eyes, and those shoulders." She gave a playful shiver. "I noticed him right away—and I'm not the only one, I can assure you. But he's not one to flirt. I learned that quite quickly. And then I heard about the two of you, and how you were in love, and everything became clear." She sighed. "It's *so* romantic."

I shook my head. "The Council doesn't think so."

"Well," said Sybil, "from their point of view, it's an unconventional match, you have to admit."

"Unconventional?"

"Well, he hasn't much money, has he? And no one knows where he comes from. And he's not exactly made a name for himself at Court. Last I heard, they nearly kicked him off the Council."

I bristled.

Sybil saw. "I'm not speaking for myself, my dear. I'm just explaining how the Council sees it. And then, of course, there's the question of children and magic. That matters very much to the Council too." She looked at me questioningly. "It doesn't matter to you?"

"I—I've never thought much about it."

"No?" Sybil dimpled. "Lucky you. I've spent half my life listening to talk about children and magic and bloodlines. Mama went on about it endlessly."

Did she, indeed? I leaned forward. Maybe it was unwise to expose my own ignorance, but how was I to learn anything if I didn't take some chances? Besides, it was time I turned the tables: I wanted to be the one asking the questions, not answering them.

"Sybil, is it true what they say?" I asked. "Can a Chantress only pass on her magic if she marries a man with Chantress blood?"

Sybil shot me a puzzled look. "You don't know? No one ever explained it to you?"

"No." My mother's brief letter had not mentioned Chantress marriage. Nor had my godmother said anything about it. Though come to think of it, Lady Helaine had taken a great interest in ancestors and bloodlines. Perhaps this was why.

I lowered my voice. "Tell me everything you can, please. I need to understand how it works."

Sybil was happy to explain matters to me. "A great deal depends on the Chantress's magic, you know. If she has a tremendous amount—as they used to, in the old days—then her daughters will have magic too, even if the father is of ordinary lineage. It won't be as strong in them, however, and that's the trouble. Eventually the blood gets so weak that the magic is lost altogether."

"Is that what happened in your family?"

"Yes. My grandmother had magic, but only a little, and when she married out, that was the end of it. Her daughters—my mother and her sister—had none."

"You mean the magic is gone from your family forever?"

She nodded. "I must say, it ate away at Mama. She married my father in part because he had Chantress lineage—quite a few old families do—and when I was born, she was convinced I would be a Chantress. But our family's ability to work magic is truly gone, even if it took Mama a long time to accept that." She took a biscuit and asked curiously, "What about you? Did your mother marry in?"

"I don't know. I don't know if *she* knew. My father died before I was born." Was it all right to tell her this? I wasn't sure. But it wasn't as if it revealed very much.

"Who was he?"

"His name was John." I only knew that because of what my mother had written in her letter. "He was a music teacher, my mother said."

Sybil's eyes widened. "A music teacher? And your mother was being raised by Lady Helaine Audelin? That *was* daring."

"She was a daring sort of woman, I think." Once again, I wished—oh, how I wished!—that I had known her better.

"She loved him?"

"Yes." That had come through in every brief word she'd written about him.

"That must have helped, then. And a musician, too: that's good. They're more likely to have Chantress blood, you know." She looked at me appraisingly. "Maybe that's why you're so powerful."

"Maybe." I had always thought of my magic as coming from

my mother. It was disconcerting to think it might have come through my father's line too.

"Anyway, you can see why the Council is so worked up about finding you the right husband. Marry the wrong man, and your daughters might have half the power you do—or possibly no power at all. It's an awful gamble, from their perspective."

"But what if I only have sons? Has the Council thought about that?"

"I suppose they would expect you to keep trying for a daughter—just as they expect a queen to keep trying for a son. But yes, sometimes a Chantress has only sons, or no children at all. And it certainly would be a disappointment to the Council if that happened." Thoughtfully she added, "It used to be, of course, that a Chantress with no daughters could choose to give her power instead to a male with Chantress blood. Mama told me that Chantresses sometimes passed on their magic to sons that way. But that doesn't happen anymore. I suppose it's another part of Chantress lore that's been lost."

"Male Chantresses?" I shook my head, not sure how much of this to believe. "I've never heard of such a thing."

"That's because they don't exist," Sybil said. "In men, the power comes out differently; they're not spell-singers, but wizards. Very powerful wizards. Or so Mama told me, anyway." She sighed. "Not that you could believe everything Mama had to say about magic. Half of it was hearsay, and the rest . . . well, she had some rather odd friends, if I do say so myself."

"Oh? Who were they?" I tried to sound as if I didn't care much about the answer, but Nat's voice was a whisper in my mind: *She and her mother lived on the Continent. . . . Nobody knows much about her. . . .*

"You mean *what* were they." Sybil grimaced. "Fortune-tellers, card-readers, conjurers, prophets, even a few alchemists. If they said they had magic, Mama made time for them. Though, of course, when it came to Chantresses, it was Mama herself who was the expert. Not just because of the family connection, you understand, but because she had made such a study of them."

As Sybil pushed the last of the biscuits my way, I went back to the word that had caught my ears. "What were the alchemists like?"

She grinned. "A rather tiresome lot, to be honest. Always going on about their metals and transitions and distillations and whatnot. And endlessly wheedling whatever money they could get from Mama for their experiments. They would have killed to get hold of Sir Isaac's crucible. I can't tell you how happy I was to leave them behind."

"And now you're surrounded by alchemists again."

She gave a wry laugh. "So I am. It seems they're my fate. Though I will say the alchemists here are a much more impressive bunch than the ones who followed Mama about. A pity they've lost their crucible, though." She touched my sleeve. "Is it true you're going to find it for them? That's what Aunt Goring says."

"That's what they'd like me to do, yes." I picked my words with care, determined not to reveal any weakness. "They were hoping I could find it instantly, but my songs . . . well, that's not the way they work."

Sybil nodded sympathetically. "I remember Grandmama telling me that all the best finding songs had been lost. People think Chantresses can do anything, though. They don't understand that our magic has limits." She stopped herself. "I mean Chantress magic, of course."

"The Council certainly doesn't," I said.

"You've only tried songs, then?" Sybil asked. "Nothing else?"

I sat back in my chair. What a peculiar question.

"What else is there to try?" I asked slowly.

CHAPTER EIGHTEEN
A VALENTINE'S VISIT

"Some Chantresses have a talent for other kinds of magic," Sybil said. "Didn't you know that?"

I hadn't. But the idea alone was encouraging. If spell-singing was barred to me, perhaps I could find some more magic elsewhere.

"Have you ever tried anything but singing?" Sybil asked.

"No. Never."

Her face lit up. "You're a novice, then? Oh, this *is* exciting. We could experiment, you and I, and see if there's anything else there."

"Experiment how?" Though I longed to hear more, I kept my voice neutral. I didn't want Sybil to guess how important her answer might be.

"Oh, I know all kinds of tricks, believe me. Most of Mama's friends were charlatans, but a few had the genuine spark, and they taught me a great deal. Nothing I could do myself, more's the pity. But I daresay I know enough to guide you." She looked about the room eagerly, as if searching for a place to start. "Here, why don't we try—"

A knock at the door cut off her suggestion.

"Oh dear." Sybil rose with a disappointed air. "That will be Joan. We'll have to stop for now."

"You don't want her to know?"

Sybil shook her head. "Joan wouldn't approve at all. She thinks it's dangerous to mess about with such things."

"*Is* it dangerous?"

"Oh, she exaggerates. It's not dangerous at all. At least, not often."

"Not often?" I echoed in concern.

Sybil was already in the vestibule, however, and didn't answer. From where I sat, I couldn't even see her—or the door.

"Oh, do let me in," I heard a man say.

"It's not a good time," Sybil murmured.

"It's always a good time. You're my valentine, remember?"

"Am I, indeed?" Sybil sounded exasperated. "Oh, come in, then. I can see I'm not going to get rid of you."

"How very kind." A young man strode in, all velvet and smiles: Lord Gabriel.

When he saw me, his smile slipped away. "Oh, er . . . I didn't realize you were here. . . ."

"No, I suppose you didn't," I said. "Not with all that talk about valentines." I spoke without rancor; I was pleased to have proof that his pursuit of me this morning had not been entirely serious.

Sybil looked at me with raised eyebrows. "You had one from him too?" was all she said, but when I nodded, she started to laugh.

Lord Gabriel looked at us both with some chagrin, and then—to my surprise—he laughed too. "Caught red-handed," he admitted. "But can you blame me? After all, who wouldn't want to claim you both, if he could?"

He gave us a slightly sheepish but admiring grin. I caught myself grinning back. Overambitious he might be, and a tad conceited, but he could laugh even when the joke was on him, and I liked that.

"So tell me, then, what have you two ladies been talking about?" He advanced into the room. "Not valentines, I hope."

"Never," I said crisply as Sybil and I sat back down by the fire.

"Or beaux, or dancing?"

"As a matter of fact," Sybil said, "we were talking about alchemists."

"Were you, indeed?" He looked at us, one to another. "And what did you have to say about them? Or should I say—*us*?"

"Oh, we weren't talking about you," I said. "I was asking Sybil some questions about alchemy, that's all."

Lord Gabriel drew up a chair. "What do you want to know?"

"Oh, anything and everything. I know so little—only what was mentioned in the Council meeting." I'd meant to learn more about it from Penebrygg, but I figured I could do worse than glean some facts here, especially if it taught me a bit more about Lord Gabriel, too.

"Be careful what you wish for, my friend," Sybil warned. "Gabriel can talk about the subject till the stars fall from the sky. The trouble is getting him to stop."

"Dear lady, you cut me to the heart." Lord Gabriel grinned at Sybil, evidently enjoying the banter. "I spent nine years studying alchemy, and now you would forbid me from so much as mentioning the subject?"

"Out of sheer self-defense, yes," Sybil said.

"Nine years?" I was surprised. "How old were you when you started, Lord Gabriel?"

"Oh, leave off the Lord bit, if you please, Chantress. Gabriel will do nicely." Still grinning, he sat back to consider. "Let's see. . . . I suppose I was not quite ten."

"And your parents didn't mind?"

"They weren't there. When Scargrave came to power, they sent me to live with family friends in Sweden; it was hoped I would be safer there. It was a strange sort of household, though. The first tutor hired for me turned out to be a closet alchemist. It took me a few months to ferret out what he was doing, but once I did, he agreed to share some of his secrets."

"There was more to it than that, I seem to recall," Sybil said.

"Well, there was a spot of blackmail involved, if that's what you're referring to," said Gabriel. "He'd never have told me anything if he hadn't been afraid of exposure."

"You were blackmailing people at nine?" I said.

"Ten, by then," said Gabriel, unruffled. "Anyway, from then on I was hooked. I didn't want to do anything else."

"Surely they made you study other subjects too?"

"Oh yes. But none of them ever interested me half as much as alchemy. After all, you don't get rich studying mathematics, do you? Or Latin, or logic, or astronomy—or any of the other things tutors tried to cram down my throat. Only alchemy can give you wealth, give you power."

"If you're lucky," I said.

"But I *am* lucky." Gabriel stretched out his booted legs with a confidence that bordered on cockiness. "I'm here in Greenwich Palace, and Sir Isaac has selected me to help him create the Philosopher's Stone. Talk about good fortune." He grinned. "Though I can't say I was overly impressed with Sir Isaac at first. He's so clumsy."

"Clumsy?" It was the first I'd heard of it.

"Oh, not in everyday things, not so you'd notice. But it's his brain that's brilliant, not the rest of him. Ask him to distill a liquid, and before you know it, he's burnt his fingers or broken an alembic." He crossed his arms with self-satisfaction. "That's where I come in, you see, with my steady hands and keen eyesight. He'd never manage to do the work by himself."

"You make it sound as if you have to do everything single-handed," Sybil chided.

"Not exactly. But I'm in the inner circle, if I do say so myself."

"The inner circle, is it?" Sybil pretended to fan herself. "Oh my!"

Afraid her teasing would make the conversation veer before I'd learned all I could, I said to Gabriel, "I have a question: What's an alembic?"

Sybil was right: it was like opening the floodgates. He launched into the answer with gusto, talking about vessels and tubes and vapor, and sketching shapes in the air with his hands. If I'd had any doubts about his enthusiasm for alchemy, they were dispelled.

The only trouble was that I couldn't quite follow what he was saying. "And a curcurbit is . . . ?"

"A *cu*curbit," he corrected. "You use it in distillation." Seeing my confusion, he rose from his chair. "Why don't we go down to the laboratory? Then I can show you everything."

I wanted to say yes. Seeing the laboratory might give me some insight into how and why the crucible had been stolen. But I wasn't sure I should embark on an expedition with only Gabriel for an escort.

"Will you come too?" I asked Sybil.

"Of course I will." She turned to Gabriel in reproach. "That is, if the invitation includes me. You never offered before."

"That's because you never showed a proper interest."

"Now there's gratitude. I listened for *hours* the night I met you."

Again that wide, devilish grin. "Was it hours? I don't remember."

"I do," Sybil said with feeling.

"Well, if I didn't invite you, that was probably because the laboratory is generally off-limits to anyone except us alchemists. But hardly anyone's around this morning. The one person who might be there is old Penebrygg, and he won't mind our coming in."

A tour of the off-limits laboratory *and* another chance to see Penebrygg?

"Shall we go now?" I said.

CHAPTER NINETEEN
EXPERIMENTS

"Are you certain about this?" Sybil murmured to me as we departed her room.

"Yes." My only misgiving was what Nat would think. Going to the alchemy laboratory with Sybil and Gabriel was a far cry from staying put in my room. But if I found out something useful, it would be worth it.

"Well, don't say I didn't warn you," Sybil whispered back.

With a dashing bow, Gabriel held the door, then offered his arms to both of us. "One for each of my valentines."

Sybil and I looked at each other and laughed.

"And what arms will you offer your other valentines?" I asked.

"Who said there were others?" Gabriel protested, but he let his arms drop.

"Anyway, there isn't enough room to walk three abreast where we're going," Sybil said. "I doubt you could even fit two."

"How did you know?" Gabriel asked.

"People talk," Sybil said.

She was right: the stairs that led down to the laboratory were narrow and winding, a slender spiral in stone. We had to go single file. Gabriel led the way, talking all the while.

"It wasn't built as a laboratory, you understand. It used to be the King's own kitchen. That was before they tripled the size of the palace, of course." He glanced back to make sure we were following. "No one quite knew what to do with the room after that, until Sir Isaac came along. He saw right away what a good room it would be for alchemy, with the big old fireplaces and the oven and the row of windows for ventilation. And it's right by the Thames, which is handy when the fires get out of control."

I thought of the moonbriar fire and winced.

We reached a door in the wall. Gabriel pulled out a key and opened it, revealing yet another door, this one with a strapping guard in front of it.

"Just bringing some guests through, Potts," Gabriel said to him.

Potts looked doubtful. "I didn't hear nothing said about that, my lord."

"No?" said Gabriel cheerfully. "Well, this is the Lady Chantress. And her friend."

"You don't say." Potts gazed at me, thunderstruck.

"She's going to work her magic and get our crucible back," Gabriel said. "But first she needs to see the room, so if you could just open the door. . . . Yes, there's a good man."

It was Gabriel at his most lofty, and he made it sound as if I were about to sing a song-spell at any moment. But I swallowed any impulse to protest. After all, what he'd said was fairly close to the truth—and it had gotten us past the guard.

The door swung shut, leaving us together in the laboratory, a cavernous space with high windows and walls stripped back to bare stone. The windows were closed now, and a pervasive stink, metallic and pungent, assaulted my nose.

Beside me, Sybil made a face. "It smells like a tannery. Or a dyeworks."

Gabriel, however, didn't seem bothered by the smell. "Doesn't look like Penebrygg's here right now," was all he said before walking us around the place. He pointed out the various fires and furnaces, then took us over to see a configuration of glass tubes and bottles used for distilling.

Finally, he guided us over to a rack of peachy-brown clay pots with triangular rims. The smallest pot was the size of an ale mug, the largest the size of a cauldron. "And these are the crucibles, of course."

"What exactly *is* a crucible?" By now I'd gotten used to the smell of the place and could talk without feeling sick. "I mean— what's it used for?"

"You don't know?" he asked.

"Have a heart," Sybil said. "She's new to alchemy."

"True enough." Gabriel gave me an ever-so-slightly patronizing smile. "A crucible, my dear Chantress, is an open vessel—one without a top—that can be heated to very high temperatures."

"How high?" I asked.

"Oh, far beyond boiling point, in some cases. Some crucibles can be cast into a veritable inferno, and yet never melt or crack. Like these." He pointed to the rack of pots. "These crucibles come from Hesse, in Europe. They're the best of their kind, barring the Golden Crucible, of course."

"And how big is the Golden Crucible?" The crucial fact hadn't been mentioned in the Council meeting.

"About the size of that one there." Gabriel pointed to one in the middle of the rack. "The Golden Crucible is very much like it, except that it's reddish-gold and it has a somewhat wider mouth."

"So you've seen it?" Sybil asked.

"Of course. I went to the Treasury with Sir Isaac himself, at his request."

I touched the crucible. "Could I hold it?"

"If you want to. But take care: if it slips from your hands, it will break as easily as any other pot. It's only in the fire that it's strong."

I picked up the crucible, hefting its weight in both my hands.

"To really appreciate it, you should see it in action." Gabriel opened a cupboard and pulled out a glass vial that looked to be almost full of water. He pried at the stopper.

"Gabriel." There was a warning in Sybil's voice. "Are you sure—?"

Pop!

Off came the stopper. In a motion so quick I hardly realized what was happening, Gabriel dropped a penny into the crucible I was holding and poured some of the liquid over it.

"Ugh." Behind me, Sybil clapped her hand to her face. "Lucy, put it down!"

I shoved the crucible onto the nearest table as the liquid inside it fizzed and frothed and turned bright green. Even Gabriel now looked alarmed.

"Keep away!" He waved us back.

A plume of red-brown smoke shot up from the crucible.

I buried my head in my sleeve to ward off the acrid air. My lungs burned, and my eyes watered. Sybil gagged and coughed.

"This way!" Gabriel herded us into a smaller, adjacent room, where the air was still sweet. The moment he shut the door behind us, Sybil gasped, "What possessed you to do that?"

"I was . . . showing you . . . what a crucible is good for . . . how an acid won't damage it," Gabriel said, hacking and panting.

"That was an acid?" I choked out.

"Aqua fortis," Gabriel said. "It's strong stuff."

"It certainly is." Catching her breath, Sybil turned on Gabriel again. "It was very wrong of you. Lucy could have been hurt. We *all* could have been hurt—"

"You're making too much of it," Gabriel protested. "Why, I've done it dozens of times."

"Dozens?" I said.

"Well, at least half a dozen." Gabriel backed down. "Though usually with just a snip of copper, and the windows open."

"They weren't open today," Sybil said.

Gabriel peeked through the keyhole into the other room. "The smoke looks to be clearing anyway. In a few minutes we can probably go back in."

Sybil still looked outraged, but now that we were well away

from that plume of smoke, I found myself growing curious about what I'd just seen. "What is aqua fortis, exactly?" I asked.

Gabriel seized on the question with something like relief. "It's Latin for 'strong water,' and it can dissolve almost any metal except gold. And you can use it to make aqua regia—'royal water'—which *will* dissolve gold. So it's tremendously useful stuff."

"You mean you need it to make the Philosopher's Stone?" I asked.

"That's right. Did you see how it changed color when it started to react with the penny?"

"It went green?"

"Yes. And that's important because—" Gabriel stopped himself. "Well, I suppose there's no need to go into detail."

"Not for my sake, anyhow," Sybil put it. "I already know about the Green Lion, the Black Crow, and the rest of the menagerie."

Gabriel's eyebrows shot up. "You surprise me."

"Good," Sybil said pleasantly.

"But what do they mean?" I asked. "Alchemists don't really make animals, do they?"

Gabriel hesitated, but Sybil happily leaped into the gap. "They're the colors you see as you make the Stone," she explained. "The first stage is black, the next white, and so forth, until at last you reach the final transformation into the Stone itself, which is the fiery Phoenix."

Gabriel eyed her warily. "Where did you learn all that?"

"Never you mind. But as to whether the Green Lion is aqua

fortis, or something quite different, I really couldn't say," Sybil admitted. "I've never actually seen an alchemist make the colors, and I've no idea how you'd go about doing it."

Still looking disconcerted, Gabriel went to the door and opened it a crack. "Look: the smoke's gone."

We filed back into the room and circled around the crucible. The worst of the red-brown fumes had cleared away, but a faint, foul haze stained the air.

"Ugh." Sybil covered her nose.

Gabriel cranked some winches on the wall, and the high windows opened.

Sybil glanced up at the haze. "It's not going."

"That's because there's no wind." Gabriel grinned at me. "Maybe you could magic one up for us, Chantress."

I felt a jolt of alarm. Was he serious?

Best to pretend he wasn't. "Use magic, when time alone will do the trick?" I said with a smile. "I could never be so wasteful."

Gabriel's grin only widened. "Magic is never a waste. Go on. Sing us a song."

"Oh, please do, Lucy," Sybil begged, eyes alight. "I haven't seen anyone work proper Chantress magic since Grandmama died. And heaven knows the air needs clearing."

They looked at me, all expectation.

I stared back at them in panic. What was I to do? The only music I could hear was a faint whisper from the river, drifting through the open windows—an infuriating blur of cracked notes that faded out and led nowhere. Even if I could tease a song-spell out of it, where would it lead me? Would it turn my bones to water? Dissolve my body into fumes?

As if she had heard my thoughts, Sybil lowered her eyes and blushed. She looked almost guilty. My skin prickled. What reason had Sybil to feel guilty? Did she know the truth of my situation? Had she, in fact, *caused* it?

Or was I misreading her completely?

A crack like a gunshot went off, and we all jerked around. The outer door had burst open. Sir Isaac stood there glowering, a metal box in his hands. "What are you doing here?" he thundered. "And what in Jove's name is that smell?"

CHAPTER TWENTY
FLAMEL'S SECRETS

Under the Chief Alchemist's furious gaze, Sybil and I froze.

Gabriel visibly deflated. "Er . . . I was merely showing the Chantress the laboratory."

"Were you indeed?" Sir Isaac's tone was biting. "A party tour for friends, with a few explosions thrown in gratis?"

Gabriel's cheeks flushed. "Not exactly, Sir Isaac."

I appreciated that he wasn't trying to put the blame on me. But honesty demanded that I own up to my part in this.

"I asked him to help me," I said to Sir Isaac. "I'm sorry. I thought if I understood more about alchemy, I might be able to help you find the crucible."

Sir Isaac's severe face softened just a little. "An honorable intention, Chantress, but we have rules here for a reason." He contemplated the scorched crucible with disdain. "Lord Gabriel, what is the source of this unseemly mess?"

"I was, er . . . demonstrating how a crucible works."

Sir Isaac's dark frown deepened. "You know that is not allowed. We will speak of this later. You will shut the windows before the place freezes and then escort Miss Dashwood upstairs."

Subdued, Gabriel winched the windows closed and offered Sybil his arm. Looking rather subdued herself, she took it.

"I should go too." I wasn't sure whether I wanted to question Sybil or avoid her, but in any case, I needed fresh air. My head ached, and I felt dizzy. The fumes of the place were wearing me down.

"No, Chantress." Sir Isaac set down the metal box he'd been carrying. "Please remain here. I wish to speak with you."

Was this good or bad? I wasn't sure, but I stayed behind as the others went out.

"Chantress, I realize you meant well," Sir Isaac said. "But if you wish to know more about alchemy, you would do better to speak to me, not Lord Gabriel. Indeed, had I known that you desired such instruction, I would have gladly made myself available. Anything that might help recover the crucible. . . ." He glanced at his pocket watch. "I am free now, if you have any questions?"

A handsome offer, indeed. No one knew more about alchemy than Sir Isaac did, not even Penebrygg. But what should I ask him? What would help me find the crucible? Hard questions to answer at any time, and even harder when I was still worrying about that look on Sybil's face: Had it been guilt? And if so, over what?

Sir Isaac tapped impatiently on the lid of his metal box.

I forced myself to focus. At the very least, I should double-check what Gabriel had told me. I pointed to the scorched crucible before me. "The Golden Crucible is about that size?"

"Roughly, yes. I can give you the exact measurements, if you like." He scribbled them down on a sheet of paper. "There. What else do you want to know?"

"What is it made of?"

"An earthen compound of some sort. I'm sorry I can't be more precise, but we haven't dared subject it to experiments. They might ruin it."

"Flamel didn't say anything about how it was made?"

Sir Isaac's long fingers drummed against the table. "Not about its composition, no. But as I believe I mentioned yesterday, he was certain it was fashioned by Hermes Trismegistus, the great originator of alchemy."

I tried to recall what else he'd told me about the crucible yesterday. "You said you found it in France? Where exactly?"

Sir Isaac's eyes narrowed. "Does it matter?"

"It might." This was a shot in the dark; I truly had no idea if it did.

"Well, if you must know, I found it in a graveyard in a small village outside Paris. There was a cipher in Flamel's papers"—he glanced at the metal box he'd set down earlier—"that revealed its location to me."

"Are they in there?" I gestured toward the box. "The papers?"

"Er . . . yes. I have to consult them regularly. But Spain and France would give their eyeteeth for them, and so would many others. This keeps them safe from theft and prying."

"May I see them?"

Sir Isaac thumbed the edge of the case. It had a combination lock, I saw—something Nat had taught me about last year, but that I had rarely seen. "No reason why you shouldn't, I suppose," he said reluctantly. "Don't expect them to make any sense to you, though. Flamel's cipher is almost impenetrable."

He opened the box, revealing a battered, black-ribboned stack of papers that stank of must. As he had warned me, they were covered with strange squiggles and symbols, none of which I could decipher.

I turned the pages with a mix of excitement and trepidation, wondering if some kind of music or magic might inhere in them. But if so, it was dead to me. The vellum was stiff and unyielding between my fingers.

I didn't protest when Sir Isaac took the papers back and closed the box.

"Is there anything else you wish to know?" he asked.

It took me a moment to recollect where we had been in our conversation. "You said you found the crucible in a graveyard?"

"Yes," Sir Isaac said. "Not in a grave, I hasten to add. But buried under a wall, just as Flamel had indicated."

"Could someone have seen you remove it? Someone who might have followed you to England?"

"I doubt it," Sir Isaac said. "I dug it up by dark of night last November. No one else was around, and I saw no one trailing me afterward. And as soon as I reached the King, the crucible went straight into the Treasury."

"Was it ever taken out again?"

"Never," Sir Isaac said. "Until it was stolen."

"And you and the King were the only ones who saw it there?"

"For the most part, yes. A week before it disappeared, I brought my assistants to see it: Dr. Penebrygg, Sir Samuel, and Lord Gabriel. I wanted them to get a feel for its weight and handling. But we left the crucible just as we found it."

This wasn't getting me anywhere.

Sir Isaac, too, appeared troubled. "Chantress, if I may say so: these seem very *mundane* questions for you to be asking."

My heart thumped. Without recourse to magic, I'd been reduced to the plodding details of ordinary investigation. But Sir Isaac was right—that wasn't the way Chantresses worked. If I didn't want to give myself away, I would have to change tactics.

"You'd be surprised how often magic hinges on mundane details, Sir Isaac," I said, trying to sound wise.

His lugubrious face continued to look doubtful.

Think like a Chantress, I told myself. *If I could still work proper magic, what would I ask?* "I wonder: could I perhaps see the Treasury? If the theft was done by magic, I might perhaps hear something useful there."

His face lit up. "Of course! If you think it would help, I would be only too happy to accompany you there."

In remarkably short order, it was arranged: the King's permission was requested and received, though he regretted he could not meet us there as he had other business to attend to. Thankful for his absence, I proceeded with Sir Isaac to the Treasury.

It was a relief to leave the stale, stinking air of the laboratory. By the time we reached the Treasury door—now guarded by four men, instead of two—my headache was gone. We were immediately admitted into the stronghold, and I was dazzled by the riches I saw there: glittering ingots, chests of jewels, shining candelabras with pearls hung thick as grapes. An entire shelf was given over to a colossal silver bowl almost big enough to bathe in. On another, a long line of gold ewers reflected my own distorted face.

I halted by a coffer studded with emeralds, rubies, and diamonds. Nat was right, I thought: there was more wealth at Court than I had imagined.

Beside me, Sir Isaac stopped too. "What is it, Chantress? Do you hear anything? Sense anything?"

Reminded why we had come, I shut my eyes, half-afraid of what I might hear. The place, however, was silent as a tomb. "No. There's nothing here."

"So you don't think it was done by magic?"

"I wouldn't go that far," I said, trying not to commit myself. "Tell me: Did you see or hear anything out of the ordinary on the night the crucible was stolen?"

"When I went to inspect the crucible, you mean? Or later, when they told me about the theft, and I came down to see what had happened?"

"Either. Both."

"No, there was nothing unusual." He wrinkled his high forehead. "Well, except perhaps for one thing . . ."

"What was that?"

"The smoke in the rooms near the Treasury," he said. "It had thinned out by the time I arrived, but a haze remained in the air. And it didn't smell quite like ordinary smoke. Or so I thought."

"What *did* it smell like?"

"That's hard for me to say, I'm afraid." He spoke with a tinge of melancholy. "When I was your age, I could have told you exactly. But I've spent so much time in alchemical fumes since then that I no longer have real acuity of smell. I know when something smells foul or fair, but not much more than that. My sense of taste has gone too." He held out his hands, which shook slightly. "And it seems the fumes have damaged my hands, also. A terrible taskmaster, alchemy." He let his hands fall. "In any case, all I can tell you is that the smoke that night didn't smell quite *right*."

Magic? I wondered. Or something else?

"Vague, I know, but it is the best I can do," Sir Isaac said. "Does it help?"

Much as I wanted and needed to act like a Chantress, I knew it was dangerous to pretend to know much more than I did. "I'm not sure it does," I admitted.

Sir Isaac looked directly at me. For a bare instant his cool, rational mask slipped, and I glimpsed the frantic anxiety that lay beneath.

"We are almost out of time," he said. "The planets align in just over forty-two hours. We must have the crucible back by then. We *must*."

Even in the worst days under Scargrave, Sir Isaac had not looked like this. But, of course, back then he had been merely one cog—if a brilliant one—in the Invisible College's machine of resistance. Now he was Chief Alchemist, in sole charge of rescuing a kingdom from starvation. The responsibility must be crushing.

"Please." From proud Sir Isaac, this was a sign of desperation. "Whatever you can do, Chantress—"

"I understand," I said.

But I could think of no way to help him.

CHAPTER TWENTY-ONE

SUSPICIONS

Sir Isaac offered to escort me back to my room, but I declined. I needed to stay free as long as I could, away from Margery's watchful eye. Only forty-two hours to find the crucible! That was hardly any time at all. I'd just spent a whole morning asking questions, and yet as far as I could see, I was not one jot closer to recovering either the crucible or my magic.

I could hear the laughter of courtiers ahead of me, the murmur of servants behind me. Trying to avoid them all, I plunged down a staircase that led to a cloisterlike passageway. Its windows looked out on a small, green courtyard, edged with rough, bare vines.

I skidded to a stop before one of these windows, telling myself that I needed to slow down, that no one was chasing after me. And yet as I stared out at the neat, green square, I truly felt haunted. If I could not find the crucible, I would be disgraced, and if the Stone could not be made, the kingdom would starve.

Add Wrexham and his spies to that, and it was hard not to feel that monsters were leaping out at me everywhere.

At that very moment, something *did* leap out at me: a tall, shadowy figure approaching from behind. I whirled around, hoping it was Nat.

It was Gabriel.

He bowed and offered me his most charming smile. "How marvelous to run across you here. I'm in a bit of a rush, I'm afraid—Sir Isaac's expecting me in the laboratory—but I did want to apologize. Not because he insisted, you understand, but of my own accord."

There was a penitent quality in his smile now, which only made it all the more appealing.

"Truth be told, I was trying to impress you," he confessed. "But I never meant to hurt you, my lady Chantress. I would never do that, not for the world. You must believe that." He spoke in a low, earnest voice, his lively eyes subdued. "Please say you forgive me."

How could I help it? "Of course I forgive you."

The spark came back into his brown eyes. "You are very kind."

Before I realized what he was doing, he clasped my nearest hand and kissed it.

I stood rooted to the spot. No brief courtly salutation, this. He lingered too long for that, his lips warm against my skin. And when he raised his head, he favored me with the most dazzling grin I'd seen from him yet.

My cheeks went hot. I'd only meant to say that I bore no grudges; I hadn't meant to encourage him.

His grin widened. "I must run, Chantress. But I will hope to see you tonight."

He rushed off without waiting for an answer, but I had one: *Not if I can help it.*

It wasn't that I disliked Gabriel. But with Nat forced to keep away, and the question of marriage staring me in the face, Gabriel's attentions were a complication I could do without. What made them especially complicated were my own reactions: he'd taken me by surprise with that kiss, and my pulse had quickened despite myself. But right now that seemed all the more reason to avoid him.

Feeling unsettled, I walked on down the passageway until I came to a door that led out to the courtyard. I pushed it open—it swung easily—and stepped onto the grass. After being so closed in, it was a relief to be outdoors in the fresh, chilly air.

But merely for a moment. As if by instinct, I found myself listening for magic, hoping against hope that it would be clearer out here in the open. But no, it was still a muddle—and after my experience this morning, the fractured sounds made my skin prickle with apprehension. I stood my ground for a minute longer, but my fear only grew, and with it came a consciousness of how very exposed I was. Too many windows looked out on this courtyard. Anyone could be watching me.

I ducked back inside and left the passageway. I needed to find a safe haven, a protected place, somewhere I could take stock and decide what to do next. But by now I was completely lost again. Unnerved, I chose routes at random, dodging anyone who came my way, racing faster and faster. Eventually I stumbled across a place I recognized: the library where Nat and I had met that morning.

As I stood there, catching my breath, I heard a fierce whisper behind me: "I thought you were going to stay in your rooms."

I spun around. Nat stood there, looking every bit as dangerous as Sybil had made him sound.

As he came closer, I saw the worry in his eyes.

"I've been looking for you everywhere," he said. "It's all over the palace that you spent the morning with Sybil Dashwood and Gabriel—the very two people I warned you about. Is that true?"

"It's all right." I rushed to reassure him. "I didn't come to any harm."

He didn't seem relieved. "You might come to harm if you go on like this—spending time with two of the likeliest suspects in the whole palace! What were you thinking?"

"I hoped I might learn something useful." I explained what Penebrygg had said about finding the crucible, and how it might change the King's mind.

Nat looked more and more alarmed. "You mean you went to see the King, too?"

"Yes, though it didn't do me any good. But if I found the crucible—"

"You mean you're serious about that? Lucy, you can't. Not when—" He stopped himself and lowered his voice, even though the library doors were shut. "Not given what's happened to you."

"I can't just sit and do nothing," I said in frustration. "And don't tell me you could, if it were you. Because I know you: you'd be out and about, trying to sort things out yourself."

Two traits I loved in Nat were his honesty and the way he treated me as an equal. Watching the struggle in his face, I thought that both were in jeopardy. Then his eyes met mine.

"Point taken," he said with a sigh. "You're right: it's not fair to ask something of you that I wouldn't do myself. It's just—" His hands balled up. "It's hard thinking of you wandering around with people who might hurt you. Who might *already* be hurting you."

"I'm being careful," I assured him. "And I'm learning things. Useful things."

His hands remained tense, but I could see he was intrigued. "Like what?"

"Well, Sybil knows a lot about Chantresses. No great surprises there, but she knows a fair amount about alchemy, too."

"Alchemy?" Nat considered this. "That *is* interesting."

"It does make you wonder, doesn't it? And there are other things too."

"Like what?"

"It's hard to describe." The more I thought about it, the less certain I was that the look she'd given me in the laboratory had meant anything. It was true that she had a relatively transparent face, but I didn't know her well enough to read it perfectly.

"Do you think she's the thief?" Nat said.

I hesitated. "On balance? No. Whoever stole the crucible is

good at keeping secrets. And Sybil, well . . . that's not her strong suit. She's always blurting out exactly what she's thinking."

"That could be an act," Nat said.

"Maybe. But she told me all about her mother's dealings with alchemists. And she really shocked Gabriel when she talked about the Green Lion and the Black Crow and the Transformation. If she truly were up to something, wouldn't she have kept all that to herself?"

"How did you know Gabriel was shocked?" Nat asked.

"I was watching him."

"I see."

That was all Nat said, but I felt my cheeks grow warm. Did he know that Gabriel had proclaimed himself my valentine? "I—I don't trust him one bit," I said.

I couldn't see Sybil as a thief and a murderer, but Gabriel . . . it was just possible. After all, he'd been a fervent disciple of alchemy for years. What if he wanted to make the Stone for himself? That would be reason enough for him to steal the crucible.

But, of course, Gabriel wasn't the only person in Greenwich who was obsessed with alchemy. And there were plenty of other people who had no witnesses as to their whereabouts on that night. If magic were involved, perhaps even those with unbreakable alibis might be involved in the theft in some way. . . .

Face it, I told myself. *You have no idea who stole the crucible. You're just going around in circles. And time keeps ticking away. . . .*

"I'm sure he's up to no good," Nat said grimly, and I realized he was still talking about Gabriel.

"What makes you say that?"

"I've been watching him this week myself, and I've seen him coming in and out of the alchemy laboratory in the middle of the night, all alone. And he spends a lot of time near Sir Isaac's rooms, even though his own are on the other side of the palace."

"That *is* strange. But maybe Sir Isaac wants him close at hand."

"He's there even when Sir Isaac's out," Nat said. "So something's up. I just don't know what."

It sounded thin to me. Maybe the truth was that Nat simply didn't like Gabriel. Whatever the answer, I wasn't about to add fuel onto any fires by leaping to Gabriel's defense. Especially not when I harbored my own vague suspicions of him as well.

"I could help keep watch on him," I offered.

"No," Nat said emphatically. "Look: I know you don't want to stay in your room, and I understand why. But there's someone very dangerous on the loose here, someone who might already have attacked you. And there's a real chance that it's Gabriel. I don't want you around him any more than is absolutely necessary."

He was so close that I could see the smoky green flecks in his warm hazel eyes. He touched my cheek with his thumb, as gentle as his voice was rough. "I mean it when I say I'd do anything to keep you safe, Lucy. If only I could get you out of this place. . . ."

I froze. Someone was calling me. "Chantress?"

It was Margery. I jerked back from Nat in panic. "You should go," I whispered. I couldn't hope to avoid Wrexham's spy forever, but it would be very bad if she discovered us together.

Instead of moving away, Nat pulled me closer and kissed me. For an instant, delight eclipsed fear. Nat, my Nat, with his arms around me . . .

"My lady Chantress? Are you here?" Margery was coming ever closer.

Fear clamped down again, and I pulled away. "Go!" I whispered.

This time Nat raced for the door behind us. I hastened the other way, hoping the heat in my cheeks and lips wouldn't show.

In the room beyond, I came across Margery. "You called?" I said.

Margery regarded me with a cool expression, but I could see anger in the folds of her mouth. "Where have you been, my lady? You're late for your fitting."

"My fitting?"

"With the seamstresses. I made the arrangements with them this morning, and they were due to arrive at your room a quarter of an hour ago. Of course, I never imagined you'd be away half the day. We'll have to hope they'll wait for you, or you'll have nothing fit to wear to the banquet tonight."

"The banquet?"

"For Valentine's Day. Had you forgotten?"

I hadn't even heard about it. Was that what Gabriel had meant when he'd talked about seeing me tonight? "Is it really necessary that I go?"

Margery looked shocked, as if I'd proposed turning down God himself. "It is a royal invitation, my lady. You cannot refuse.

Not without giving offense to the King. And it will be an offense to him, too, if you are not properly dressed."

That settled matters, then. I could not afford to offend the King. Like it or not, I would have to go with Margery now. And I would have to go to the banquet, too.

And all the while, the hours would keep slipping away.

CHAPTER TWENTY-TWO
THE BANQUET

Within an hour, I had come to the frustrating conclusion that it is impossible to move, let alone escape anywhere, when you are surrounded by seamstresses sticking pins into you. In desperation, I claimed to be faint, but that got me nowhere. Margery just stood over me, making me sip water, while the seamstresses trotted out samples of cloth and trimmings until I thought I would scream.

Four hours later, I stood in the anteroom of the Great Hall, trussed up like a Christmas goose. The seamstresses had done their best, but it had proved impossible to make an entire new costume at such short notice. Instead, to my embarrassment, I was wearing someone else's dress. Hearing of my difficulties—through Joan, who was friendly with the seamstresses—Sybil had sent some of her own garments to me, with a message that I was to alter them as I saw fit, for she no longer had need of them.

A gracious gesture, but Sybil was taller and shapelier than I was, and it had been necessary to rip out seams and baste in new ones to keep the bodice from falling off me. The skirts, too, had required pinning and tucking. In spite of these efforts, the fabric still slid around and crumpled in odd places—a fault that grew more marked by the moment.

My fingers went up to the pins at my shoulder. I had terrible visions of the silken folds unraveling midbanquet. Perhaps I should just retreat now . . . though what retreat could there be, with Margery standing over me? Even now, she was watching me from the nearest doorway. But truly, while I was wearing this dress and the high-heeled slippers that matched it, there was no need for her to bother. I was as tethered as a staked goat.

Just as I was about to totter into the Great Hall, Sybil swished up to me, a vision in strawberry-red satin. Her bodice made the most of every curve, and pearls glowed against her shell-pink skin. Her face radiated nothing but pleasure in seeing me; I wondered again if I had only imagined that look of guilt earlier.

She linked her arm in mine. "Dear Lucy, you look wonderful."

I look absurd, I wanted to say, but since the dress was hers, I thought that might be rude.

Apparently my face gave me away, however, for she laughed and said, "Really, you do, whatever you might think. That sea green suits you. Indeed, it looks far better on you than it ever did on me. And no need to worry that anyone here has seen it either; I haven't worn it in ages. I honestly don't know why Joan packed it, but now I'm glad she did."

It was hard not to be moved by her kindness. "You're very generous—"

She cut me off with a smile. "Nonsense. I was only too happy to help. Especially after having made such a misstep this afternoon."

"A misstep?" I wasn't sure what she meant.

"Asking you to do magic for us like that." Again she had the expression I'd seen in the laboratory: eyes abashed, a faint blush. "Chantress magic isn't a plaything—that's what Grandmama always used to say. I shouldn't have asked you to use it for such a silly reason. It wasn't right."

So I'd read the signs right: Sybil *had* felt guilty. But not for the reasons I'd feared. And if she wasn't going to demand I do magic anymore, then my life would be easier. I relaxed a little despite the benighted pins at my shoulder. "No need to say another word about it. I'm glad you understand."

"Oh, I do, believe me." Lowering her voice, she said, "I hope I didn't offend you with the other things I said either."

"What other things?"

"About trying other kinds of magic. I truly meant only to help."

"It was good of you to offer—"

"You mean you would like to try them?" Sybil bounced on her toes in anticipation. "Oh, I do hope so. It would be such a thrill to assist you."

Much as I liked Sybil, I wasn't prepared to dabble in strange magic with her. "It's very kind of you, but—"

"Oh no," Sybil interrupted. "Steel yourself. Gabriel's making a beeline for you."

"For us, you mean."

"No, *you*," Sybil said. "He's fond of me, in his own way. But there's something different about the way he looks at you. I think he's smitten." Seeing my expression, she laughed. "Oh, don't look so horrified, Lucy. I know how you feel about Nat, but Gabriel's a fine man in his own right. Most girls would congratulate themselves if they attracted his interest."

Maybe. But I wasn't most girls.

Yet the moment of meeting was not as awkward as I'd feared. Gabriel was merely the vanguard of what turned out to be an army of courtiers. With cheers and huzzahs, they surrounded Sybil and me like a phalanx and carried us off to the banquet.

†   †   †

Such a wonder that banquet was! The Great Hall, blanketed in hothouse flowers, was a vast room, and yet the crush of people was so great that it almost seemed too small to hold them. Every corner was packed with courtiers and councillors—though Nat was not among them, at least not that I could see.

Eventually I found myself seated at the far end of the King's table, pinned in between Lord Gabriel and Lord Ffoulkes, Wrexham's florid ally, who had been one of my more surprising bouquet-bringers. Not my ideal choice of dining companions—Gabriel had steered me toward the chair before I'd quite realized what was happening—but it hardly mattered. The din of the crowd was so loud that it was difficult to make conversation.

The table itself, however, could not be faulted. China and

173

silver gleamed against spotless linen, and candlelight danced in a thousand pieces of crystal, from the pendants on the vases to the glass in my hand. But what stunned me most of all was the food. Platter after platter appeared, each with a different offering.

Two seats down from me, on the far side of Lord Ffoulkes, Sybil ladled oysters from a golden bowl. The gooseberry-eyed Aunt Goring, to whom I had been briefly introduced, sat across from her, filling a plate with roast swan and asparagus. On my right, Lord Ffoulkes partook of ham and roast beef. On my left, Gabriel passed me an enormous tureen of strawberries. And those were only a few of the sixty dishes being served tonight, or so Lord Ffoulkes told me.

My mouth watered on seeing the strawberries—an extraordinary sight in the middle of February. I piled them onto my plate, along with a dollop of cream and several oysters, and picked up my spoon. I couldn't wait to dig in. I'd eaten very little that day, and I was famished.

Famished . . .

I thought of the children I'd seen on the road from Norfolk. That was what *famished* meant. I put my spoon down.

"Eat up, my lady, eat up!" Lord Ffoulkes was right beside me, but he almost had to shout to be heard. "No need to be dainty. There are victuals enough to feed a crowd twice this size."

I raised my voice in turn. "Lord Ffoulkes, where does all this food come from?"

"Come from? No need to bother your pretty head about that,

Chantress. Just eat and enjoy." He tried to load more strawberries onto my plate.

I held up my hand. "No, thank you." *Your pretty head?* Did he think such words would please me?

Apparently so. Looking hurt, he dabbed at his mouth with his napkin. "Perhaps the spirit of the occasion has escaped you, my lady. A banquet is meant to be a celebration."

"I'm not sure there's much to celebrate," I said, but Lord Ffoulkes had already turned to Sybil.

On my other side, Gabriel leaned over and said, "You wish to know where the food comes from?"

"Yes." I bent toward him, hoping he would have an answer for me. "There's so much of it, and so many kinds. Is it English? Did they import it?"

"I couldn't tell you myself. But ask Wrexham. He'll know. He sees to everything around here." He drained his glass. "A finger in every pie, that's Wrexham for you." Glancing up the table, he gave a sour laugh.

I followed his gaze and saw Wrexham at the King's right hand, looking like a demigod in the splendor of candles. His plate was loaded high with every kind of delicacy, and he was spearing a slice of venison with his knife. Evidently he was not troubled by the specter of hunger beyond these palace walls.

Knife in midair, Wrexham looked down the table, eyes narrowing as he caught sight of me. The animosity in his face made me lose what little appetite I had left.

I pushed my plate away.

"He's a beast," Gabriel said in my ear.

I was astonished by his venom—and by how closely his feelings mirrored mine.

"They say his father was even worse," Gabriel went on. "But I find that hard to believe. Though they say he broke any man who crossed him, even his own son. He almost beat the life out of Wrexham once." He added vehemently, "Wish I'd been there to see it."

Not sure how to respond, I said, "You know the family well?"

"Know them? I should think so," Gabriel said. "I'm Wrexham's ward."

His easygoing confidence had deserted him; he looked touchy and tense. I put my next question to him with care. "What does that mean, exactly?"

"It means that when my father died last year, the courts named Wrexham guardian of my person and of all the property I am to inherit. For a fee."

I had been at Court long enough to have heard about fees. "You mean he bribed them?"

"Of course." Gabriel scraped his plate with his knife. "It's how it's done, by everyone. Wardships are a good way for men to make money; they can manage the lands for their own profit until their wards come of age. It was just my bad luck to end up with Wrexham. I doubt there will be anything left of the estate by the time I'm twenty-one."

No wonder the Philosopher's Stone appealed to him. And then, with some dismay, I wondered: Did he think marriage to me would solve his money problems as well?

As if he'd sensed my thoughts, Gabriel's lazy grin reappeared. "But how did we get onto this gloomy subject anyway?" He leaned slightly closer. "Let's talk about you instead."

"I'd rather hear more about Wrexham," I said. "What has he done with your money? Do you know?"

"Used it to make himself richer." Gabriel downed a new glass of wine and poured himself yet another. Brown eyes a little unsteady, he murmured to me, "He rules the borderlands like a king. Only he's not, you know. Not king. Not yet."

I murmured back in surprise. "Not *yet*?"

"His ambition has no end," Gabriel said softly, gazing at Wrexham with a mix of malice and fear. "But he's merely third in line to the throne now—there are two cousins of Henry's before him—and his position will worsen once Henry has sons. His only hope is to take the crown by force."

However much I hated Wrexham, I found this hard to swallow. "He saved the King's life in battle," I protested.

"And made himself into a hero—the King's most trusted man, the power behind the throne," Gabriel said in my ear. "Putting himself in a perfect position to knife him in the back. He wants the King dead, I tell you. He's plotting it right now."

I shook my head, still skeptical. "You have proof of this?"

Gabriel thumbed his wineglass and looked warily up and down the table. "Nothing I can talk about. Nothing I can take to the King." He took another sip of wine and whispered, "But it's true."

Before I could question him further, the King surged up from his chair. "Help! In Heaven's name, help!"

As we all rose in alarm, the King turned to the man on his left, who had collapsed over his plate. I could just make out who it was: Sir Isaac, in a dreadful state.

"What's wrong?" Gabriel exclaimed.

"Some sort of fit," Lord Ffoulkes guessed.

But it was Wrexham who riveted us all.

"Poison!" He roared out the word, and the room went still.

CHAPTER TWENTY-THREE
A QUESTION OF TRUST

"Someone has poisoned the Chief Alchemist," Wrexham bellowed over our heads. "Fetch the Head Cook at once."

"Send first for the Royal Physician." Unlike Wrexham, the King did not bellow, but nonetheless his voice carried. "Sir Isaac still breathes. Perhaps he can be saved."

Gabriel leaped unsteadily from his chair. "Your Majesty, I have some knowledge of medical matters—"

"And I!"

"And I!"

As half a dozen men converged on Sir Isaac and argued noisily about what was to be done, Wrexham stalked off, still shouting for the cook. Over the bedlam, the King called out, "Perhaps the Lady Chantress will come to our aid."

"Of course, Your Majesty." I gathered my errant silk skirts and went forward anxiously. What did the King expect from me? Did he believe I could cure Sir Isaac with song?

"Whatever you can do, Chantress," the King said to me.

I went up to Sir Isaac, still collapsed over his plate. His face was flushed; his thin-lipped mouth gaped open; his hands trembled like November leaves. Whatever had done this—illness, fit, or poison—he was in a very bad way.

Even at the best of times, I would have found it a challenge to help him, since I had no specific magic for healing. And this was far from the best of times. But Sir Isaac might be dying: I couldn't bear to stand here and do nothing.

Of course I couldn't even think of singing, not given what had happened this morning. But there was less danger in listening. I knew that all things—even poisons—had a characteristic music, a Wild Magic all their own. Perhaps desperate need would sharpen my hearing, and I would be able to tell if poison were present—or even which kind.

This was Sir Isaac, my old ally and colleague; I had to try.

I knelt by his slack mouth and listened. Yes, there was something there . . . but there was too much noise from the crowd to hear what it was.

"Please," I said to the King, "can you quiet them?"

"Silence," the King commanded. "Silence, all of you, for the Chantress."

The moment they went still, I realized I'd made a mistake. All eyes were on me now. People were expecting miracles. Yet strain as I might, I heard only the faintest slivers of sound, sharp and meaningless as a packet of pins.

I rose and faced the King. "I'm afraid magic cannot cure this, Your Majesty. We must trust to medicine instead."

Was that anger I saw in his face, or merely agitation? The crowd began to buzz behind me.

"You did send for the Royal Physician, didn't you, Your Majesty?" I said.

"Yes. Yes, I did—"

"Tut, tut." The Royal Physician himself, bewhiskered and bustling, pushed forward, eyeing me with a superior air. "Your incantations not up to the job, eh? Well, never bring a woman in to do a man's job, they say."

My cheeks burned with anger and embarrassment, but what could I say? It was true that I had failed.

Elbowing me out of the way, the Royal Physician checked the patient's pulse, lifted his eyelids, and smelled his breath. "Poison, most definitely. Perhaps in the wine?"

"No. He hasn't drunk any," the King said. "Or eaten anything either. He came in late, and he wanted to tell me something about Flamel's cipher first. I couldn't quite follow it, I'm afraid. There were too many people speaking at once."

The Royal Physician frowned. "So neither the wine nor the food poisoned him. . . ."

Sir Isaac gagged. As I reached to steady him, a small packet fell from his coat, scattering little white balls everywhere.

"What are these?" I picked up the half-empty packet.

"Mint comfits," Gabriel said. "He keeps a great supply in his room."

"Here, give that to me." The Royal Physician snatched the packet from my hand. After crushing a single comfit between his teeth, he smelled it and tested it on his tongue. "A nasty dose of belladonna," he pronounced. "And perhaps something else, too. I wonder Sir Isaac didn't detect it."

"He hasn't much sense of taste," I said, remembering our conversation in the Treasury.

"No, he hasn't," Penebrygg agreed. "More's the pity."

Very quietly the King asked the Royal Physician, "Will he die?"

"At this point, I cannot tell." The Royal Physician pressed his thumb to Sir Isaac's wrist again. "I will do my best to revive him. There are antidotes I can try, and purgatives. Their effect is not pretty to see, but they may do the trick. First, however, he should be moved to another room—one with a fire and a bed."

"Of course," the King said. Again, Gabriel and the others were quick to offer their services. With the King and the Royal Physician leading the way, they carried Sir Isaac out of the room.

Once they left, the banquet disintegrated into hubbub. Even though the poison had been in the mints, the incident had put most people off their food. They would not eat; they wanted to leave. But as they made their way out, they could and would talk about the poisoning, and what it might portend. I heard the gossip rising up around me.

"Did you see his face? White as a flounder. He'll never survive."

"Someone's trying to stop him from making the Philosopher's Stone, you mark my words."

"A woman's trick, poison."

"God's vengeance, for aiming so high."

"No, no. He's doing God's work, can't you see? He's trying to save the kingdom."

I looked around, trying to identify who had said what.

A fist closed around my arm.

"Chantress." Wrexham pulled me close. "You will come with me."

He marched me to a far alcove, where we were alone.

"You have failed us again." Wrexham's face was flushed and angry, and he did not release me. "God's blood, but you have failed us most miserably. You have not found the crucible. And now you have allowed harm to come to our Chief Alchemist."

"Not for the world would I have seen him harmed—"

"No? And yet he was. Which makes me wonder, Chantress." Above his wide cheekbones, his flat eyes narrowed, and he tightened his grip on my arm. "Whose side are you on?"

"The King's side," I said as steadily as I could. "Always the King's."

"Then prove it," Wrexham growled. "Find the crucible. Guard the King and his alchemists from harm." His iron hand was like a vise on my arm, pressing so hard that I feared the bone would break. "Do it, I tell you—or by God, I will deal with you myself, as you deserve."

Just as I thought my arm would snap, he thrust me away.

"As you deserve," he repeated. Hand on his dagger, he stalked off.

† † †

After he left, I stood very still in the shadowy alcove, fingering my throbbing arm. Fear churned my stomach, and yet I felt fury, too.

How dare he lay hands on me? How dare he make threats? *If I had my powers, I would make him pay. . . .*

My arm throbbed again, reminding me that such vengeful thoughts were pure fantasy. The reality was this: I was a seventeen-year-old girl with a sore arm, and few friends, and no magic to speak of.

I could reason, however; I could try to think things through. I sat down on a bench in the deepest recesses of the alcove. What did it mean that Wrexham had dared hurt me like that? Was it merely that he was so used to meting out violence that he thought nothing of it? Or did he know that there was no way for me to get back at him—know it because he had crippled my magic?

Much as I knew him to be my enemy, I wasn't convinced of that last charge. He had appeared truly enraged that I wasn't helping the King. If he had known I had no magic to offer, he wouldn't have acted that way. Unless, of course, he was playing a much more devious game than I would have thought possible. . . .

But perhaps Wrexham was quite good at deception. He would have to be if Gabriel's suspicions were right, and he was secretly aiming at the throne.

How was I to protect myself against such a man?

Oh, if only my magic would come back!

As if by a miracle, silvery notes cascaded around me, the clearest music I'd heard in days. Magic? I shot up from the bench.

Even before the notes broke up, however, I realized the truth: it was only a flute player out in the anteroom—probably here to provide music for the banquet. I sank back onto the bench.

Such a stupid mistake to have made. How could I have thought, even for a moment, that a flute was magic? How could my ear have failed me so? How could I have lost so much in a matter of days?

Magic, where are you? I need you!

"Lucy, are you all right?" Sybil advanced on me, looking worried. "I waited outside for you, but you didn't come. Someone said Wrexham was with you—"

"He was, but that's done." *Until he chooses to come after me.* "Thank you for looking for me."

"Of course," she said simply. "I was worried." She lowered her voice. "He's a vicious man, Lucy. He didn't hurt you, did he?"

The concern in her face decided me. It was time to set aside the small doubts that still niggled at me—time to trust her and ask for her help.

"Sybil?"

"Yes?" She looked at me, still worried.

"That other magic you talked about," I whispered. "Can we try it?"

CHAPTER TWENTY-FOUR
A TERRIBLE EMBRACE

Midnight, Sybil said. I was to meet her at midnight, in a small chamber not far from my rooms, where I could attempt the new magic without being disturbed.

Now, having waited for what felt like forever for Margery to fall asleep, I was here in the appointed chamber, with only a single candle to illuminate the gloom. By the frail light of its wick, I watched the glimmering face of the golden clock on the mantel.

Ten past midnight—and Sybil was nowhere to be seen. I pulled my nightgown tighter around me, wishing I had more than my thin shift underneath it. I had been waiting here in the cold and dark for twenty minutes. Should I give up and go back to bed?

The door creaked open. Another candle gleamed in the gap, with Sybil's bright eyes above it. Spying me, she slipped in. Dressed in a nightgown far more elaborate than mine, she pushed the door shut.

"Oh my dear! I'm sorry I took so long. I gave Aunt Goring a bromide in her tea—"

"You put *what* in her tea?"

"A bromide," Sybil said calmly, "to make her sleep. I've done it before, especially after any great excitement or distress. And having a poisoner in our midst has certainly distressed her."

It distressed me, too, even though it seemed likely now that Sir Isaac would survive. Before I'd gone to bed, I'd heard that the Royal Physician's purgatives had proved effective. Sir Isaac was too weak to leave his bed, or even to sit up in it, but he was holding his own. He'd fallen into what everyone hoped would be a healing sleep.

Sybil was still talking about her aunt. "She was having hysterics until the bromide took effect, and then she nodded off quite easily. But Joan was another story entirely. She wanted to stay up half the night sewing. I finally had to send her to bed, then wait till she slept."

"I had to wait a long time for Margery, too."

"Yes, she has sharp eyes and ears, that girl. Joan does too, more's the pity. I was so afraid I'd wake her, especially carrying all this." She hefted a pillowcase onto the table. "I wrapped everything in a spare petticoat to muffle the sound, but it's an awkward bundle."

The pillowcase fell on its side, and I heard a soft clank.

I reached out for it. "What's in there?"

With a crooked smile, she waved me away. "That's my secret." When I didn't withdraw my hand, she frowned and pulled the case toward her. "Seriously, Lucy, you shouldn't look. It will only ruin your concentration. One kind of magic at a time, that's all you should be thinking about."

What she said about concentration made some sort of sense, but I didn't like secrets at the best of times, and I liked them even less in a strange room at midnight, coming from someone I still wasn't absolutely certain I should be trusting. "You're not going to have me reading the stars or calling up spirits, are you? All I want to do is find the crucible." Well, perhaps not *all*. But locating the crucible would go a long way toward improving matters.

"We'll only do magic for finding things, I promise." I must have looked doubtful, because Sybil leaned forward earnestly. "Cross my heart, Lucy. *Three* times."

That childhood vow again—and she sounded sincere. "All right, then. What do we start with?"

"This." From the linen case, Sybil drew out a crystal pendant on a cord.

I set my candle down and took it from her. "What is it?"

"A dowsing pendulum. It's used to find water, especially, but if you have the gift, you can use it to find almost anything. I've already buried it in earth and passed it through flame, so it's ready for you to use."

I threaded the cord through my fingers.

"No, not like that." She looped the cord so that I grasped it between my thumb and forefinger. "Don't grip it so tightly. You need a little looseness there, so you can feel the vibrations."

"The vibrations?"

"Well, some say it's more of a pull, really. You walk about, concentrating on the object you want to find, and as you get close to it, the pendulum twitches in your hand. When you're very close, the pendulum might even dive straight down. I saw it do that once in France, in the hands of a man dowsing for water. It turned out he was standing over an underground river."

I circled the small, dim chamber, trying not to stumble against any furniture. The table was easy to see, but there were cane-backed chairs, too, and an elaborate high cabinet at the end of the room. "I don't feel anything."

"Are you thinking about the crucible?"

"As hard as I can. But I still don't feel anything."

"Perhaps that just means the crucible isn't anywhere near us," Sybil said. "If you were closer to it, the pendulum might work."

I let my hand fall. "I can't walk all over the palace like this, Sybil. Not in the dark. And not by daylight, either."

"No, I suppose not. Well, never mind." She took the pendulum from me and rummaged in the case again. "I have other kinds of magic we can try."

"Such as?"

She frowned. "I'd try a dowsing rod if I had one, but I don't. And there are cards, but I've never heard of a Chantress being good at reading those. Anyway, they're not the best way to find things. Palm-reading isn't likely to help us find the crucible, either. I did bring something else, though." From the case, she pulled out a luminous glass sphere no bigger than a cooking apple. "Here, take this."

I cupped it in my hands. It was beautiful, but what made it magic? "What does it do?"

"You can scry with it," Sybil said.

"Scry?"

"It means *see*. It's for seeing the future, or the past, or another place entirely. Some people can even use it to spy on others—"

Spying by proxy? It was an intriguing idea.

"And, of course, you can also use it to find things," Sybil went on. "You look into the crystal, and you ask it to show you what you seek. And the glass will reveal where it is. If you have the gift, that is."

"Let's hope I do." I rolled the ball from my left hand to my right. "How do I start?"

She pulled a chair out from the table. "Sit down first. You can keep it steadier that way."

Once we were both seated, she adjusted my hands so that they loosely cupped the bottom of the sphere, then tilted them toward the candle. "It shouldn't be too bright, but you want to have enough light to see by," she explained.

Cool against my fingers, the ball glowed in the flickering light.

"Now look past its surface and into its depths," Sybil said. "Look into the heart of it. And when you have gone as deep as you can, then ask, 'Where is the crucible?'"

I fixed my eyes on the crystal. Deep inside it, I could see tiny flecks of light. As I stared at them, bright constellations jumped out at me. A single bright spot like the North Star, a glowing cluster like the Pleiades. The lights multiplied, until it was like looking out into the heavens, with stars upon stars upon stars, as far as one could see.

"Now ask," Sybil prompted.

Her voice jarred me. What was it I was supposed to ask? Oh yes . . .

"Where is the crucible?" My voice echoed in the dark night sky of the ball.

"Now relax and clear your mind of everything," Sybil whispered. "Gaze into the ball, and breathe, and visions may come to you."

Clear your mind. Breathe. Wait for what may come. A familiar litany, for this was how one listened for song-spells. It felt odd to approach scrying the same way, yet it was comforting, too—as if I were merely translating what I already knew into some other language.

I let myself fall deeper into the glass, just as I would let myself fall into a song, and something shimmered inside the ball. For a bare instant it blossomed: a red-gold circle against a night-black sky.

My fingers tightened, and the ball shook in my hand. The vision vanished.

"Oh," I said in disappointment.

"What is it?" Sybil's excitement was plain to see. "What did you see?"

I described the red circle.

"The rim of the crucible," Sybil said. "Surely that's what it was."

"Perhaps," I said doubtfully.

"Do it again," Sybil urged. "You might see more this time."

Try as I might, however, the magic wouldn't work for me again. My eyes kept tracing the surface of the glass and the curving flame reflected in it. I couldn't see the stars at all.

"Still, *something* happened," Sybil said, taking the ball from me. "That's a good sign. You have some kind of ability here; it's just a matter of drawing it out."

"Draw it out how?" I glanced at the lumpy case. "Do you have another ball?"

"No, but I have something that might serve you just as well. Perhaps even better." Rising from her chair, she put the ball back in the case and drew out a shallow copper bowl. "Not everyone scries with a ball. Some find that mirrors work better—and some use water."

Water. Hope flared inside me. The element I best understood. The magic that came most easily to me.

But that was Chantress magic, I reminded myself. Scrying magic—that was something else altogether. Water might not make any difference there.

Sybil handed me the bowl and plunged her hand back into the case again.

"Now, where . . . ah yes, there it is." Looking quite pleased with herself, she pulled out a glass vessel.

I looked askance at it. "A perfume bottle?"

"Not anymore," Sybil said, "I finished the last of it the other day, and I dunked the bottle into my handbasin when Joan wasn't looking."

When Sybil poured the water into the bowl, the faint scent of lilies splashed out too. "Oh dear. I thought it would be more."

The water only just covered the bottom of the bowl. "Does it matter?" I asked.

"Perhaps not," Sybil said after a moment. "There's still something to catch the light, and something for you to gaze at. Give it a try, won't you?"

She slid the bowl across the glossy table toward me. "It's just like the ball, you see," she said. "You look, and then you ask, and then you wait for the answer."

Perched on the edge of my chair, I stared at the water. It was no more than half an inch deep, and through it I could see a pattern incised into the center of the bowl: a figure almost like a flower.

Sybil sat back down beside me again. "Hmm . . . the light's not quite right, is it?"

She pulled back the candle, and suddenly it was the water I saw, and not the bowl. The surface held me first, rippling with both the light of the candle and the dark of the room, and then something deeper called to me. The water barely covered the bottom of the bowl—I knew that—and yet somehow it seemed to go down and down and down, slippery and cold as the sea.

"Ask," Sybil whispered.

"Where is the crucible?" My voice sounded slurred, almost the voice of a stranger.

Something almost like music rang in my head. I breathed in with delight, and the water stirred. Truly, it stirred, though nothing else moved—stirred and whorled and took monstrous shape before my eyes. In its depths I saw a king and queen locked in a terrible embrace. Their hands clawed each other's necks. They were choking the life out of each other. Beneath their golden crowns, their throats bled from crimson gashes.

As their faces turned blue, something closed around my neck too, a sharp, strangling cord biting into my skin, bringing up the blood. I could not get air; I was drowning—

The bowl rippled. Suddenly the water was only water, with no pictures in it. Air rushed into my lungs.

"Lucy? Are you all right?" Sybil bent over me, her eyes wide with alarm. "You were making the most dreadful sounds."

I put my hand to my throat. No cord, no blood. And yet it had felt so real. . . .

"What happened?" Sybil still looked agitated. "Did you see something?"

It was impossible to forget the vision. When I shut my eyes against it, the picture only became brighter.

"What was it?" Sybil asked again.

Perhaps putting the picture into words would exorcise it. "A king and queen, attacking each other, choking each other—"

"*Our* king?"

"I didn't recognize the faces." They'd looked like stained glass, or the kings and queens on playing cards.

"What do you think it means?" Sybil asked.

"I have no idea."

"Well, it must mean something." She nudged the bowl of

water toward me. "Try it again. See if the water will show you anything else."

I tried again and again, but either I'd lost the trick of it or the water didn't have anything else to communicate. My head started to pound. My body craved sleep.

At last, after nearly half an hour of fruitless effort, I said, "I think we should stop."

"Shhhh!" Sybil put her finger to her lips.

I thought at first that she wanted me to keep working. But then I heard what she'd heard: dim shouts echoing out in the corridor, beyond the closed door.

"They're looking for us," Sybil said.

I bolted from my chair. "We'd better hide."

"No." Sybil grabbed the linen case and dumped the water from the copper bowl into a great vase by the window. "We'll clear everything away, and then we'll go."

"Go?"

"To meet the searchers. Best to brazen it out, I think, rather than be caught here." She shoved the bowl into the pillowcase and bundled the whole thing into the ornate cabinet. "You can tell them you heard a sound outside your door and you found me sleepwalking. You followed me to keep me safe."

A very neat story. I was surprised that she had come up with it so quickly.

"Come on, Lucy." Her hand was on the doorknob. "If they find us here, they might find the case, too. And that will be hard to explain."

Out in the corridor, the shouts were louder. But it turned out they were nothing to do with us at all.

"The King! The King!"

As Sybil and I looked at each other, Gabriel came round the corner and rushed toward us. "Chantress, Miss Dashwood, have you heard? The King's been attacked!"

"Attacked?" I repeated. A terrible dread crept over me.

"Yes," Gabriel said. "Someone tried to strangle him."

CHAPTER TWENTY-FIVE

AN ATTACK AND A LIE

"Someone strangled the King?" Sybil sounded horrified, but at least she could speak. My own voice had left me, and visions of the murderous king and queen flickered in my head.

"He was attacked with a garrote, from the look of it," Gabriel said. "He's lucky to be alive."

So the King had survived. Sybil looked as relieved as I felt. Indeed, she looked almost ready to cry.

"You're quite certain?" she asked urgently. "Have you seen him?"

"Yes." Gabriel spoke with more than his usual self-importance. "I woke to the sound of someone wailing, and when I went out to see what was wrong, I saw them carrying the King past on a bier. For a moment, I thought the worst, but then I heard the rasp of his breath. He's sitting up now, with the Royal Physician and Wrexham in attendance. And now the order's gone out that everyone is to be woken and questioned."

"So the King doesn't know who did it?" I said.

Gabriel shook his head.

"Does he remember anything?" Sybil asked.

"He can't say much; his voice is too raw," Gabriel said. "But he can write, and it seems he was attacked on the way back from a late meeting with Wrexham and Roxburgh. Wrexham confirmed that the meeting took place; he says he'd received dispatches saying that Boudicca now has over two thousand followers, some of them marching in formation like an army. He wanted the King to give the order to attack, but the King wouldn't. He can't seem to believe the woman really means him harm.

"After some debate, Wrexham says, the King left. And the rest of the story comes from the King's own written account. He says that as he made his way back to his room, he heard a thump behind a door on the east side of the palace. And so he went in to investigate."

"By himself?" Sybil was surprised. "He didn't call out an alarm?"

"No," Gabriel said. "He had his dagger, he said. That was enough."

Unwise, but who could blame him? His life was a weary round of meetings and diplomacy and compromise; it was probably a welcome change to be wielding a dagger on his own—especially after an argument with Wrexham.

"All appeared to be well at first," Gabriel went on, "and then he saw by the light of his candle that a piece of the paneling was out of joint. When he pushed on it, a little cupboard in the wall opened up—and there was the crucible."

"The crucible!" I was astonished.

"Yes. He started to call out then, but he'd barely made a sound before the cord closed his throat. That's the last he remembers, until a guardsman found him some time later, crumpled on the floor."

"And the crucible?"

"The guards have searched the room and found the cupboard. But the crucible is gone."

"But it was here," I said. "Here in the palace."

"And most likely still is," Gabriel said. "They're searching every room now."

While he was speaking, Nat appeared around the corner, his eyes lighting up with relief as he saw me. When he took in my companions, however, he backed away.

Left to myself, I would have gone after him, but with the others there I couldn't. Sybil and Gabriel were facing me; they had missed both his sudden arrival and his disappearance. I didn't want to be the one to give him away.

I wasn't quite the blank slate I wanted to be, though.

"Chantress?" Gabriel glanced at me oddly. "Is something wrong?"

"No, nothing." I shook my head and pulled my cloak tighter around me. "I'm just uneasy, that's all."

"So am I." Sybil shivered. "First Sir Isaac, and now the King. That's two attempts at murder in one night."

"Are there any clues?" I asked Gabriel. "Anything that could point to who did this?"

"Nothing very much," Gabriel said. "It's given a few people alibis. Wrexham and Roxburgh, for instance. They both swear they were together from the end of the meeting until they heard the guards raise the alarm. For what it's worth."

He clearly wasn't convinced, and neither was I. But even if the alibi turned out to be true, Wrexham wasn't in the clear, since he could have asked one of his spies to do the dirty work for him . . .

"Where were you?" Sybil asked Gabriel.

"I was asleep. Though I'm afraid there aren't any witnesses. What about you?" he asked Sybil. "I passed by your room, and your maid was shouting that you were missing."

Sybil blushed in a charmingly sheepish way. "I was sleep-walking," she told Gabriel. "And Lucy was following me. I don't remember anything about it myself. But I'm afraid I've done it before; it's a bad habit of mine." Her blush deepened. "So very embarrassing."

Gabriel looked as if he wasn't quite sure what to make of this. "You're a sleepwalker?"

Time for me to back Sybil up. "I woke up and there she was, right by my bed," I told him. "But she couldn't seem to see me. After a bit I realized she was asleep. When she started to walk off, I thought I'd better follow."

"I've led her a merry dance for the last hour, she tells me." Sybil looked utterly mortified.

An hour? Well, that would cover us nicely, I supposed, especially if her maid had missed her some time ago. Yet even as I nodded, part of me was taken aback by the calculation that had gone into Sybil's lies. I hadn't realized she had such a talent for deception.

"She was afraid to wake me," Sybil went on. "Don't they say you can frighten the life out of sleepwalkers that way? But in the end I came out of it myself."

At that moment, Aunt Goring came upon us, pop-eyed in her nightdress and a bizarre assortment of furs. "Sybil! What are you doing up here—and in such company?" She pursed her lips and glared at Gabriel.

It was not as if Gabriel could see anything through our heavy woolen nightgowns, I thought. Still, her outraged stare made me aware of quite how improper the scene must look.

Gabriel, however, was unruffled. "I was only making sure they were safe, Lady Goring. And now I must be on my way."

He dashed off as Aunt Goring clamped a no-nonsense arm around Sybil and propelled her toward the nearest staircase. "Come with me, young lady."

Lady Goring seemed to want nothing to do with me, so I hung back, wondering if Nat was still nearby. Almost the instant they were out of sight, he flew back around the corner and caught my hand.

"Over here," he whispered. He tugged me back toward the room where I had done the scrying.

Once we were inside, he shut the door and turned to me. "Tell me what you were doing with Sybil Dashwood." His hazel eyes were fierce and unblinking in the light of my candle. "And this time tell the truth."

CHAPTER TWENTY-SIX
A NEW PLAN

We stood barely a foot apart; the candle, burning bright between us, revealed everything. I couldn't keep lying now, even if I had wanted to. "What gave me away?"

"Your voice was too flat. It didn't sound like you."

"Do you think Gabriel noticed?"

"Gabriel?" The shadows sharpened the angle of Nat's jaw. "Why are you so concerned about him?"

I was surprised I had to spell it out. "Because I don't trust him."

"Oh." Nat looked mollified. "No, I don't think he noticed. But you haven't answered my question: What were you doing with Sybil?"

I told him everything, even describing the terrible vision I had seen.

When I finished, he did not speak.

"Nat?"

"I can't believe it," he said slowly.

"I know it sounds impossible, but I really did see it." The faint scent of lilies still perfumed the air. "I was sitting here, in that chair—"

"I don't mean the vision. If you say you saw it, you saw it." He looked at me across the candle flame. "What I can't believe is that you trusted Sybil like that. You put yourself completely in her hands."

"I needed help, Nat."

"Help? From her?"

Was it worry driving him, or anger? In the dim light, I couldn't tell, but I could feel my temper fraying, in part because I was trying to squelch my own doubts about Sybil. "You don't understand what it's like. I feel like I've lost myself—"

"You haven't." He spoke more gently now. "Whatever's going on, you're still you, Lucy."

"But it's frightening not being able to defend myself. That's why I went to Sybil. Any kind of magic is better than none."

"I don't know about that," Nat said. "Look here: Are you sure you were the one doing the magic tonight?"

I looked at him, bewildered. "What do you mean?"

"Could it have been Sybil who put the pictures in your head?"

"I—no. No, it couldn't have been." I rejected the idea out of hand.

"She wasn't working some dark magic through you?"

"She doesn't have magic—"

Nat shook his head. "You saw a king choking to death. And

at the very same hour, King Henry is strangled. I don't like the coincidence."

"I saw things, yes. But I didn't *do* anything."

"You say that, but how do you know?"

I shook my head, but his questions tore me up inside. Had I made a terrible mistake in trusting Sybil?

He must have seen the pain in my face, because his voice softened again. "I'm not blaming you, Lucy. If harm was done, you were innocent. But Sybil could be using you for her own ends. She might even be the reason why you can't sing magic anymore. Maybe she's cast some enchantment of her own against you—"

"We don't know that."

"No. But these are dangerous waters, don't you see?"

I did. Even if I hated to admit it.

"But it's going to be all right, Lucy." His voice deepened and grew eager. "I have good news. That's why I came looking for you. I've found a way out of here."

All thought of Sybil fled from my mind. "A way out?"

"Yes. I've been looking for one since you came here."

"You never told me." He'd talked about wanting me far away from here, but I hadn't expected this.

"I didn't want to get your hopes up," Nat said. "But it's real, Lucy. It'll bring us out farther down the Thames. And I have everything in readiness: a bit of food, some money, disguises. We can go this very night. In fact, I think we'd better."

"You mean now?" I missed Norfolk terribly, but the suddenness of his plans disconcerted me. The candle wobbled in my hand.

"There's no better time. The whole palace is in an uproar because of the attack on the King. It will be a while before anyone can take stock and count heads. And by then, we'll be well on our way to—well, to where we're going."

"And where is that?"

Nat's voice, already low, dipped still lower. "Holland, I think. At least at first. I have friends there—botanists and engineers that I've corresponded with, and others I met when I was there, and some merchants, too. They're good men; I'm sure they'd help us. And I've picked up some of the language, which will be useful."

"But Holland, Nat. It's a long way to go."

"Well, it's not as if I can bring you back to Norfolk. That's the first place they'll look."

He was right; I realized that as soon as he said it. But the truth was that Norfolk was the only place I wanted to go—to my own small home by the sea. The home that I owed to the King's grace and favor, I thought with a sinking heart. One that he might well take away from me, if I escaped in the night mere hours after he himself had been attacked.

"We could go somewhere else on the Continent, if you'd rather," Nat said. "In fact, we'll almost certainly need to move around a fair amount at first, to shake off any pursuit. But I think Holland's the best place to start."

He was so determined, so certain. Which made it all the harder for me to clear my throat and say, "Nat, I'm not sure about this."

He looked at me, startled. "Not sure about what?"

"About the whole plan. Not just Holland, but running away. I'm not sure it makes sense."

"It makes perfect sense," he said heatedly.

"But if we run now, they might suspect us of trying to murder the King."

"They might suspect us of that anyway," Nat said. "Especially you. That sleepwalking story is bad enough, but if Sybil tells them what really happened—"

"She won't."

"She might, if they put enough pressure on her. Or if that's part of her plan."

It was an uncomfortable thought. "But what if we go, and she tells it to everyone then? I won't be able to defend myself, and they'll have every reason to blame me. We'll be outlaws, Nat. We'll be hunted."

"I'll keep you safe," Nat promised. "I swear I will. And once you're out of here, I'll bet anything that your magic comes back."

"And what if it doesn't?"

"It will," Nat said again. "Maybe not at first, but after a while. And when it does, you'll have other ways of staying hidden."

"Maybe so," I said doubtfully. "But I don't want a life where I have to hide all the time. Where I daren't show my face in my own country." A new thought smote me. "And Norrie—oh, Nat, what about Norrie? I can't leave her behind."

"She would understand," Nat said, but I heard the first note of uncertainty in his voice.

"I'm not sure she would. And anyway, it doesn't matter

whether she understands or not. The point is I don't want to go without her."

"She could follow us," Nat suggested.

I shook my head. "If we go, she'd be the first person they'd track down. They'd never let her leave the country."

"Maybe so," Nat conceded. "But it wouldn't be forever. Eventually they'll find the real culprit, and then we could come back."

"You think they'd have us back?" I looked at him in disbelief. He was so intent on running that he was willfully ignoring every problem that stood in the way. "If we go, we'd be leaving them in the lurch. We'd be disobeying the King. And if they don't find the crucible in time, they'd blame us all our lives. Wrexham would have us branded traitors outright."

"We can work all that out," Nat said. "Wrexham's influence won't last forever, and neither will this alchemy craze. What's important is that we get you out of here alive." In the penumbra of the candle's flame, his eyes burned. "Someone in this palace tried to do murder tonight. And that same someone might try to murder you." His voice grew more desperate. "I have to take you somewhere safe, Lucy."

It was impossible not to be moved by his words, and even more by the love I knew lay behind them. But I couldn't go along with a plan that would make us outlaws for life. A plan that would leave Norrie to face old age alone. A plan that—for all Nat's certainty—might not even get us safely to the Continent.

I set the candle on the table, stalling for time as I tried to find the right words. But what was there to say, except the plain truth?

"I can't do it, Nat. I can't run away."

"Lucy—" He reached out a hand.

I wanted to take it, to feel his strong fingers against mine. Instead, I twisted my hands behind my back. "Please, Nat. Don't ask this of me. I can't go."

He let his hand drop. I felt a shift in the air between us.

"You really mean it," he said. "You won't go."

"I can't."

"You'd rather stay here than go with me."

Did I imagine it, or was there a slight emphasis on 'me'? "Nat, if things were different, I would go anywhere with you—"

"And yet you don't." His eyes were guarded now, his face pale. "Even with a murderer on the loose. Even with the Council trying to marry you off. You'd rather face all that than run away with me." A flash of pain crossed his face. "I guess that tells me where I stand."

"It's not like that," I said. "You know it isn't."

He was already striding toward the door.

This time I was the one who put out a hand. "Nat!"

He left without looking back.

CHAPTER TWENTY-SEVEN
EVERY INCH A CHANTRESS

After Nat walked out, I stood stunned. I hadn't seen any of it coming—not Nat's proposal, not the argument, and not the pain in his eyes when I'd turned him down.

Was there any way to make him understand that it was his plan I was rejecting, not him? Perhaps not, but I needed to try. I ran out of the room, then stopped. Which way had he gone?

"My lady!" Margery burst in on me. "Where have you been? You must come. They want to see you."

Her eyes snapped with anger—or was it with fear?

Pulse racing, I asked, "Who commands it?"

"The Earl of Wrexham, my lady, and the Council. They've ordered the guards to bring you to the East Tower for questioning."

I stiffened. Wrexham wanted to question me? And in the East Tower, the most heavily fortified part of the palace? That couldn't be anything but bad news.

Margery's eyes narrowed as she regarded my disheveled nightclothes. "But you can't go looking like that."

I couldn't believe it. A moment as grave as this, and her first thought was for clothes.

Before I could respond, two guards darted into the adjoining room. "There she is!"

That settled it. I had no hope of finding Nat now. I could only face Wrexham and the Council with as much confidence as I could muster. And there was some justice in that, I supposed, for wasn't that what I had told Nat—that I must stay and demonstrate my loyalty?

It was easier said than done.

Taking a deep breath to fortify myself, I held up my hand as the guards approached me. They stopped short and looked at me uncertainly. Did they fear I would work a song-spell on them?

If only I could. . . .

I tried to disguise my lack of magic with poise. "I am going to the East Tower," I said serenely. "Will you kindly accompany me there?"

After that, the guards treated me with a measure of respect—a victory, if a small one. They even allowed me to stop in my rooms. There Margery covered my nightgown with a velvet cloak the seamstresses had hastily sewn for me that afternoon.

Perhaps it is as simple as that, I told myself. *If I am bold, if I speak bravely, if I am every inch a Chantress . . . then everything will be fine.*

My confidence disintegrated, however, as we reached the East Tower. Behind its thick doors, I heard Sybil's voice raised high in distress.

What were they doing to her? And what was she telling them?

It cost me a great effort to hold my head high as the guards closed in behind me. In front of me, another set of guards opened the Tower doors.

The King, it seemed, was too injured to preside over this Council himself. Instead, it was Wrexham who was in charge. Although he did not sit on the throne, he stood on a dais just in front of it, his face full of wrath. A small throng of Council members had gathered before him, and I could just make out Sybil's golden curls at their center.

"Chantress." Wrexham practically spat out the word as I was ushered in.

The Council members turned, and I saw they were mostly Wrexham's cronies. Gabriel was there, too, perhaps as a witness, but Penebrygg and Sir Samuel were absent. Were they with Sir Isaac? Or had Wrexham simply not wanted them there?

"My lords and gentlemen." I greeted them with due decorum, standing tall in my velvet cloak. Margery's concern about clothes had been justified, I had to admit. Even though it was the middle of the night, Wrexham was dressed in all his usual grandeur, as were the other Council members. I would not have wanted to appear before them in only my nightclothes, as Sybil did.

As the Council members parted and allowed me into their circle, I could see her plainly: the curls hanging down, the nightgown askew, the fear writ large on her face. She looked at me as if she were drowning, and I were the branch that could save her.

All my instincts yearned to help. But at the same time Nat's question rang like a warning bell inside me: *Could it have been Sybil who put the pictures in your head?*

Wrexham beckoned me forward. "Our King has been attacked in the dead of night. What have you to say to that?"

"How does he fare?"

"He will recover, but that is not the point." Wrexham did not shout, but I could hear his rage. "When the King was attacked, where were you?"

Be careful. "I do not know when the attack happened, my lord. Not exactly. If you could tell me—"

"Half past midnight or shortly thereafter, by the King's own reckoning. And now I hear from Lord Gabriel that you and Miss Dashwood were up and about at that same hour."

What story had Sybil told him? The truth or the lie? I must be careful, very careful, to say as little as possible till I knew. "Yes, my lord. We were."

"And what were you doing?"

I feigned surprise. "Did Miss Dashwood not tell you?"

Wrexham stared me down. "Her account leaves a great deal to be desired. And in any case, I should like to hear it in your own words."

I was cornered. *Which story?*

Behind me, I heard a sudden commotion.

"Miss Dashwood has fainted!" someone cried.

I looked back and saw Sybil pulling herself up from the floor, looking wan. She caught my eye for the barest fraction of a second, then bowed her head to Wrexham. "Forgive me, my lord. I was dizzy, and my leg fell asleep. It will not happen again."

Fell asleep? That settled it. I turned back to Wrexham. "Miss Dashwood came to my room, my lord. She behaved strangely, and after a time I realized she was sleepwalking . . ."

I kept the tale simple, fearing that embroidery could get us into trouble.

"A most peculiar story," Wrexham said coldly when I was done. "In all that time you saw no one? You heard nothing?"

"Nothing, my lord."

"And you *did* nothing?"

The room went quiet. I straightened my shoulders. "What do you mean?"

"Exactly what I say. While you were abroad in the night, our King was attacked."

"I would *never* harm the King." I could hear my voice rising higher. I forced it down again, and lifted my chin. "How dare you even suggest such a thing?"

Wrexham's cold eyes watched me, unmoving. No one spoke for me, not even Gabriel. Did Wrexham hold them all in the palm of his hand? Did they dare not speak against him? Or was it even worse than that—did they truly have doubts about my loyalty?

I appealed to them. "My lords, gentlemen, this is nonsense.

What possible reason could I have to attack the King? Remember, please, that I am the one who restored his kingdom to him, not twelve months ago." There was no room for modesty here; I had to fight with everything I had.

"Yes, you did," Lord Roxburgh agreed, his beady eyes spiteful. "And look what has happened since then. The country is coming apart at the seams. The people are in open revolt."

He was blaming me for this? "My lord, magic cannot fix everything."

As I spoke, Wrexham's eyes flared. "Not if it is wielded by an enemy to the Crown."

An enemy to the Crown? Indignation choked me at first, and then—as I watched his face—fear. He was serious.

"My lords, let us not be too hasty." Gabriel came to my defense. I turned to him, trying not to show how relieved I was to have his support.

Gabriel spread his hands wide, appealing to the whole Council. "The Chantress has pleaded innocence. Shall we not allow her a chance to show her loyalty?" He gave me a brief, earnest glance, as if to say, *I'm doing all I can to help.* "I know you weren't able to find the thief when you arrived, Chantress, but by then the crime was some days old. Perhaps now, when the trail is so fresh, more can be done." He turned to Wrexham. "Surely we must allow her to try."

My stomach flipped. Gabriel had gone out on a limb for me—but what a limb. Now I was in greater danger than ever, for Wrexham was nodding.

"Yes," he said. "A most excellent test."

"My lord—" I began.

Wrexham cut me off. "No more words, Chantress. Only deeds." His eyes glittered, hard and brilliant as the jewels in his rings. "You will use your magic, here and now, to find the King's assassin. Otherwise, we will know you for a traitor."

CHAPTER TWENTY-EIGHT
OUT OF THIN AIR

Swallowing hard, I struggled to speak. "You want me to work magic? Now?"

"Yes." Wrexham's face might have been chiseled from stone. Could he sense my fear?

My mind skittered here and there, trying to find a way to evade him. "My lord, it is the middle of the night—"

"Are you saying you cannot do magic at night?" Lord Roxburgh said in disbelief.

Even Sybil looked surprised.

I flushed. "No, I am not. I am only saying . . ." What *could* I say? Nothing about scrying, that much was clear. It was singing they wanted. Anything else would not satisfy—and might raise questions I did not want to answer. Besides, the power in scrying still frightened me, for I did not know where it came from, or what it might do.

"God's blood, Chantress!" Wrexham shouted. "It is just as I

suspected: You will not do magic—not for us, not for your King. Not even when your life depends upon it."

My life? Did he really mean that? I looked straight at him, and saw the cold light in his eyes.

Yes, he really did.

Panicked, I said, "My lord, please understand: magic is not as simple as asking and getting."

"It seems simple enough from where I stand," Wrexham said. "If you value your life, you will find the assassin for us. *Now*."

Fear cinched my throat. My godmother had been right. *We are hunted; we are prey.* I was surrounded by men who hated me, who would kill me without pity if I showed any weakness.

Even if I confessed that I had no magic, they would never believe me. They would say I was lying, that my very denial proved me a traitor. I was well and truly trapped. I had to sing; I had to be seen to work magic. . . .

Be bold, be brave, be every inch a Chantress . . .

Through the haze of panic in my head, a rough plan started to take shape. It was a gamble, at best. But a gamble was better than nothing.

My cape swirled as I drew myself upward. "Very well. I will sing for you," I said. "But first we must go to the room where the King was attacked. If the magic is to work, it must be done there."

† † †

Wrexham ordered me to walk in front of him. "For your safety, Chantress," he said, but it was like having a dagger drawn at my back.

With torches lighting our way, we trailed out of the East Tower, all of us in company. No one wanted to miss the possibility of magic. Unless perhaps it was my downfall that some of them hoped to see? Even Sybil came with us, for Wrexham was loath to let her go.

At first I did not recognize the route we traveled, but when we stopped, I saw we were in a chamber very close to the one that held Nat's secret room. Its paneled walls shone like polished ebony against the blazing torches.

It was not a large room, and it felt even smaller when the entire company had assembled inside it. As they settled themselves, I studied the walls and windows and floor, searching for any clues I might use in my "magic." There was little to work with.

"So, Chantress." Even without the dais, Wrexham still towered over me. "We are here. Prove your loyalty."

"So I shall," I said, pretending to a confidence I did not have. "But first may I remind you: magic has its limits. No matter what you or I may wish, I cannot find the crucible out of thin air. Neither can I pluck out assassins and poisoners and present them to you on a plate."

A murmur of dissatisfaction ran through the crowd.

I raised my voice. "It is possible, however, that by magic means I may be able to learn something of what occurred here tonight. The crime is so recent and the struggle so brutal that an impression of it may yet remain in the very fabric of the place. I will use my magic to discover what I can. May it lead us to the villain."

Silence—but this time an encouraging one.

Taking that as my cue, I stepped away from Wrexham and waved them all back. "Give me space and quiet."

When they all obeyed, even Wrexham, I felt a small glow of satisfaction.

Now, however, came the hard part. I must sing.

I did not want to close my eyes. Indeed, with Wrexham standing so close, hand on hilt, I could hardly bear to. But I knew I must, to have any hope of hearing whatever real music was in the room—for I was still hoping, desperately, that a miracle would occur, and my magic would come back in time to save me.

I listened long and hard. Every time I was about to open my eyes, I heard faint fragments of discord, so ghostly I feared they might be coming from my own imagination. I pursued them anyway, to no avail.

Eyes still closed, I heard sighs and the shuffling of feet. The audience was growing restive.

My heart thudded. I must sing something—if not real magic, then something that sounded like it. Yet where was I to begin? Always before it was the song that had told me where to start. Now I had only the evasive notes in the air around me, and I did not dare to use even those. My experience with the mist song had reminded me that Wild Magic was as wild as its name; it had a violent energy that could destroy everything in its path—including me.

Instead, I drew on my memory of the drills and exercises my godmother had forced me to learn last year as part of my training. They were not themselves magic; they were meant simply to build my strength and teach me technique. I had loathed them at the time. Now I patched bits and pieces of them together and concocted something I hoped would pass as a Chantress song.

The melody I improvised had nothing of the strength of a true song-spell, or its beauty, or its complexity, and as I sang it, my fears began to grow. Would Wrexham see through me? Would the Council know me for a fraud? Did I have any hope of fooling them?

The notes wobbled in my throat. I cut the song off and opened my eyes.

They were all watching me, fear and awe in every face. Even Sybil watched me with wide eyes.

"The room holds tight to its secrets," I said. "But I have charmed something from it." I walked to the wall, my cloak sweeping behind me, and pressed my hand to a place I had spied earlier, where the joinery was slightly out of line. To my relief, the panel gave way, revealing a small cupboard in the wall. "It happened here."

A few in the crowd looked impressed, but not Wrexham and his closest allies.

"This is your magic?" Lord Roxburgh sneered. "You tell us nothing but what is already known."

"Ah, but did you know this?" I took a deep breath. "The attacker was the thief who stole the crucible." I was only guessing, but it seemed a reasonable deduction. "And he—or she—was acting on someone else's behalf."

"Someone else?" My words caught Wrexham by surprise. "Who?"

"I cannot say for certain; the magic is not so exact. I can only tell you this: there is a queen involved, a queen who wants to do the King harm."

It was the best I could do with the picture I had seen in the scrying water. Was it enough?

"Which queen?" someone cried.

"That I do not know . . . ," I began.

The room dissolved into bedlam.

"The Queen of France!" someone shouted. "She's intriguing with the Scots again, and she's sent her spy into our court."

"What about the Queen of Spain?" another argued. "Those Spaniards have always had it in for us."

"Depend upon it, it's Queen Mariana," someone else agreed. "She wants the Philosopher's Stone for herself, to cure her sickly son."

"What about Christina of Sweden?" Lord Roxburgh suggested. "She's a devotee of alchemy, we all know that. And the Swedish treasury is almost as depleted as ours is."

"Queen Christina?" Gabriel shook his head. "Never. She's always been the King's friend."

Lord Roxburgh's beady eyes flickered over him. "You are quick to defend her, Lord Gabriel. But then you spent a great deal of time at her court. Four years, was it?"

"And what of it?" Gabriel sounded flustered. As others turned to stare at him, all with the same considering look in their eyes, he added heatedly, "I trained with the alchemists in Queen Christina's court, it's true. But that doesn't make me her spy. I'm the King's man, I swear."

Gabriel, a traitor working for the Swedish queen? Was that the truth that lay behind the picture I'd seen?

Others evidently thought so. Wrexham wheeled on Gabriel, as if ready to wrestle him to the ground.

"Is this the traitor, Chantress?" he asked.

"I do not know." For all my suspicions about Gabriel, I wasn't prepared to condemn him on such flimsy evidence. "The magic could not give me a name."

Next to Lord Roxburgh, a bewigged man spoke up: my dinner companion, Lord Ffoulkes. "It could be the girl."

At first I thought he meant me, but he pointed to Sybil. "She was brought up in France, wasn't she? She could be working for the French queen."

Sybil gasped. "I'm not. I swear I'm not. I've never even *met* the queen."

"Miss Dashwood was sleepwalking when the King was attacked," Lord Roxburgh pointed out. "Or so the Chantress says." He looked at me.

"Yes." I couldn't back away from that lie now; I was in too deep. But Ffoulkes's suspicions chimed with my own doubts about Sybil. It seemed all too possible that she might be a French spy.

The others, however, had gone back to watching Gabriel.

"Don't look at me like that," he snapped, all trace of his lazy grin gone. "I'm not the man you want."

"Then who is?" Lord Roxburgh demanded.

"It could be anyone." His eyes almost black in the torchlight, Gabriel pointed at his accusers. "One of you standing here, perhaps. Or perhaps none of us at all. It could be a servant—"

"A foreign queen choosing an English servant as her agent?" Lord Roxburgh inquired. "That seems most unlikely."

"They could be masquerading," Gabriel argued. He stopped short, as if a new thought had struck him. "Or perhaps what the Chantress saw wasn't a foreign queen at all. Perhaps it was Boudicca. I've heard that's what some of her followers call her: the Queen of the People."

Boudicca? From the expressions on the faces around me, I wasn't the only one surprised by the suggestion.

"Is that possible, Chantress?" Wrexham demanded.

I thought back to the picture I had seen. Neither figure had looked like anyone I knew, so what had made me so certain the woman was a queen? The gold circlet on her head, no doubt— but that did not mean she was a queen by blood. She might be merely a self-proclaimed queen, like Boudicca. "I suppose it is possible, yes."

A tense quiet settled over the room.

Wrexham eyed Gabriel, then scowled at me. "It is not enough, Chantress. We need to know more."

My stomach tightened. I had no more to offer. "That is all I saw, my lord."

"Then sing again."

"My lord, I don't think—"

"I'm not asking you to think!" he shouted. "You will sing for us, do you understand? You will sing your throat raw, if that's what it takes to find the traitor."

Panic robbed me of breath. He wanted the impossible, and he was willing to break me to get it. And this time I truly could see no way out. Having forced me to work "magic" once, he would ask for it again and again, until at last the truth would become plain. I would be revealed as a lying Chantress, a Chantress who had worked false magic, a Chantress who had no true power.

What would Wrexham do to me then?

"My lord Earl!" A guard shot into the room.

"Not now," Wrexham snarled, barely sparing him a glance.

He didn't fall back. "Begging your pardon, my lord, but you asked us to find Nathaniel Walbrook."

I'd been relieved by the interruption, but now I tensed in apprehension. Wrexham had sent guards after Nat?

The pale Viking eyes swung away from me. The guard had Wrexham's attention now.

"You mean you've found him?" Wrexham asked.

"No . . . that is, not quite, my lord. We have one witness— a footman—who saw him headed in this direction. That was some time ago, but it's all we have to go on. I've given my men orders to search the rooms here. Including this one, with your permission."

"What is there to search?" Wrexham demanded irritably. "We'd have seen Walbrook if he were here."

The guard looked abashed.

"Unless—" Wrexham's eyes narrowed as he looked again at the cupboard where the King had seen the crucible. "Unless there are other hidden compartments in this part of the palace, ones big enough to conceal a person. Yes, that is a possibility we must consider. Order your men to knock on all the walls!"

"We'll help you," Gabriel cried. Within moments half the Council was tapping at the walls. Less than a minute later, at the guard's command, the pounding began next door. It was as if a regiment of carpenters had descended on us.

Nat's secret room, I thought in a panic. *They'll find it. What if he's in it?*

Of course, he could be anywhere. But if he had been seen running this way. . . .

"My lord, we've found something!" a guard called from the next room.

When we rushed in, several guards were clustered around the place where Nat's secret room was hidden.

"It's hollow here," one of them said. "And if you look in the chamber next door, the walls don't join up quite right."

"Then what are you waiting for?" Wrexham roared. "Bash the wall in."

The guards were more than willing to follow his order. Two pikes smashed into the wall. The panel splintered, revealing Nat's dark hideaway.

"Light!" Wrexham shouted. "Bring the torches!"

Please don't let Nat be there, I prayed.

But as the flames came close, I saw him. He was crouched against the farthest reaches of the wall, and his eyes, wild and hunted, searched out mine.

Beside him, glowing red-gold in the torch light, was the crucible.

CHAPTER TWENTY-NINE
RED-HANDED

The guards pushed forward, blocking Nat's way out—and blocking my view of him. "I didn't steal it!" I heard him protest. "It was already here when I came in."

"Arrest him!" Wrexham ordered.

The room erupted into a shouting mass of men.

"No!" I cried out. "He didn't do it."

No one heard me. Guards, lords, gentlemen—they were all shoving forward and crying out for Nat's blood.

"Get the traitor!"

"Hang him!"

"Hie there, you—bring us some rope!"

Rope? Dear heaven, were they planning to hang him right here? Surely they only meant to take him prisoner. . . .

I had to save him somehow. But what could I do without magic?

In a frenzy of frustration, I pushed at the backs of the men who stood in my way. The men did not budge. *I can't even see him,* I thought. *They'll kill him for a traitor, and I can't even see what's happening.*

"They've got him!" someone shouted.

The men in front of me shuffled forward, and through a gap I glimpsed Nat. Two guards had him pinioned and were marching him toward the door. Just before they reached the threshold, he stumbled. Blood on his cheek glistened in the torchlight.

"Nat!" I cried out. What had they done to him?

He didn't rise. The guards leaned over him.

Quick as a hare, he jerked up and knocked the guards off balance. Dodging their flailing arms, he ran free.

"Stop him!" Wrexham cried. But the two guards were still getting their footing. When the others rushed forward, they tripped over them, blocking the doorway for everyone else. By the time the tangle was undone, Nat was out of sight.

"Find him!" Wrexham shouted.

As the guards fanned out, Wrexham wheeled toward me, the crucible in his massive grasp. His free hand came down on my shoulder. "You. Come with me." He turned to one of the guards. "Alert the soldiers outside. They must keep watch for the traitor on the walls, in the park, on the river—"

"Yes, my lord."

"And summon the full Council to the Crimson Chamber. Bring the man Penebrygg there under guard. I don't want him slipping away." His hand tightened on my shoulder. "The Chantress and I will meet you there."

† † †

Whatever the guards said to the Council members, it made them act quickly. Within a quarter hour, almost everyone was assembled in the Crimson Chamber, including Penebrygg. Spectacles askew, cap missing, he had been marched into the room by two guards who now stood behind his chair. I was too far away to say anything to him. Indeed, I hardly dared meet his eyes, for Wrexham was watching every move I made.

It was Sir Isaac's entrance, however, that caused the most stir. White-faced, he tottered through the door.

Sir Samuel rushed up to steady him. "You oughtn't to have come here, old friend. Not in your condition."

Sir Isaac grabbed Sir Samuel's arm for support. "Bother my condition. Wrexham, is it true? Have you found the crucible?"

"We have," Wrexham said. "And I swear to you, it will be ringed with guards from this night onward, until your work is done."

"But where is it?"

Wrexham beckoned forth a cohort of men who had been standing in the corner. "Show the crucible to Sir Isaac."

The men trotted around the table, carrying a chest. When they opened this before Sir Isaac, he looked as if he were about to faint.

"It *is* the crucible. It truly is. God be thanked." As he touched its smooth side, his voice shook. "Where did you find it?"

Wrexham recounted what had happened. Those who had

not witnessed the turn of events for themselves—Sir Isaac, Sir Samuel, and Penebrygg—looked shocked.

"I can hardly believe it," Sir Isaac said. "I know Nat was no fan of alchemy, but to stoop to such infamy . . ."

"He wouldn't." Penebrygg shook his head vehemently. "I raised the lad; I know him through and through. He's not a murderer. And he wouldn't steal the crucible."

Sir Samuel looked torn. "But what about the evidence? He was caught red-handed—"

"He didn't do it!" I had to speak, even though I was half-afraid Wrexham would muzzle me. "Dr. Penebrygg is right. We know him, none better, and he wouldn't do this."

"Nonsense," Lord Roxburgh said. "He was found with the crucible. We all saw it. And everyone knows he was against the alchemy work."

"But he told you he was," I said. "The real thief would never dare be so open. Nat is innocent. He must be."

"He's guilty as Judas, Chantress." Wrexham pounded the table as he delivered his verdict. "You saw him there with the crucible."

"It could have been planted on him," Penebrygg said.

Wrexham dismissed this. "How, when no one else knew the room existed?"

"What about the queen?" I said, scrambling for any point in Nat's favor. "The magic told me there was a queen involved."

"And who's to say there isn't?" Lord Roxburgh put in. "Perhaps the boy is working for a foreign queen—or for Boudicca. Of the two, I'd say Boudicca is more likely. We all know he comes from base blood himself."

"His blood has nothing to do with it!" I rose from my chair in anger. "I tell you he isn't working for any queen. If he were, I would know it—"

"Would you, Chantress? And how exactly would you know?" Wrexham leaned in close, and I saw rage in his eyes. "Have you been seeing him in secret?"

I opened my mouth, but no words came out.

"God's bloody bones!" Wrexham's rage spread, reddening his cheeks, twisting his mouth. "Understand this, Chantress: you will not be seeing him again. Not until you see him put to death like the traitor he is. For we will hunt him down, have no doubt about that. We will hunt him and capture him; he will be drawn and quartered. And you will be there to see his head tarred and spiked and set high on London Bridge."

"No." I would not listen. I would not let myself picture it. "No."

"You will be there because I tell you to be." Wrexham's fist slammed into the table again. "The women of my house do not disobey me."

My mouth went dry. Surely I had not heard him right. Surely I had misunderstood. "The women . . . of your house?" I repeated.

"Has no one told you yet?" Wrexham leaned close, his breath hot on my cheek, his eyes burning with malice. "The Council has come to an agreement about your marriage: you are to become my wife."

CHAPTER THIRTY
CONJURINGS

I stared back at Wrexham in disbelief.

"I recall no such decision by the Council," Penebrygg protested from far down the table.

"The Inner Council settled the matter this very night," Wrexham said without taking his eyes off me. "We are agreed: in these dangerous times, the Chantress requires the protection and steadiness that a man of my years and position can offer."

The room was quiet.

So it was true. They were marrying me off to Wrexham. The horror of it nearly swallowed me whole.

"You don't even like me," I whispered, looking into his perfect, hateful face.

"Liking has nothing to do with it," he said coldly. "I had thought to save you for my son, but we need a more immediate solution. The kingdom has a pressing need for Chantresses who respect authority—as I assure you our daughters will do."

Our daughters? I wanted to retch.

"You can't do this," I said.

"I can, and I will. And I will not suffer you to disobey me." Wrexham's fists tightened as he motioned to the men standing at the door. "Guards, I fear the Chantress is unwell. Escort her to her rooms—and watch over her."

† † †

The guards delivered me to my rooms, where I found Margery waiting up for me. When the guards made as if to accompany me, she pointed them firmly to the door. "It isn't proper for you men to be here, not when the Lady Chantress is about to take her rest. You can take up your post outside. I'll watch over her in here."

The guards looked at each other, then did as she asked. Was that because of her implacable manner—or because they knew she was Wrexham's spy?

Well, if she was his spy, what did it matter now? Wearily, I sank before the fire. As Wrexham's wife, I could expect to be surrounded by his spies for the rest of my life.

Wrexham's wife. Was it possible? Exhausted and defeated, and still terrified for Nat, I watched the fire through blurred and aching eyes.

"You cannot sleep there by the fire, my lady," Margery said.

"Did you know?" I asked dully.

"Know what, my lady?"

"That I was to be married to Wrexham."

"My lady!" Her shock appeared genuine. "Surely not—"

"He told me so himself. Before the Council. There can be no doubt." Despite my best efforts, my voice shook.

"Oh, my lady." She was silent for a moment, then said, "He has wanted another wife for some time. But I did not think it would be you."

I didn't want to keep talking with someone who was in Wrexham's pay. "It is very late, Margery. You should go to bed."

Her voice grew wooden again. "I must help you into your own bed first, my lady."

"No. Just leave me." I was fighting now for self-control. "Please."

For once, she let me have my way. "Yes, my lady." I heard her soft footsteps tread back and forth behind me. She placed a blanket around my shoulders. "Good night, my lady."

I heard her walk into her own small room and climb into bed. She left the door between our rooms open, but once I was sure she was asleep, I allowed the scalding tears to fall.

If only I had run away with Nat when he'd asked me to! Guilt and regret gnawed at me. I'd been so certain that I knew a better way forward—and look at the result: I was to be married to Wrexham, and Nat was to be hunted down and hanged for a traitor. And I had no way to prevent any of it. The only magic I could do now was to see strange visions. And what kind of power was that? A paltry one at best.

Unless I could somehow use it to see the face of the true culprit....

My tears dried as I considered this. When I had scried with Sybil, the faces of the king and queen had been blurred. But if I tried it again on my own, I might see more clearly and be able to identify the queen. Or perhaps I would see an altogether different picture, one that would reveal some other clue.

Scrying would tell me something else, too: if I were successful, I'd know that the scrying magic was my own, and that Sybil didn't control it—or me.

Of course, even if Sybil were innocent, there remained the danger that the visions were more than visions, that they somehow worked harm in the real world. What if I scried a picture of Nat being captured—and it happened? My whole body tensed. Perhaps I ought not to try scrying after all.

Yet what else could I do? Lie here and hope for my Chantress magic to come back—knowing, all the while, that Wrexham was drawing his net tighter and tighter? And that if he found Nat, he would condemn him to torture and death?

No. To do nothing was intolerable.

After listening to be sure Margery was still asleep, I crept over to the chest in the corner. On it stood the floral offerings from my erstwhile valentines, which Margery had arranged in vases. I tried not to make a sound as I pulled the nosegays from the shallowest bowl. Made of fine, gilded porcelain, it was quite different from the bowl Sybil had used, but it was the only reasonable container I had.

I carried the bowl, nearly full of water, over to the fire. How to get the light right? I tried several different arrangements, but nothing worked.

Just as I was about to give up, a log in the hearth broke in two, sending up a shower of sparks. I saw their fire reflected in the water, and then, beneath that, another swirl of light diving down and down and down . . .

Ask, some small part of my mind said. *Ask the question.*

"Who stole the crucible?" I did no more than breathe the words. "Who pinned the blame on Nat?"

Deeper and deeper I fell, and then all at once I saw colors rich as stained glass. They whorled and shifted and then resolved into the picture I'd seen before: the murderous king and queen. Again, to my horror, they fought their life-or-death battle, clawing at each other's throats until their blurred faces turned blue.

But this time the picture twisted, and a new image appeared before me: a circlet of gold crowning a faceless head, and a hand with a pearl ring grasping a knife. A flash of blue light, and the knife sliced between crown and head. Blood spurted. Another slash, and the crown tore away. And now it felt as if I could not breathe, as if I myself were dying. . . .

My hand flailed, rocking the cup, and the picture vanished. I was left sitting before the fire, a half-spilt bowl of water before me, and a spreading puddle on my cloak. Dread filled every inch of me.

I knew now that the magic was mine and not Sybil's. But what did the pictures mean? Whose hand had wielded the knife? Could it be Wrexham? I was fairly sure that one of his rings had a pearl. But then why hadn't I seen his other rings too?

So many questions! But the worst one was this: By conjuring these pictures up, had I somehow harmed the King?

"My lady?" Margery appeared at my side. "Did you cry out?" Sharp-eyed as always, she swooped down on the cup. "What's this?"

"There was a mark on my cloak," I said. "I . . . I wanted to get it out."

"You ought to have left that to me, my lady. Velvet needs special care." She started mopping at the wet cloth. "Anyway, you ought to be sleeping now."

"I can't."

She looked up from her mopping and surveyed my face. "Syrup of roses and saffron, that's what you need, my lady. I could send to the kitchen—"

"No." I had a sudden thought. "Could you send someone to check on the King instead? That's part of why I can't sleep. I worry he's taken a turn for the worse."

Her eyes widened. "It's the *King* you're worried about? I thought—" She cut herself off and asked quickly, "Is your magic telling you something?"

"No." I didn't want to bring magic into this at all. "It's just ordinary worry. But if I knew the King was doing well, I might be able to sleep."

Margery's face had turned unreadable again. "All right, my lady. I'll ask a guard to find out."

It took nearly half an hour for the answer to come back. During all that time, Margery sat up with me, her presence fraying my nerves still further. But when the guard reappeared, the news was good.

"The King's condition has improved, my lady," Margery reported, giving me a severe look. "He is sleeping peacefully, as you yourself should be."

This time she gave me no quarter, shepherding me toward my bed like a collie. But I climbed in willingly enough, for I wanted to be left alone with my thoughts. After Margery went back to her own room, I lay there in the dark, plotting out what to do next.

The scrying hadn't told me much, but thankfully it hadn't done any harm, either. Which meant that I could trust Sybil's good intentions. She wasn't working black magic through me; she was truly trying to help.

What I wanted to know now was this: Did she have any other magic to offer me? Something stronger than scrying? Something that would help me foil Wrexham's dreadful plans? Something that would allow me to clear Nat's name?

First thing tomorrow, I would find Sybil and ask.

CHAPTER THIRTY-ONE
PRISONER

Exhausted in body and mind, I eventually sank into a deep sleep. When I woke, it was almost noon, and Margery was out. Given her distress at my wanderings yesterday, I suspected she wouldn't be gone for long. But if I was quick, perhaps I could dash out to see Sybil before she returned.

I hurried into my clothes—the blue woolen skirts and bodice that I had worn on my travels, now cleaned and pressed. But when I slipped into the vestibule and tried to open the outer door, it wouldn't budge.

Outside I heard voices.

I pounded on the door. "It's the Chantress. Let me out!"

Metal clanked. The voices grew louder. But no one answered me.

A good quarter hour later, I was still calling for help when the door opened sharply, almost knocking me down.

"My lady Chantress." Wrexham's enormous frame filled the doorway. Behind him, out in the corridor, stood a line of men with pikes and swords. I stepped back, and he pushed the door shut behind him. "I hear you have been making trouble for the guards."

The mere sight of him filled me with loathing. "I want to go out."

"You will stay here until Walbrook is found."

So Nat was still free? Relief washed over me—and then fear, for this was only the first day, and the hunt was far from over.

I have to get help from Sybil.

"And you will have no visitors," Wrexham went on, "until we are certain the danger is over."

No visitors? "You mean you're locking me away?"

"I am protecting you, Chantress. The Council agrees with me on this: you are young and confused, and for your own safety we must guard you until all danger is over."

"And the King? Does he agree too?"

"The King is not well, but I have explained matters to him," Wrexham said carefully. "He agrees we must keep you safe."

His eyes didn't quite meet mine, and that gave me hope. Perhaps the King did not know that I was being treated as a captive. "I want to see the King myself."

Even this small protest made anger flare in his eyes. "I have already told you, Chantress: you will not be seeing anyone."

"I insist."

"You will do as you're told!" His fist flew past my face and slammed into the wall beside me.

His rings splintered the wood. They could so easily have scarred my skin. Shaken, I backed out of his reach.

He took another step toward me, fists still bunched, the

knuckles on one hand bleeding. "My wife will not disobey me."

My wife. The words made me sick. But I did not want those rings to split my face. Though it made the bile rise into my throat, I bowed my head to him. "Yes, my lord."

His breath rasped. "That is better."

I must not raise my head. I must not look him in the eye. Instead, I stared down at his huge hands, at the blood on his knuckles, at the golden hairs on his fingers, at the gaudy rings that glinted in the light. And that's when I saw the truth: Only one of his rings—the pearl one—bore a conventional jewel. The other stones, though beautiful, were something else entirely.

They were the stones of dead Chantresses.

My breath stopped.

I shut my eyes. The crazed pattern of cracking on the stones was unmistakable, and so was the odd way that the light refracted inside them. I'd only seen such a thing once before, in Lady Helaine's stone after she died, but I had never forgotten it.

It was all I could do not to reach for my own ruby, slung under my bodice on its long, thin chain. It, too, had a crack in it—a different pattern, signifying that I had lost the power to do Proven Magic yet was still living. Would it, too, decorate Wrexham's fingers one day?

My head was still bent when I heard Wrexham heave the door open. At the sound, I sprang forward, hoping to catch the door before it closed.

Wrexham was too quick for me. The door slammed in my face.

"Bar the rooms shut!" he commanded the guards. "For her own safety."

The bar came clunking down.

† † †

I was pacing the room, caught between fear and fury, when the door opened again. Margery walked in past the guards, an enormous bundle of bloodred cloth in her arms. The moment she was through, the guards slammed the door shut again.

I looked at Margery. "So they'll let you in and out, but not me?"

Pink-faced, Margery hugged the bundle closer to her. "I had duties to see to, my lady."

Duties that included reporting to Wrexham, no doubt.

"And those men out there are only trying to do *their* duty," Margery added. "My lord Wrexham gave strict orders to them. You'll find he guards his possessions most carefully, my lady."

His *possessions*? Did she mean me?

"When the Countess was alive, he never let her stir without guards at her side." Margery spread the cloth out on the bed, her back turned to me.

I didn't like what I was hearing. "You mean Wrexham's wife? She never went out on her own?"

"No. And by the time I served her, she mostly kept to her rooms."

"Was she ill?"

"No." Margery's hands stilled over the cloth. "Just . . . fragile."

A fragile woman, completely under Wrexham's brutal control.

Something made me ask the question: "Margery, you never told me: How did she die?"

"She had a bad fall, my lady." She kept her back to me. "But we shouldn't speak of such sad things. It will not make your confinement any easier to bear. Let us turn to more cheerful subjects." She turned, tugging out a length of the cloth to show me. "Only look at this: the very best Venetian silk, and there's enough to make an entire gown. My lord Wrexham gave it to me this morning—"

So she *had* seen Wrexham. And his hands, covered in dead Chantresses' stones, had touched this cloth. I looked at the cascade of shining silk with revulsion.

Margery faltered as she took in my expression. "It's a gift for your betrothal, my lady."

"I do not accept it," I said.

"But you must, my lady," She fingered the cloth anxiously. "My lord Wrexham will be most offended if you do not. He says you must be properly dressed—"

"Because I am his possession?" I said softly.

The cloth fluttered down from Margery's hand. Her face was carefully blank. "My lady, it is the very best silk. And the color suits you. Only allow me to make it up, and you will see—"

"I tell you I will not wear it."

She looked at me for a long moment, her face drawn. Then the blank mask came down. Without another word, she scooped up the cloth and removed it to her room, out of sight.

† † †

When Margery returned, her hands were empty, and there was no more talk of Wrexham or silk or betrothals. Indeed, for most of the afternoon there was hardly any talk at all. Margery busied herself about the room, and I sat silently by the window, blindly turning the pages of a book, seeing Wrexham's rings in my mind's eye.

I listened to every sigh and sound and squeak in the room, willing them to become music, to become magic. If determination and desperation sufficed to summon song-spells, I would have had them at my beck and call. But it seemed that Wild Magic could not even be bothered to toy with me today. Just once, when I leaned my head against the drafty window frame, did I hear a single shaky note on the wind. And it was gone almost as soon as it came.

Worn out by listening, yet unwilling to stop, I lost all track of time that afternoon. I only knew that whenever I looked up, Margery's watchful eyes were on me.

Something, it seemed, was bothering her, and the longer I stayed at the window, the more restless she became. Perhaps it was only the dress that was on her mind, but I found myself tensing, wondering what else might be in store for me.

"Won't you eat, my lady?" she asked, not once, but twice, and then again.

Each time I turned her down. Even as the light began to fade from the sky, I continued to sit at the window, looking out at the garden, where soldiers paraded. Did their maneuvers have something to do with the hunt for Nat?

With my eyes I traced the boundaries of the garden and what I could see of the walls of Greenwich Park. *Let Nat escape*, I prayed. *Please let him escape. And let me find a way to reach Sybil. . . .*

"You really must eat something, my lady," Margery said once more as she lit the lamps. "Such a beautiful platter they sent up for you, and you haven't tasted anything on it."

The platter overflowed with delicacies from last night's banquet. Merely glancing at it made me sick. "No, thank you."

"Just a bit of the roast chicken," Margery suggested, "or a few of the sugared grapes . . ."

"No, thank you," I said again, this time more forcefully. "I don't want anything."

"But you must eat." Margery looked pained. Was she hoping that food would sweeten my temper, and make me change my mind about the silk? "I remember the Countess—"

"Enough, Margery." I couldn't bear to hear another word about Wrexham's first wife. "I'm nothing like your Countess. I'll never be like her."

"But that's just it, my lady." Margery's voice was sharp with anxiety. "You *are* like her. She used to stand by the window, just like that, and she wouldn't eat either. That's how she became so frail. She wasted away, my lady; she had no strength to stand up when he—"

She stopped abruptly.

"He?" I repeated. "You mean Wrexham? He did something to her?"

She shrank back. "I oughtn't to have said anything, my lady. Please, please don't tell him what I said."

The dread in her eyes horrified me—not only for what it told me about Wrexham as a master, but also for what it told me about myself. In all the time that I had feared Margery, I had never once stopped to think that she, too, might be living in fear. I had never tried to step into her shoes, never wondered if she served Wrexham because she had no other choice.

"I promise I will not say anything, Margery."

The naked relief in her face shamed me.

"Would he punish you, then?" I asked. "If he knew?"

A mute nod.

I took a deep breath and left my post by the window. "Then we'll have to do everything we can to keep you safe from him."

Her mouth trembled. And then, impossibly, my stoic maid began to cry.

"It's Mam I worry about," she choked out, so soft I could barely hear her. "Mam and the girls. My lord Wrexham said they'd be fed if I pleased him, but he'll see them starve if I don't. And Mam's been ill, and the girls are so young, and I haven't known what to do . . ."

My own throat tightened. I had thought myself powerless, but Margery was vulnerable in ways I hadn't even dreamed of. I felt as if I were seeing her for the first time. Behind her implacable mask was a girl who was younger than I'd thought, perhaps even younger than me—young and scared and worried out of her mind.

The painful whisper went on. "And he hasn't been happy with me as it is, for I haven't had much to report—" She shot me a panicked look. "I mean, I—"

"Never mind," I said. "I already know."

"Know w-what?"

"That you're Wrexham's spy."

Her face went an ugly red.

"One of his spies, that is," I added. A spy who had been forced into the job. A spy who I might have turned into an ally, if I'd been wiser and more compassionate. But maybe it wasn't too late. . . .

"I expect it wasn't a job you much wanted," I said. "But never mind. Your secret is safe with me."

She gaped at me.

"Tell me," I said. "Have you had anything to eat today?"

"N-not much. But—"

"Then let's both eat." I broke off some of the sugared grapes and handed them to her. "You're right: we need our strength. And while we eat, we can talk."

"Talk?" she said faintly. "About what?"

"Well, about the cloth, for one. The silk." I took some grapes myself. "Will Wrexham be angry with you if I don't wear it?"

"Very much so, my lady. I'm to see that you are turned out correctly, so that you are a credit to him. And I was told particularly to have the silk made up for you right away."

"I see. Well, we can't have him punishing you for that."

"You mean you'll wear it?"

I popped a grape into my mouth, savoring its sweet coating and tart juice while I considered the matter. "I'll have it made up, at least. That should satisfy him."

"Yes, my lady." She hesitated. "At least—for a while."

For a while, and what then? I saw again Wrexham's fist whistling past my face. If he became my husband, I might not last as long as Margery's Countess had.

I must not let that happen.

"Do what you can to see the work goes slowly," I told Margery. "Now, about your mother. I want to help you there—"

Hope suffused her face. "With your magic?"

What could I say? It was impossible to tell her the truth, not when there was a risk she might turn around and tell everything to Wrexham. "Yes."

"You would help her? Truly?"

I nodded, praying I wasn't building up false hopes. "I'll do everything I can, Margery. I give you my word."

"Oh, my lady." She was trying to keep back tears. "You aren't anything like he said. You're not high and mighty, or mad for power, or anything like that. It was all lies, wasn't it?"

"That's what Wrexham told you about me?"

She nodded. "And I believed him. But you're not like that at all."

"I should hope I'm not," I said lightly, trying to conceal my distress. How many other minds had Wrexham poisoned against me?

Something clanked on the other side of the door.

My heart skipped a beat. Was it Wrexham, come to check on me again? Beside me, Margery turned pale.

"Of course I have permission to see her." A proud voice, smooth and fluid. "From Wrexham? No, from the King himself. Look—here's his seal upon it."

The outer door opened, and Sir Isaac strode into the room.

CHAPTER THIRTY-TWO
A POWERFUL WOMAN

"Your guards are rather more zealous than I expected," Sir Isaac said as I led him to the fire.

"The Earl of Wrexham has ordered them to refuse all visitors." I gestured to a chair and took the one next to it.

Sir Isaac frowned as he sat, his dark brows a marked contrast to his too-white face. "Yes, but I had the King's permission to enter. As I told the guards—"

Whatever he was about to say was lost as a great tremor passed through him. He clutched at the chair arms.

"Sir Isaac!" I rose in alarm.

"It's nothing," he gasped. "Merely the aftereffects of the poison."

"You ought to be resting."

"No, no." The fit, whatever it was, seemed to be passing. Or was it merely that he had found the strength to fight it? At any rate, he was sitting up straighter, and his breathing was easier. "It is nothing, I swear. And it is vital—absolutely vital—that I meet with you now. Pray, sit down again and let me speak to you."

I sank into my chair again and glanced back at Margery, who was retreating to her own room.

Following my gaze, Sir Isaac said softly, "Do not be troubled if she overhears. The Council never would have allowed her to serve you if she could not be trusted. Wrexham himself has vouched for her discretion and judgment and absolute loyalty."

No wonder he had, given his hold over her family.

"What is it you wish to tell me?" I asked.

"Only this." His bloodshot eyes beseeched me. "At dawn tomorrow, when we make the Philosopher's Stone, I must have you by my side."

"Me? But why? I'm no alchemist, Sir Isaac—"

"That matters not at all. Let me explain." Sir Isaac pressed his fingers to his temple, as if warding off a headache. "It's to do with the papers, you see. Flamel's papers. Even if one understands the cipher he used, their meaning can still be cryptic."

I nodded, remembering what I'd seen of them.

"And there is a passage in them," Sir Isaac continued, "that I have struggled with again and again, for the symbols it contained did not entirely make sense to me. Nevertheless, I was fairly certain that what they called for was this: an assistant to hold the crucible during the last stages of the work, a man powerful and incorruptible. At least that's what I believed—until yesterday."

"And now?"

"Now I have worked out what those extra symbols mean. I

was almost right. I do need someone with those qualities. But what the symbols reveal is this: she must be a woman."

"A woman?" I looked at him in frank surprise. "Are you sure?"

"Beyond all doubt. I ought to have worked it out before. There have long been rumors that Flamel's wife, Pernelle, helped him in his work. And many alchemists through the ages have maintained that women's energies are vital to the Great Work. An erroneous belief, I thought, and yet it seems they are correct. Flamel says we must have a woman—powerful and pure in heart—to make the Stone. And that is why I come to you."

Because I was powerful? Not with my magic gone. "Sir Isaac, I'm not the best choice—"

"Chantress, there is not a woman in the kingdom who can match you for sheer power. And in using that power to restore the rightful King to his throne, you showed yourself to be incorruptible." He leaned toward me, his gray eyes fervent. "My lady, believe me: there can be no one better for the task."

"But why should any qualities of mine matter? How could they possibly affect the result?"

"Would that I knew! It is one of the great mysteries of alchemy. I can only assure you that all the sages agree: boiling and burning change the nature of matter, and so, too, do the invisible auras of our intentions and purposes. An unworthy practitioner, no matter how skilled, cannot succeed in making the Philosopher's Stone. God will not allow it."

His explanation chilled me. If I agreed to help with the Great Work when my power was gone, would the experiment fail?

I tried to smile. "Truly, Sir Isaac, it sounds as if you require a saint."

"We require *you*." Another small tremor passed through him. "Rest assured, the entire Council agrees with me: you are the woman we need."

"Surely there is someone else, someone older and wiser—"

"My dear lady, no false modesty, please! It must be you." Sir Isaac was unbending. "The Council agrees, and they will compel you to serve. Given your great heart, however, I should hope that conscience alone would be persuasion enough. Without your help, we will fail, and the country will starve."

It seemed I had no choice, not if the Council was determined to drag me to the task. Best to give in gracefully—and hope what little power I had would see the work through. "If you truly need me, I will help."

Sir Isaac gave me one of his rare smiles. It lightened his whole face. "My lady, we are grateful. *I* am grateful."

"I am to hold the crucible? That is all?"

"That and a few other minor tasks. We alchemists will do the rest."

I saw a chance to break free of my prison. "Even so, I would like to practice. If you could only arrange it, I will gladly go to the laboratory—"

"There is no need, my lady. They are simple tasks, and I have no doubt you will manage them to perfection at the appointed hour. Until then, the Council thinks it best that both you and the crucible remain under guard. If anything happens to you, all our efforts will be for nothing."

"But you are at least as crucial to the success of the enterprise," I pointed out, "and you are not living under guard."

"My dear lady, I am a grown man. I do have an escort—they are waiting for me outside—but that is sufficient."

"I am a Chantress. It would be sufficient for me, too."

"The Council thinks not. Nat is drawn to you. He is desperate; we fear he may find a way to take you hostage."

"But that's mad," I said. "He would never do that."

"I understand the impulse to defend him, believe me." Sir Isaac regarded me with some sympathy. "Despite our differences over alchemy, I have always held Nat in the highest regard. But even you must admit that the facts are entirely against him."

"I admit no such thing."

Sir Isaac sighed. "Facts are facts, my dear Chantress. We get nowhere by ignoring the evidence." He rested his shaky hands on the chair arms. "That said, all this talk of drawing and quartering is unnecessarily bloodthirsty. And, of course, I would be the first to agree that the boy deserves a fair trial."

"Yes, but I don't see how he will get a fair trial—"

"Chantress, we should not keep talking about this." His tone was not unkind, but he spoke right through me, drowning me out. "It is an unhappy subject, and dwelling on it will sap your strength at a time when we must have you well and strong."

"But—"

"Please try to turn your mind to happier thoughts. In less than twelve hours, we must begin the Great Work, and we need you to be in the best possible state of health for it. Indeed, you ought to be resting right now." He rose from his chair.

He wasn't going to listen to me. At least not about Nat. But there was another matter he might take in better spirit, if I approached it the right way.

"Sir Isaac, it is hard to rest with these sad thoughts whirring in my head. It would help so much if I could see a friend. If Miss Dashwood could visit—"

"Impossible, I'm afraid." Sir Isaac shook his head, his face grave. "A necessary visit like mine is one thing, but social calls must wait for less perilous times." He offered me a brief but courteous bow. "No, no, don't get up. Rest, please. The guards will bring you to the laboratory at four tomorrow morning."

He was already passing into the vestibule. I stood. "Sir Isaac—"

"I must run, my dear Chantress. There is so much to prepare." He knocked at the outer door, alerting the guards, who ushered him over the threshold while barring my own way out.

When the door closed behind him, I felt more imprisoned than ever. A rich prison, this, with gilded ornaments and a warm fire burning, yet the very tapestries on the walls seemed to smother me.

"My lady?"

I looked up, startled, to see Margery coming toward me. In truth, I had half forgotten she was there. "Yes, Margery?"

She bent toward my ear like a conspirator. "You wish to see Miss Dashwood?"

"Yes. Yes, I do."

"I might be able to help," she whispered.

CHAPTER THIRTY-THREE
SECRETS

The unexpected offer buoyed me up. "What did you have in mind?" I whispered back.

"I could carry a message to her." Margery's voice was soft but intent. "The guards search me when I go in and out, so it can't be written down. But if you tell me what you want to say, I will find her."

It was a magnificent offer, especially from someone who had as much to fear from discovery as Margery did. Yet I hesitated. In person, I could have asked Sybil point-blank about other magic. But any messages relayed through Margery had to be much more discreet.

"It's very kind of you," I said at last. "But I'm afraid what I have to say is too complicated. If I could see her myself—"

"You need to see her?" Margery interrupted. "I'll tell her that, then."

"But she could never get in."

"She might, if she had a letter from the King."

"The way Sir Isaac did?" I shook my head. "Sybil couldn't get a letter like that."

"I wouldn't be so sure, my lady. Her aunt says that Miss Dashwood and the King knew each other when they were small. Indeed, Lady Goring remarks upon it often. And ever since Miss Dashwood arrived, she's received kind attentions from His Majesty. He looks favorably upon her."

Sybil had the ear of the King? She hadn't mentioned that to me. But now that I thought about it, there had been that basket of fruit in her room, and the pineapple . . . and she had been so deeply upset when he'd been attacked. . . .

"All right," I whispered back to Margery. "Ask her to seek the King's permission to visit me. If you're willing."

"I am," Margery said. "And I'll go right now. I'll tell the guards I have to see the seamstresses about the silk that my lord Wrexham sent you. That part's the truth, anyway."

"The seamstresses work so late?"

She shook her head at my ignorance. "My lady, we *all* work late here."

I should have known. "Thank you, Margery. Thank you for everything."

She acknowledged my gratitude with a determined nod. "I'll gather up the cloth and go, then."

But when she returned from her room, her arms wrapped around the silk, she came toward me, not the door. "My lady?"

"Yes?"

"You said you would help Mam with your magic. Will you—"

Her eyes shone fearfully above the red cloth. "Could you do that *now*?"

Seeing the hope in her face, my heart sank. "No." What else could I say? There were no explanations that were safe. "Not now. But later, I promise . . ."

Margery hardly moved at all, except to become more still. Yet the ease between us vanished. "Yes, my lady. I understand, my lady." She curtsied and backed away, all life gone from her face.

Was she angry with me? Was she trying not to cry? Or was it simply that *later* wasn't good enough, not when Wrexham had a chokehold on her family? She had retreated so far from me that I could not tell what she was thinking.

"Margery, please don't go—"

"I must see about that silk, my lady." She rapped on the door, and the guards let her out.

Was she going to the seamstresses and to Sybil? Or had she decided that she could best protect her family by going to Wrexham instead?

Keep calm, I told myself. It wasn't as if I'd given much away to Margery, except for my need to see Sybil. But that might be damning enough to Wrexham. Would he interrogate Sybil again? Would he come after me?

I sat there for a long time, my ear open to every sound: the spatter of rain at the windows, the snap of the fire, the moan of the wind outside. What I heard most of all, however, was an absence: the absence of music, of magic, of the power I so desperately needed.

† † †

One hour, two—and still Margery did not return. She *must* be with Wrexham.

I was pacing the room, wondering what to do, when I heard soft laughter ripple out from the other side of the door. It sounded exactly like Sybil.

Deeper laughter joined it—my guards?

The door opened, and the laughter streamed in. "So kind of you," Sybil was saying. "I am so very much obliged. Oh dear, have my skirts caught *again*?"

More laughter, and then she was in, blue eyes merry and bright. But the laughter vanished from her face the instant the door shut. She hurried over and embraced me. "Oh, Lucy, I was so afraid they wouldn't let me see you! It took the King's letter to get me in."

"So Margery found you?"

"Margery?" Sybil pulled back from me, confused. "No."

"I sent her out to look for you. She still isn't back."

"I did see her," Sybil said thoughtfully. "At least, I think it was Margery. She was lurking just outside Wrexham's rooms."

So Margery had gone straight to Wrexham. My heart plummeted.

"I wanted to speak to her," Sybil said, "just to find out how you were, but she slipped away before I could reach her. Are you sure she's trustworthy?"

"No," I said. "I'm not."

Sybil's brow furrowed. "What message did you mean her to give me?"

"That if you sought the King's permission, you might be able to visit me. But it seems you worked that out for yourself?"

"I did. It took me nearly all day, though, to be admitted to his presence. But he was kind." Her color deepened. "He always is."

Not always, I thought. But Sybil's unexpected blush told me—even more than her words—that she saw a different side to him.

"You knew him when he was small?" I led her over to the fire, where we pulled our chairs close.

"Long before he was King, yes. Back when he was merely Lord Henry Seymour. Our fathers were friends, and I can remember dancing with him and playing hide-and-seek when we were small. He was two years older, and I used to trail him around the gardens, asking him to pick daisies for my daisy chains." Her eyes were bright with affection. "It must have been most dreadfully annoying, but he never said so. He was kind even then."

Sybil and the King? It was not a pairing that could come to anything, not when the King was determined to marry as the Council directed. But still the attachment was there—at least on Sybil's side.

"He looked dreadful today, though." Sybil's eyes lost some of their brightness. "Poor man. He's hoarse as a crow, and his neck is a mass of bruises. And yet he continues to drive himself hard. The doctors told him to rest this morning, but he still insisted on meeting with Wrexham. And then a new report came in about

Boudicca, and since then he's been cloistered with his war leaders for hours at a time."

"What report about Boudicca?"

"Oh my dear," Sybil said. "Has no one told you? More men than ever are flocking to her banner; some say she's assembling an army. And she's coming closer to us every day. It's quite alarming. Between that and the search for your Nat, the Court's in an uproar."

My hand tensed on the damask of the chair. "They still haven't found him?"

"Nat? No."

Such relief!

"That's part of why it took me so long to see the King," Sybil said. "When he wasn't with the Inner Council, he was arguing with Wrexham about the best way to handle matters. And I thought it best to wait till Wrexham had gone. If he'd gotten wind of what I wanted, he'd have quashed the visit. He's scary, Lucy. Last night, before you came in, when he was questioning me . . ." Sybil trailed off and shuddered. "I don't want to see you married to a brute like that."

"He's even worse than you imagine," I said. "That's why I had to see you. I need your help to get away from him."

Sybil turned wise eyes on me. "Because you've lost your magic?"

My breath stopped. I tried to shape a denial, but nothing came out.

Although her gaze was sympathetic, she missed nothing. "So it's true. I thought so."

I gave up. "How did you guess?"

"Your song. My grandmother taught me how to recognize Chantress music—and whatever you sang, it wasn't that. And I knew you'd already seen the queen by scrying."

"But when I sang, you looked as impressed as everyone else."

"Did you think I would give you away?" Sybil said indignantly. "I'm a better friend than that."

"You haven't told anyone?"

"Of course not," she said with fierce kindness. "I *can* keep a secret sometimes, you know. Especially when it's as important as this. But how did it happen? How did you lose your magic?"

I decided I might as well tell her everything. Maybe she could help.

"It simply disappeared," I said. "Somewhere on the journey to Greenwich, I think. Or possibly right after I arrived." I summed up the circumstances as quickly as I could, worried that Margery might return at any moment.

When I finished, Sybil thoughtfully prodded at the carpet with her slipper. "There are only so many ways a Chantress can lose her powers, you know."

"What are they?"

"You might have done it to yourself, singing the wrong Wild Magic. Or else someone's done this *to* you, with some magic of their own."

"Wrexham said—back when I arrived—that he had a way of protecting himself against my magic. Is that possible? Could he have done this to me?"

Sybil tucked her slippers under her chair, considering this. "With some kind of talisman, you mean?"

"Do such things really exist?"

"Maybe," Sybil said. "Mama thought so, anyway. And it certainly would explain why Wrexham was such a good Chantress-hunter."

"Why wouldn't he have told Scargrave about it?" I wondered.

"Because if he had, Scargrave would have taken it," Sybil guessed. "And I expect he wouldn't have wanted anyone to know he had an unfair advantage."

I clasped my arms restlessly. "So you think he's the one who's done this to me?"

Sybil shook her head. "I'm not sure about that. In a couple of Mama's old books, there were stories about talismans that could protect their owners from Chantress song-spells. But their power was limited. They could only make a single person safe from Chantress magic; they couldn't destroy a Chantress's magic entirely. So even if Wrexham does have a talisman, I think there must be some other magic at work here—either some mistake of yours, or an enemy's spell."

"Then we're back where we started," I said, discouraged.

"Oh, it doesn't matter which it is," Sybil said cheerfully. "Either way, the solution is the same."

"There's a solution?" I was elated.

"Yes. Ordinarily the best way to fix things would be to go to another Chantress for help—"

"I can't do that. There's no one to go to." My voice rose in panic. Was there no way to get my magic back?

As Sybil put her finger to her lips, a great banging and thumping came from the door.

Wrexham? Margery? Heart racing, I held my breath, but the door didn't open. Instead, after some more insistent hammering, everything went quiet again.

Unnerved, I turned to Sybil. "What else can I do? Tell me quickly."

"Well, that's the wonderful thing," Sybil said. "There's another cure that's said to be infallible: the Philosopher's Stone. But you have to be the first one to touch it."

"What?" I stared at her in consternation. "The alchemists never said any such thing—"

"That's because they don't know." Sybil gave me a conspiratorial grin. "It's a Chantress secret. I only know because my grandmother told my mother, and my mother told me. Mama always harbored the hope that if I were to touch a Philosopher's Stone, I would find my Chantress powers; that's why she spent so much time with alchemists. But Grandmama said it didn't work that way. The Stone only restores power to those who had it in the first place."

"Are you sure?"

Sybil nodded. "Grandmama explained it this way: an ordinary human who touches the Stone will find himself healed of any illness affecting his body or mind. And it's much the same for someone with magic: if your magic has been damaged or broken, the Stone heals that, too. But for that, you have to touch it first, before anyone else has. Otherwise, the Stone won't have enough power in it." She looked at me anxiously. "Do you think you could do that?"

I seesawed between hope and dread. "I've got a fighting chance, I think. Provided we succeed in making the Stone."

"I shouldn't worry about that," Sybil said. "Now that the crucible is back, Sir Isaac has everything well in hand. Or so I hear."

"But he needs my help." I told Sybil about his request and the reason for it. "He thinks I'm powerful, you see—and I can't tell him how weak I am; I can't tell him the truth. The whole experiment may fail because of me."

Sybil frowned and twined a curl around her finger, so tight the tip turned almost purple. "What exactly did Flamel ask for?"

"A powerful woman, Sir Isaac said. Powerful and incorruptible."

"Did Flamel say anything about her having magic?"

"No, I don't think so. Not specifically—"

Sybil released the curl and relaxed. "Then we don't need to worry."

"But—"

"We don't need to worry," Sybil repeated. "Lucy, you're the most powerful woman I know, and that's true whether you have magic or not. Look at the way you've kept your weakness hidden. You fooled everyone but me last night. You had those men hanging on every word you said."

"But it was a trick," I said. "It wasn't real power."

"That's as real as it gets for most of us," Sybil said with uncharacteristic soberness. "Most power's an illusion, Grandmama used to say. But you need courage and strength of character to carry it off—and that, my dear, you have in spades." She tilted her head.

"Although in your case, I think you must still have a bit of magic left, given how the scrying went."

"I tried it again," I said, "last night. And I saw—" I looked up and stopped short.

The door between Margery's room and my own was open a crack. Surely it had been closed earlier. Was someone there?

Without another word, I leaped for the door and yanked it open.

Behind it stood Margery.

CHAPTER THIRTY-FOUR

SURROUNDED

My hand flew to my heart. "Margery! How did you get in?"

How long had she been there? I thought frantically. And how much had she heard?

Looking less composed than usual, Margery stepped into the room. Her cheeks were pink, and wisps of hair had fallen out from her neat cap. "I came through the other door, my lady."

"There's another door?" I peered into the dark room. "Where? I never saw it."

"You wouldn't have, my lady." Margery pointed to the far end wall. "It's behind the tapestry there. It locks on the outside, and it's not often used. They only opened it for me because the usual door is stuck shut. Didn't you hear them hammering at it?"

I remembered the banging. "We didn't know what it was."

"The bar's wedged fast," Margery said. "Someone's been summoned to fix it, but until then we have to use this door. I'm sorry if I disturbed you."

"Oh, you didn't disturb us," Sybil said, rising from her place by the fire. "Why, we didn't even hear you coming."

"That would've been the tapestry, Miss Dashwood," Margery said. "It muffles the sound. And the guards kept everything quiet. They wanted their bit of fun and laughed to think I might come upon you unawares. Although, in fact, it's you who've surprised me. I was looking all over the palace for you, Miss Dashwood, without any luck, only to find you here."

"It's a terrible maze of a place, isn't it?" Sybil said. "Though I believe I saw *you*. At least it looked like you, waiting just outside the Earl of Wrexham's rooms."

"Outside his rooms?" Margery shook her head sharply. "Oh no, miss. I had no call to be there."

Sybil and I exchanged a quick glance.

"Well, never mind," Sybil said. "I'm here, and that's what matters."

"Yes, miss." Margery dipped a small curtsy. "I'll just straighten up the room now, if you please."

Sybil prolonged her visit for another few minutes, but it did us no good. With Margery there—twitching at the draperies, clearing crumbs from the table—we couldn't say anything of significance. But when Sybil took her leave of me, she hinted at what was really on her mind. "I hope she didn't hear," she whispered in my ear.

I didn't dare whisper back; Margery was watching me.

Had she overheard what we had said about the Philosopher's Stone? Was she planning to report it to Wrexham? After Sybil left, it was all I could think about.

My fears increased as the hours passed, for Margery grew ever more remote and preoccupied, and her eyes kept wandering to the door. It was not until after supper, however, that she actually tried to leave.

"I must see the seamstresses again, my lady," she said.

"Oh, please don't go!" I clutched at my stomach. "Stay with me, please, Margery. I—I'm not feeling well." Anything to keep her from going to Wrexham before we made the Stone.

Margery came back from the door. "You're not well? What's wrong?"

"Queasiness." I passed a hand over my eyes. "And a headache."

Margery looked alarmed. "I'll fetch the Royal Physician."

Now I was alarmed. "No, no. Please, Margery—I truly couldn't bear having that man look me over. I don't think it's serious. It's just that I don't want to be alone when I'm feeling ill."

Margery's lips tightened. "Very well, my lady. I will stay. But why don't you go to bed, my lady? Sleep is what you need."

"No, no." I stayed seated in my chair. "Lying down would only make the queasiness worse."

Still tight-lipped, Margery brought out some mending and sat down across from me.

"I'll help you," I said. It was as good a way as any to keep a close watch on her.

"It's not your place, my lady." She stopped threading her needle and gave me a sharp look. "And I thought you said you had a headache. Sewing will only make it worse."

"I'm not sure that's true," I said, but I didn't offer again to help. Instead, I watched her work and wondered what she was thinking. As the time passed, it got harder not to yawn, harder not to lean my head against the pillows that Margery insisted on bringing to me.

"You look so tired, my lady. And it's growing late. Really, you ought to go to bed."

"No, no," I said. "I'll feel better if I stay upright."

Even if I hadn't been determined to keep watch over Margery, I couldn't have slept. I had too much on my mind. Besides Margery, there was so much else to worry about: the Great Work and the Stone and Wrexham and Nat . . .

. . . and yet somehow I fell asleep anyway, right there in my chair. The next thing I knew, someone was shaking me awake.

I blinked sleepily. "Margery?"

"She's not here," a man said roughly. "You must get up, Chantress."

"Margery's gone?"

Snapping awake, I saw Rowan Knollys and four guards standing before me. Candlelight gleamed on their pikes and illuminated the clock behind them. It was half past three.

"The King and the Earl of Wrexham wish to see you," Knollys said. "You must come at once."

The King and Wrexham? I shrank back in my chair. Margery must have betrayed me. "No. I—I cannot."

"My lady Chantress, you must. They await you downstairs." Knollys raised the candle higher. "We are here to escort you."

Even as I flinched, four of the men came and surrounded me.

It was true: I had no choice but to go with them. I wrapped myself in my velvet cloak, and they marched me off.

At first, as we tramped through grand rooms of state and down dim gilded staircases, I could hear only the sound of their boots. But when we neared the Great Hall, my heart slammed into my throat, for I could hear Wrexham shouting.

"The woman is a traitor, Your Majesty. She deserves to die!"

There was no time to think, no chance to run. The doors to the Great Hall stood open. Propelled by the guards, I flew straight through them. Torches blazed everywhere. The guards halted and fanned out.

I stood alone before the dais where Wrexham and the King awaited me. They stood shoulder to shoulder, like comrades in battle, although only Wrexham was dressed in armor. Margery was nowhere to be seen.

The King motioned me forward. Willing myself to be strong, I stepped onto the dais.

"My lady Chantress," the King said hoarsely, "we have been waiting for you."

Whatever Margery and Wrexham had said about me, I was determined to stand up for myself. "I have done nothing wrong, Your Majesty. I swear it."

I saw surprise in the King's face. "No one suggested you had."

Next to him, Wrexham narrowed his eyes, but spoke no words of accusation.

Was my secret safe, then? Was this about something else entirely? "Then why have I been brought here?"

"Because we have an enemy at our throats." Wrexham spat the name out: "Boudicca."

Not me. That was all I could think at first, with relief so powerful it overwhelmed everything. Margery must have kept her own counsel after all. Or perhaps she hadn't overheard anything in the first place.

The King was speaking to me.

"Lord Wrexham's scouts report that she has been using black magic against us," he was saying. "They say also that she aims at the throne."

"Black magic?" I was startled. "Are you sure?"

"Do you doubt my scouts?" Wrexham growled. "They say whole villages empty out and follow her as she passes—as if she were the Devil, and they were dancing to her tune. And she's used her magic to creep up on us too. There was much fog along the river today, perfect cover for their crossing. An hour ago, our scouts spied her only two miles from here—with over three thousand men."

Proof of magic? Not to me. Hunger and desperation might account for the followers, and fog was hardly unknown on these reaches of the Thames.

The King looked a little doubtful too.

"Do you have any other evidence of magic?" I asked Wrexham. I was wary of setting off his temper, but I hoped he would keep himself in check in front of the King.

"What more do you need?" Wrexham's armored fist clenched. "We ought to have crushed her right at the start." He turned to the King. "But better late than never, Your Majesty. Now that you've given me leave, I'll give her the beating she deserves. Her magic will be no match for my strength."

"You must not be the first to attack, Wrexham," the King rasped out. "I don't doubt your courage or your skill, but I meant what I said. Perhaps there is still a possibility of parley."

"Parley? At this stage, when she has us nearly surrounded?" Wrexham could barely restrain his temper. "Your Majesty, this is a war—"

"We cannot be sure of that," the King said, his words ragged but emphatic. "Lady Chantress, is there anything you can do to bring Boudicca to the table?"

As he and Wrexham looked to me for an answer, Sir Isaac mounted the dais and joined us.

"Not at such a distance," I temporized.

"If you were closer, perhaps," the King suggested.

"There is no time for that, Your Majesty." Sir Isaac still looked rather white and drawn, but his hands had a firm grip on the metal box that held Flamel's papers. "It is almost time to begin the Great Work. We cannot spare her."

The King nodded reluctantly. "No, I suppose we cannot."

Wrexham pressed his case. "Your Majesty, trust me: Boudicca means to kill you. My agents are not mistaken on that point. If we cannot dispatch her, we look like fools indeed."

"If we shoot her in cold blood, we look like tyrants," the King said. Dark welts and bruises ringed his throat like shadows. "Do not fire first. If it's food she's after and not the throne, then all will be well. When the Great Work succeeds, we should have more than enough to make all parties happy."

"Very well," Wrexham conceded. "Instead of killing her, I'll capture her."

The King eyed him with concern. "Perhaps I should ride with you."

Both Wrexham and Sir Isaac looked alarmed.

"Your Majesty, your life is far too valuable to be risked this way," Sir Isaac said. "And you will only inflate Boudicca's pretensions if you yourself battle her."

"And they are already too great as it is," Wrexham said. "We'll soon show the old woman who's master. She may have the advantage of numbers, but we are trained warriors. Truly, Your Majesty, the battle will be over before it's begun. There is no need for you to be there."

"Whereas we could indeed use your talents in the laboratory," Sir Isaac said. "I must bring the Chantress there now. Will you not accompany us?"

The King inclined his head; the circle of bruises darkened. "If you need me, I will come."

Sir Isaac bowed. "We should be grateful, Your Majesty."

"Wrexham." The King put his hand to the man's plated shoulder. "I wish you Godspeed. Is there anything more you need from me?"

"One thing only," Wrexham said. "I want a word with the Chantress."

"Ah." The king seemed disconcerted as he looked from Wrexham to me, but then he stepped back, all politeness. "Of course."

He and Sir Isaac walked to the edge of the dais to confer with

Gabriel, who had just arrived. I was left alone with Wrexham, who closed the gap between us and took my hand, pressing it so hard the bones hurt.

"We shall make our betrothal vows this very day, after my victory," he said. "And we shall be wed within the week."

I shuddered. "So soon?"

Wrexham's cold eyes traced my face. "I am not a patient man, Chantress." To my astonishment, he jerked my hand up and rammed a thick metal band onto my finger, bruising the tender flesh at the base. "This will do for a ring."

It was the ring from his own little finger, set with a dead Chantress's cracked, green stone.

Unable to hide my revulsion, I wrenched my hand away, but I couldn't claw the ring off. It jammed against my knuckle and sliced into my skin. With a wolfish half smile, Wrexham watched me struggle.

I yanked at the ring again, and this time it twisted off my finger. As I handed it back to him, I saw that he knew exactly how much I hated him, and that the knowledge gave him a strange sort of pleasure.

"Next time you'll wear it for good," he said. "The Council approves of my plan, and I know a bishop who will issue the licenses."

Everyone with power was on his side, I thought in despair. But then I realized there was one person he'd omitted to mention. "And what of His Majesty? Does he approve?"

"He will, once he knows," Wrexham said robustly. "We've had

more pressing matters to discuss. But once I return in triumph, he will deny me nothing."

He sounded very sure of himself—and why not? Once he'd defeated Boudicca, how could the King turn him down?

But I had a plan too, I reminded myself. If we could make the Stone and it restored my magic, I would have the power to end this dreadful match and to protect Nat, too.

If, if, if . . .

Wrexham turned away from me and saluted the King. Striding out of the hall, he called his men to his side. The entire palace was awake now, a hive of activity despite the darkness. Through the windows came the high whinny of horses being prepared for battle, and then a great shout from Wrexham himself.

"For God!" he bellowed. "For King! For Country!"

His men roared their approval, a sound that shook the palace. They knew, better than anyone, that victory was almost theirs.

"I don't understand it," Gabriel said.

I started. I hadn't realized he was close behind me. "Understand what?"

He gave me a bitter look. "How you could agree to marry Wrexham."

He thinks I have a choice. And I mustn't tell him I don't, or he'll work out that I have no magic. "Let's not waste our time discussing it," I said. "Aren't we supposed to be starting the Great Work?"

"Yes." At the mention of alchemy, Gabriel's bitterness ebbed slightly. "That's why I came up here—to fetch you and Sir Isaac. Time's growing short."

Evidently Sir Isaac had reached the same conclusion, because he broke away from the King's side. "Chantress, I must bring you to the laboratory now. We cannot waste another minute."

He was in too much of a hurry to allow the King to lead the way, but instead ushered me toward the laboratory himself. The King did not seem to mind not taking precedence. Lagging behind, he spoke of alchemical matters with Gabriel, their boots tapping against the clay-tiled floors.

Looking up as we came through a door, I glimpsed Margery in a gallery above me. At the same instant she saw me and turned tail. I stifled an exclamation.

"Are you all right, Chantress?" Sir Isaac asked me.

"I . . . I almost tripped."

Sir Isaac offered me his arm, but we were approaching the stairs to the laboratory, and my only thought was to get there quickly. Leaving Sir Isaac behind, I raced down the steps.

I was not going to let Margery—or anyone else—stop me.

CHAPTER THIRTY-FIVE
THE GREAT WORK

When the guard saw us coming, he opened the laboratory door. Sir Isaac breezed past him and escorted me into the room.

It was like walking into the Devil's own dominion. The place reeked worse than ever, and in the vast darkness the great central furnace burned bright as infernal flame. Sweating in a leather smock, Sir Samuel manned the enormous bellows. They wheezed like a mythical beast, as if the fiery furnace were a dragon that might at any moment consume us all.

Sir Isaac set down the box of Flamel's papers. "Is Dr. Penebrygg here?"

"Up there," Sir Samuel gasped, pumping hard at the bellows.

At the top of a ladder, Penebrygg was shutting the high windows. Even before they closed, I could hear nothing from the Thames. Had I lost what little hearing I had left? Would my dwindling power put the Great Work in jeopardy?

Please let Sybil be right, I prayed. *Please let what power I have be enough.*

Here and there, the panes of glass caught the red light of the fire, and when Penebrygg waved at us in greeting, his spectacles glowed strangely.

"I have made the necessary observations," he called out to Sir Isaac. "The conjunction of the planets is almost upon us."

"Just as I predicted." Sir Isaac consulted his pocket watch. "We must lose no more time. Lord Gabriel, will you take Sir Samuel's place at the bellows?"

After Gabriel stripped off his doublet and rolled back his shirt-sleeves, Sir Samuel yielded his position with evident relief. Under Gabriel's steady hands, the bellows rasped faster and faster, and the fire leaped up in response.

Sir Isaac held a candle to the flames with a shaking hand. "We must be able to see the work perfectly."

He set the lighted candle on a table, and in the bright circle of its light I saw the Golden Crucible. Beside it were other, plainer crucibles, as well as an assemblage of bottles and vials containing mysterious substances.

Sir Isaac saw me looking. "The first part of the Great Work will be done in the ordinary crucibles," he explained. "It is only the last part—the fourth stage—that requires the Golden Crucible."

"And that's when you'll need me?"

"Precisely. I will require your assistance at a few other points too. Attend closely, and be ready to act as I direct." He ran a discerning eye over the substances on the table, then called on Sir Samuel to assist him with decanting one bottle into another.

Penebrygg came down from his ladder and joined me as I watched, his spectacles still glowing in the firelight. "My dear," he said under his breath, "I am so sorry about what has happened. You and Nat—"

"They haven't found him?" I whispered in alarm.

"No, no," Penebrygg said. "There's a report that he was sighted in London, but he's not been discovered yet."

I'd expected him to head to Holland, not London. But perhaps the report was wrong. *Wherever he is, please let him stay safe. Let him stay safe until I can protect him.*

"All is in readiness," Sir Isaac announced. "Your Majesty, will you prepare the copper?"

The King bent to the task, using pincers to place strips of copper in a crucible with Sir Samuel's help.

"Lord Gabriel, you may leave off pumping," Sir Isaac said. "The fire is hot enough, and we need you here. Of all of us, you have the steadiest hands." His own, I saw, were shaking worse than ever. "It is the first stage," he said as Gabriel came up to us. "You know what to do."

Gabriel picked up a bottle containing a liquid that looked like water, but that probably wasn't. With deft hands, he poured a small amount into a marked beaker, then brought the beaker to the copper-filled crucible.

"Wait." Sir Isaac stopped him. "The Chantress must pour it in. That is what Flamel says: all the female elements must be added by the woman."

So the watery substance was supposed to be female? It made no sense to me. There was an acrid smell in the air, however, that I thought I remembered.

"Is it aqua fortis?" I asked.

Looking a bit surprised, Sir Isaac nodded. "It is indeed. Lord Gabriel, hand her the beaker."

Gabriel surrendered it, but only reluctantly. Was he still angry about my supposed arrangement with Wrexham? Or did he simply fear I would ruin the experiment?

Well, I might ruin it, at that. And it could well be my hands that failed me first, and not my lack of magic. The beaker was slippery. What if I dropped it?

"Pour it into the crucible," Sir Isaac commanded.

This work was second nature to him, but it wasn't to me. "All at once," I asked, "or little by little?"

"All at once," Sir Isaac said, a trifle impatiently. "Take care, however, that you don't pour so fast that it splashes. It must all stay inside the crucible."

"If it dribbles over the edge of the beaker," Sir Samuel added, "it will burn your skin. And once you are done, be sure to step away, for a devilish smoke will rise up from the crucible."

I hesitated, remembering the fumes from Lord Gabriel's experiment.

Penebrygg gave me a reassuring smile over his spectacles. "Never fear, my dear. Just put it in, and we'll pull you back ourselves if need be."

Bracing myself, I poured the acid. It fizzed when it hit the copper, and a putrid green cloud funneled upward. I ducked back, nearly bumping into the King.

"Cover your face," Penebrygg said, raising his sleeve. "Don't breathe the smoke in."

The others covered their faces too, except for Sir Isaac, who took the empty beaker from my hand. "Sir Samuel, are you ready?"

Cloaking his nose, Sir Samuel tossed something into the crucible that immediately lessened the smoke.

"Now for your part, Lord Gabriel," Sir Isaac ordered. "Bring the crucible to the fire."

With a heavy set of tongs, Lord Gabriel placed the vessel in the furnace. The smoke thickened for a few moments, then died out.

"One minute," Sir Isaac counted, timing the operation with his pocket watch. "Two . . . three . . . four . . . Now take it out!"

Gabriel yanked the crucible from the fire and secured it in an iron stand—not an easy task, when done with tongs. The other alchemists crowded round the table. When I joined them, I saw a coal-black powder at the bottom of the crucible.

"The Black Crow," Penebrygg said in satisfaction.

"Black as night." Sir Samuel smoothed his apprentice's apron as if it were fine silk.

"Yes, we have accomplished the first stage." Sir Isaac glanced back at the furnace. "But there is much more to do. We must move quickly. Sir Samuel, will you add the powder?"

This next stage was like the first, in that I was asked to add all the liquids to the crucible, while the men added the other compounds. This time, however, there was no terrible smoke at the end. Instead, after a short wait, we witnessed an almost miraculous transformation, as the black powder turned white.

"The White Swan," Sir Samuel breathed.

"White as snow," the King said, astonished.

"On to the next stage," Sir Isaac urged. "Citrinitas, the yellowing."

More liquids and powders, another firing, a distillation, and yet more mixing . . . and the contents of the crucible became thick and yellow, like a bowl of beaten egg yolks.

"The Golden Sun," Gabriel exulted.

Penebrygg blinked down at the bowl as if dazzled. "We are getting very close now."

You could feel the excitement rising in the room. Indeed, I felt it rising in me. The work was so captivating that I had almost forgotten my fear.

You must be the first to touch it, I reminded myself. *You must be the first to touch the Stone.* But surely that would be easy enough, if I were the one holding the crucible?

"Now for the fourth and last stage." So far, Sir Isaac had been the most dispassionate of all of us, but now his voice trembled with emotion. "Chantress, you must hold the Golden Crucible. Lift it up firmly with both hands. Lord Gabriel, you must pour the yellow fluid into it."

The crucible was heavier than it looked. I spread my hands wide, cupping it as best I could, but its smooth sides made it surprisingly difficult to hold. I began to worry again that I would ruin the experiment with a simple slip of the fingers. Gripping the crucible more firmly, I worked hard to keep it steady as Gabriel poured.

"There," Sir Isaac said, his voice still quivering slightly. "Dr. Penebrygg, will you add the contents of that green flask? Sir Samuel, if you will be so good as to stir?"

I held on to the crucible so tightly that my fingers ached. Soon, however, I was distracted from the pain by the magic of what was happening inside the crucible: the yellow liquid thinned out and turned a rich orange. As Penebrygg brought the candle close, I saw flashes of shimmering blue-green spread across the surface.

"The Peacock's Tail," Gabriel said in wonder.

"Amazing!" Penebrygg, too, was filled with awe. "I've never seen anything like it."

We stood around the crucible for several minutes, completely engrossed. Then Sir Isaac pulled back, his long face furrowing.

"Is something wrong?" I was hoping the answer was *no*, and that Sir Isaac would say that our work was almost done, for the ache in my hands was creeping upward now, into my arms and neck.

"The transformation is not complete." Sir Isaac's frown deepened. "The color ought to be changing again."

"Yes, to a deep and most perfect red." Gabriel watched the liquid closely.

The King, too, stared into the crucible. "I don't see any red myself. Only orange and blue and green."

"Did we make a mistake?" Penebrygg wondered aloud. "Perhaps we mistimed things?"

Sir Isaac consulted his pocket watch and shook his head. "The timing is perfect."

"The ingredients, then," Penebrygg said. "Perhaps we measured out the wrong ones?"

Again Sir Isaac shook his head. "All the ingredients were

checked and double-checked. They are exactly what Flamel called for."

"Well, we must have done *something* wrong," Sir Samuel said. "Because nothing is happening."

"It might be the auras," Sir Isaac said slowly. "An imperfection or imbalance in the qualities each of us brings to the work."

Could it be me? Was it my weakness that was holding back the Great Work? The mere thought was paralyzing, and the crucible slipped down in my hands.

CHAPTER THIRTY-SIX
CRUCIBLE

"Careful there!" Sir Isaac warned as I regained my purchase on the crucible.

"She's tiring," Gabriel said.

"Yes." Sir Isaac scrutinized me for a moment. My cheeks flamed, and not from the furnace. Did he suspect that I was the weak link?

Apparently not, for he turned to the others and said, "Your Majesty, gentlemen—you must leave the room."

The King's shoulders went back. "Leave the room? Why?"

"Are you suggesting we are at fault?" Gabriel said angrily.

"No, no," Sir Isaac said. "You must not take offense. It is merely a matter of balance, as I said. Flamel, you see, calls only for an alchemist and an assistant—a man and a woman—to finish the work. I thought it wouldn't matter if there were more people, but perhaps it does. Perhaps the energies are skewed with so many extra men in the room."

"I don't see why it should matter," Gabriel began, but he stopped when the King held up his hand.

"If you think it would help," the King said with dignity, "then of course we will leave."

"You needn't go far," Sir Isaac said. "If you could just wait on the other side of the door with the guard, that will be sufficient."

With the King leading the way, the others followed without further objection, though frustration was writ large on Gabriel's face. As they walked out the door, I felt a faint surge of strength, and with it a leap of hope. Could Sir Isaac be right? Was the fault not with me, but with the balance in the room?

After the men passed through the door, Sir Isaac closed it behind them, then bolted it shut and set the dead bar across it.

"Just in case they are tempted to peek," he said, answering my look of surprise. "In their place, I would find it hard to resist, but an interruption at the wrong moment could be fatal for the enterprise."

He crossed back over to me and gazed into the crucible. "Ah, I see something is happening—excellent!"

Something was indeed happening—and I could not only see it, but also feel it as well. The weight of the crucible lightened ever so slightly, and inside its bowl, the liquid began to swirl and then give off a very light steam, like mist.

"It looks like the ocean," I said, for beneath the mist, the liquid had turned a deep blue-green.

"Indeed." Sir Isaac seemed enraptured by the sight.

"But wasn't it supposed to turn red?" The more I stared at the liquid, the dizzier I felt.

"Give it time," Sir Isaac murmured. "Give it time."

I nodded, but the dizzy feeling was growing worse by the moment. Was it the smell of the mist that was doing this to me? Or the power of the Great Work itself? Or was it just exhaustion?

Whatever you do, don't let go of the crucible, I told myself. But then the dizziness worsened into outright nausea, and I lurched forward.

"Don't drop it!" Sir Isaac shouted. His hands shot out to cover mine, pressing them against the crucible.

Perhaps they heard his shout outside, for there was some commotion behind the door. I could not make out exactly what it was, though; it was too muffled for that, and I was too sick. My head was spinning, and the crucible would have fallen if Sir Isaac hadn't been standing across from me, supporting my hands with his own.

"Not much longer now." As Sir Isaac spoke, a tremor ran through him, but his fingers remained strong as wire against mine. "The change has begun."

Could I hold out till the Great Work was done? Through the high windows above us, the sky was dimming from black to deep blue; dawn was near. I looked down into the bowl, hoping to see at least a touch of crimson this time. But the liquid was still the same blue-green, and the steam above it was thickening, like a sea mist on a stormy day . . .

. . . and then all at once the steam swirled like the sea itself, and I was falling down into it with my mind, deeper and deeper, the fall I now associated with scrying. I tried to pull back, but

I couldn't. Indeed, the dizziness only made me fall faster and harder.

What's wrong?

I didn't ask the question out loud, but it resounded inside me like a tolling bell: *What's wrong?*

As if in answer, a picture formed in the shimmering liquid. I almost groaned to see it, for it was the same one I'd seen twice before: the bloodthirsty king and queen, choking each other in all their finery. Only this time, as I stared at them, their blue faces shifted into something horribly recognizable: the king had Sir Isaac's face, and the queen, my own. As I watched in sick shock, the tiny Sir Isaac quenched the life out of me and hacked off my coronet with a knife. My blood spurted over his pearl-bedecked hand.

The liquid sloshed in the crucible.

"Take care!" Sir Isaac shouted.

My head snapped up. "You," I said, still in the grip of what I'd seen. "You're what's wrong. You're doing something to me. Something awful."

Sir Isaac's face was all puzzlement. "My dear Chantress, you're not making any sense."

A small snake of doubt crept through me. But the picture had been so clear. I couldn't ignore it.

"Something's wrong," I said. "I want to stop."

The moment I tried to pull away, Sir Isaac's mask of puzzlement vanished. For that's all it had been—a mask. Beneath it, he had the blood-maddened look of the murderous king of my visions.

"Oh no." He tightened his hands like a vise, flattening my fingers against the crucible. "You're not stopping now. Not until we're done. There, look! It's changing now. We've done it!"

The liquid had indeed changed: it was now a bright, pure blue.

"It's not red," I said. "It's not the Philosopher's Stone."

"No," Sir Isaac said. "It's something far more precious: a Chantress Elixir."

"What?"

As I stared at him, dumbfounded, he seized the crucible for himself. Cradling it in one arm, he pulled an astonishingly luminous pearl out of his coat. Before I could duck away, he touched my hand with it. My head swam, and my muscles flagged. I sank toward the floor.

"You have done such an excellent job convincing everyone that you can still do magic," Sir Isaac said softly. "But I know the truth. This talisman makes it impossible for you to hear music clearly; it confuses your senses. And when I hold it to your skin, it weakens you fatally. You cannot oppose me."

Horrified, I tried to roll away from him. Waves of nausea pulsed through me.

"Look at you, cowering there on the floor." He nestled the crucible closer to his chest. "You did not know the talisman existed, did you? Wrexham had the stone for years, you know; he told no one about it, but eventually I recognized it for what it was. A very rare object, indeed, though he did not know a tenth of what it could do."

"You and Wrexham?" I gasped. "You plotted against me?"

"I, plot with that clod?" Sir Isaac spoke with disdain. "I should think not. I gave him a sleeping draught a fortnight ago and took the stone. He believes the talisman is still on his finger; I put an ordinary pearl in its place, and he never noticed the difference. And he never guessed that his talisman's powers could be augmented through alchemy. Solely by a true adept, of course—and even then I only achieved my end a week ago." He loomed over me with a superior smile, holding the pearl high. "And you were ignorant all the while. You never even heard the drone."

The drone? The sound I'd heard by the sea in Norfolk, and in the river by the King's hunting lodge—that was the talisman?

"I heard it," I choked out.

"You did?" He looked faintly surprised. "Well, well. The process of creating the talisman is long and arduous, and it greatly disturbs the elements; the effects can ripple out for hundreds of miles. When the process is done, a Chantress will be deafened to it, but while it is happening, she may occasionally hear a drone, as you did. If so, it ought to serve as a warning to her."

I wish it had, I thought groggily, trying to push myself up from the floor.

He leered down at me. "But you didn't know what to do about it, did you? Clear proof that a foolish girl like you does not deserve magic. Much better that it should be in the hands of a man like me, a man with judgment and discernment and wisdom. After all, I am the genius of my age; men everywhere acknowledge it." He gave me a manic smile. "Genius and magic—what a combination it will be!"

Was he mad? I hoped so. But dimly, I remembered something Sybil had said once, about there being a way of transferring Chantress powers to a man. The way had been lost, she had said. . . .

"You know how to do it," I said, feeling sick again. "How to claim a Chantress's magic."

"I do," Sir Isaac acknowledged, with a touch of boastfulness. "The papers put me on to it. There were several pages that made no sense, at least not at first. But gradually I began to piece it together, step by step. It was so obscure I doubt anyone else could have decoded it; yet everything was there. Of course, the transfer of powers cannot succeed unless the man in question has Chantress blood, however faint. But fortunately, I do."

He did? "You never said so."

He shrugged. "What was the point, when I had no power to show for it? A terrible injustice, I always thought, that the male line was excluded from magic. But I shall redress that soon enough."

Lying on the floor, my head by my knees, I remembered something else that Sybil had said. "I wouldn't be so sure about that. I have to give the power willingly, that's what the old lore says. And that I will never do."

"But you already have." His eyes glowed in triumph. "You helped make the elixir of your own free will. Your moments of struggle came too late; the transformation was already taking place. The proof lies before you: the elixir exists. It need only ripen for another minute, and then I will claim your magic for myself."

CHAPTER THIRTY-SEVEN
THE ELIXIR

Sir Isaac circled my prone body, the sharp tips of his boots coming within inches of my face. When he held the talisman before me, it multiplied before my eyes.

"It is an effective little ball, you must admit," he mused. "Yet even with it, my success was far from assured. I thought I would never be able to lure you down here, or near any laboratory good enough to do the necessary work. Despite all the Council's arguments, the King insisted you must be allowed to remain in Norfolk if you wished, that he had granted you safe haven there. And I feared that if I told him you were crucial to the Great Work, he might insist on seeing the papers for himself—and then Nat and Penebrygg and the others would begin to ask awkward questions." He gave me another one of his manic smiles. "But finally I hit on the idea of stealing the crucible, and that worked like a charm. The King had to bring you here then—and it meant, too, that he would not let you leave, even when you wanted to."

I stared up at him in dizzy disbelief. "You stole the crucible?"

"I did. And I spoiled the moonbriar seeds, too, although I did that much earlier, in case you came to Court before I was ready for you." He spoke with evident pride in his own ingenuity. "Later I planted the crucible in Nat's room. You all thought I was sleeping off the poison. But I'd done the poisoning myself—a much smaller dose than it looked. Once everyone left me, I took my chance to rid myself of Nat. Too clever, that boy."

"And the King?"

Sir Isaac shrugged. "He got in my way. But never mind that now. The time has come." Hugging the crucible close, he leaned over me, reaching for my hand. "The elixir is ready. All that remains is for us both to dip our fingers into it, and then your magic will flow to me."

"That will never happen." With a strength born of panic, I surged up from the floor.

"Oh, no you don't!" He lashed out with the talisman. It glinted across my skin, and the world heaved under my feet again. I fell back, gasping, against the table. As the sickness washed over me, bottles smashed against the floor.

Bottles . . . tiny bottles . . .

He lunged for me just as my fingers found the right one: aqua fortis.

"Don't you dare!" he shouted.

I hurled the bottle at him. It broke against the crucible, spurting acid onto Sir Isaac's hand, the hand that held the talisman. Sir Isaac screamed—as much from rage as pain, it seemed, for when the acid hit the talisman, it vanished into smoke.

The moment it was gone, music flooded the world. With joy and relief and awe, I heard Wild Magic swirling around me, every note luminous and clear: the busy melodies of the potions in their bottles, the crackling cadence of the fire, the hypnotic canticle of the blue elixir itself. And wrapping around all these songs, running under them and over them and through them, I heard the toll of the River Thames outside the open windows— old London River, now at high tide.

Yet even as I opened myself up to the music, Sir Isaac's hand locked around my wrist. He was bigger than I, and stronger than I, and half-mad with the desire for power. Even without the talisman, he could win, and he knew it.

But I knew my own strength now. I drew on the power that pulsed in the Wild Magic around me; I drew on the power I'd found in myself. And I sang.

Back in Norfolk, I hadn't fully trusted myself. I'd usually gone for what was safe and easy. Now I trusted my deepest instincts, and the song I chose was the most powerful I could hear: a song that called upon the great river to defend me from my enemies.

It was a wild and fathomless music, as ancient as the river itself. As it surged through me, the river and I gained strength from each other.

But Sir Isaac, too, had found a new strength: the strength of desperation. Even as I sang, he forced my hand down toward the elixir. Our locked fingers neared the surface.

I gathered everything I had, calling the river to me . . .

. . . and it came, slamming through the walls and ceiling, gushing through the broken stone. Mighty and purposeful, it cleaved together like a living thing, a towering wave of water that barreled straight for Sir Isaac and me.

Wood splintered, stones rumbled, pots smashed on the floor. Then there was only the roar of the river itself—the roar and the splash and the muck and the brine—as the wave closed over us.

I thought at first it would drown us both, but it sluiced between our joined hands, knocking me aside. It wanted only one of us. As I held on to an iron ring in the wall, the wave washed over Sir Isaac, crucible and all, and dragged him back to the riverbed.

Choking and spluttering, my garments drenched, I rushed to the broken walls and saw the Thames sink back between its banks in the pale light of dawn. The whole river shuddered, as if thrashing in its sleep. And then the Thames was itself again, flowing strong to the sea, with only the broken walls and the wet trails on the floor to show it had ever done anything else.

† † †

It felt like an age, but might merely have been a minute, before I heard my name.

"Lucy!"

"Nat?" Still in shock, I turned and saw a crack in the door, and Nat's aghast face above it. Behind him crowded the King, Penebrygg, Sir Samuel, Gabriel, and the guard named Potts, all gazing at me and the shattered wall in stunned silence.

I straightened my spine. "You saw?" I said.

"We saw." Reaching through the broken wood, Nat threw the deadbolt, lifted the bar, and shoved the battered door open. There was a small cut on his cheek, and a yellowing bruise on his jaw, but otherwise, he had no injuries. "Are you all right? I thought—"

He stopped short, a pained look in his eyes. The others filed out behind him, still watching me in silence. They were all keeping their distance. And why not? They had just seen me call up a wall of water and destroy one of their own.

"I had to do it," I said. "He wasn't making the Philosopher's Stone—"

"We know," the King said. "Nat showed us the book. We were already growing anxious by then. We could not hear what you were saying, but you sounded distressed."

I turned to Nat with a questioning look. "The book?"

"It's all in here." Nat held up a palm-size volume. "In Gabriel's writing."

"Gabriel?" I was instantly on my guard. Was he part of the plot too?

"I didn't know." Gabriel's brown eyes pleaded with me to believe him. "I merely copied what I saw. I didn't mean to hurt you, I promise."

I heard the ring of truth in his voice, and what's more, a note of fear. *He's afraid of me*, I realized. They were all at least a little afraid.

Except, perhaps, for Nat. He gave Gabriel a hard look. "Yes. We've had it out with him, and it seems he was only copying from Sir Isaac's papers. And from what I've seen of his attempts at translation, he didn't understand a word of it."

Gabriel looked as if he wanted to knock Nat down. But he checked himself.

"A spy?" I repeated, startled. "For the Queen of Sweden?"

"For himself," Nat said.

Gabriel flushed, but he did not deny it. "And why not?" he said with a pale imitation of his old swagger. "If you stood to lose your entire fortune, your lands, your home, you would act too."

Nat ignored this. "He wanted to make his own Philosopher's Stone. That's what his own notes say. And when he found where Sir Isaac hid his metal box at night, and worked out the combination, he thought he'd found the way to do it. But it turned out he couldn't read the papers inside, or at least not well enough to glean what he needed."

"They were in the most devilish code ever devised," Gabriel said bitterly. "All I could do was copy them." He pointed an accusing finger at Nat. "And then you stole my book."

"I saw him hide it," Nat said to me. "After we, well . . . on that last night, just before I was found with the crucible."

My cheeks went hot, remembering what we had said to each other then: how I'd refused to go with him, and he had left me because he thought I didn't care for him.

"I thought I'd better find out what was so interesting to him," Nat said, "so I took the book out to look—but the next thing I knew, the whole palace was chasing after me. You know how that ended."

"I know some of it," I said. "You managed to escape?"

"I did. I got the book and myself to a hideaway in the Greenwich cellars."

"You've been here all the time?" I was amazed. "How did you keep hidden?"

"I have a friend or two in the kitchens. And a few in the guards." He and Potts exchanged the ghost of a smile. "That helped a lot."

I nodded. It made sense that Nat would have allies in unusual places. Rank didn't matter to him. He'd as soon strike up a friendship with a servant as a king—a trait I loved in him.

"After I went into hiding, I worked on cracking the cipher," Nat said. "And when I finally figured it out, I discovered that Sir Isaac wasn't making the Philosopher's Stone, but an elixir to steal away Chantress powers."

"I didn't know," Gabriel said again. He opened his hands to me, as if to plead that he'd meant no harm.

"I came up from the cellars then," Nat said to me. "It was almost dawn, and I was afraid I was going to be too late. My only chance was to come straight here. Because everything was in an uproar, I had no real trouble till I approached the stairs. There was a bit of a scuffle then, but fortunately, Sergeant Potts here was on duty, so I got through to the King. And thanks be, he listened."

The King took up the tale. "When he showed us the book, we could hardly believe it. But we thought it odd, the way Sir Isaac had barred the door, and then we heard the sound of shouting. And then Nat appeared with an explanation that made sense of it all."

"So we started to smash the door down," Sir Samuel said. I looked up and saw the hatch marks in the wood.

Behind his spectacles, Penebrygg's eyes were distressed. "We wanted to save you, my dear."

"But you saved yourself," Nat said.

I did, I thought. *I did. I found my power.*

Nat's eyes were steady on me, and I thought I saw both pride and regret in them—but we were too far apart for me to read more. Before I could step closer, the King said, "Where are Flamel's papers?"

"I doubt they're Flamel's," Nat said. "They're more ancient than that."

"Sir Isaac brought them down here," I said. "I think the river took them."

For a long moment, we all looked at the wreck of what had been the best alchemy laboratory in Europe. There was no sign of the box that had held the papers. Even the great fire-breathing furnace had been humbled into a heap of broken bricks and twisted metal. The bottles and crucibles and beakers had been dashed to pieces.

"Even so," the King said, "I think we had better search Sir Isaac's rooms. Who knows what else may turn up?"

† † †

The King led the way upstairs, with the rest of us following behind. I had thought Nat might speak to me then, but instead, he lagged at the back. Perhaps he was still keeping watch over Gabriel. Or perhaps he was waiting until we had more privacy.

"You are cold, Chantress?" the King asked.

I was shivering. "I'm afraid the wave soaked me through."

The King took in my sopping clothes for the first time. "So it has. You must change."

He insisted on escorting me to my rooms. As we traversed the palace, people moved out of our way. I heard whispers echoing around us: "Chantress . . . wave . . . rose right out of the Thames . . . taller than the East Tower . . . magic."

When we reached my door, the King ordered the guards to stand down. They did so immediately. From the look on their faces, they too had heard about the great wave.

"Come and find us when you are ready," the King said to me.

The room was empty, but I didn't need a maid's help to dress. Instead, I shrugged myself into the only clothes I could find—my mulberry silk—and wrapped my plain traveling cloak around me to keep warm.

By the time I reached Sir Isaac's room, the place had been well and truly gone over. It was Nat and Gabriel who had made the chief discoveries: two secret boxes shaped like books. One contained various poisons and their antidotes. The other held keys swaddled in wool, including all the keys needed to open the moonbriar casket.

"He must have had copies made," Nat said to me. "And we're guessing that he might have used the poisons on Sir Barnaby, to keep him out of the way. Of all of us, Sir Barnaby knew Sir

Isaac the best, and he might have noticed something was wrong."

"Can anything be done to help Sir Barnaby now?" I asked.

"I don't know." Nat closed the doors to the cabinet at the foot of Sir Isaac's bed. "I hope so."

"How could he stoop to such things?" Penebrygg shook his head, his eyes dimming behind his spectacles. "And how could I have been so blind? My dear," he said, turning to me, "I am so very sorry."

"He made fools of all of us," Sir Samuel said indignantly.

"Only because we let him," the King said in a low voice.

Blustering, Sir Samuel started to deny this, but Penebrygg cut across him. "The King is right. Sir Isaac told us what we wanted to hear, and we believed him. We ought to have guessed he was promising us something too good to be true."

"One of us guessed it," the King said, looking at Nat. "I will not forget that."

Before Nat could reply, Lord Roxburgh shot into the room. "Your Majesty!" He scuttled to the King's side, distraught. "I have been searching for you everywhere. What are we to do? Boudicca has scattered our army. And she's captured Lord Wrexham."

CHAPTER THIRTY-EIGHT
BOUDICCA

I stared at Lord Roxburgh. Wrexham was captured?

"It cannot be!" the King said.

Roxburgh wrung his hands. "It is true. I was out there. I rode back to tell you." His eyes were terrified. "It happened right at dawn, a bare mile from here, on the banks of the Thames. We'd cornered Boudicca—she was on her own, with just a few of her men—and Wrexham gave the order to fire. But then a mist rose up from the river and threw everything into confusion." He finished bitterly, "Boudicca must have summoned it."

"So she does have magic?" the King exclaimed.

"No one saw her do anything," Roxburgh admitted. "But she must have called that mist up somehow, Your Majesty. It came so suddenly—and when it cleared, she had the high ground, and her army was massing behind her. And she had captured Wrexham, too. One of our men saw him being dragged away. How could a woman like that have accomplished such a thing without magic?"

With luck and leadership, I thought. And yes, magic might have been involved too. But whose? Boudicca's—or mine?

Defend me from my enemies. That was what I'd sung to the river, just as dawn was breaking. Had it not only dispatched Sir Isaac, but delivered me from Wrexham as well? Did my magic extend that far? Remembering the power of the river's song, I thought it might. Yet magic or no magic, Boudicca was clearly formidable.

"And it doesn't end there," Roxburgh was saying. "Our line broke in the mist, and others were captured too. When our men saw how many were gone, and what a great host Boudicca had arrayed against them, they fled. Have no doubt of it: Boudicca will soon be at the gates."

Only then did he seem to take in his surroundings. "But why are you gathered here in Sir Isaac's room? Is it to do with the Stone? Have you made it?"

"No," the King said heavily. "There is no Stone. Nor will there ever be."

"No Stone?" Roxburgh cried out. "But then what is to be done? Boudicca will attack, and we have nothing to bargain with. Our men are in disarray, and her followers outnumber us."

"You forget that we have a Chantress on our side." With an anxious face, the King turned to me. "You said if you were close enough, you could defeat Boudicca with magic. You must help defend us."

"Yes." Roxburgh turned to me, his small eyes beseeching. "Do it! Put an end to that viper Boudicca once and for all."

I almost told them the truth: calling up the great wave had tired me. My power had not faded entirely—I could still hear the river's music, even though Sir Isaac's windows were closed—but it could be hours or even days before it returned in full force. Even had I wanted to, I doubted I had it in me right now to defeat a whole army.

Instead, I took a deep breath. If I had power—or even the illusion of it—then I must use it wisely.

"No," I said.

The King stiffened.

Roxburgh's cheeks bulged with rage. "You do not refuse your King!"

Ignoring him, I spoke only to King Henry. "Of course I will do what I can to protect you, Your Majesty. But as you yourself have often said, it is better to talk than to fight. Offer to meet with her, and I will go with you. Let us see if we can make peace."

"No!" Roxburgh shouted.

The King focused not on him, but on me. "What can I possibly say to her? Without the Stone, I have nothing to give her."

"You have more to give than you think," I said. "You can sell houses and jewels. You can tell your Court to do likewise. And you can stop draining the Treasury to build fortifications."

The King looked worried, especially by this last. "Wrexham would have something to say about that."

"He's not in a position to protest right now," I said. "And as you yourself have said, everyone must compromise."

"But how can we know that Boudicca will accept our compromises?" the King asked. "What if she expects more? And what will we do next year, if the harvest fails again?"

Standing behind us, Nat at last raised his voice. "I have something that will help with that, Your Majesty."

† † †

Three hours later, the King and Boudicca met at the top of Greenwich Hill. By negotiation, their armies remained on the low ground, well apart from each other—the King's better armed, but Boudicca's substantially outnumbering it.

Fewer than fifty of us gathered at the summit. I was among them, and so was Nat. As we climbed up to the meeting point, I glimpsed Wrexham below, bound with ropes behind Boudicca's lines, red-faced with impotent fury.

It had taken half the morning and a host of white flags to arrange the conference. It took the other half of the morning and a great deal of talking for the meeting to reach a conclusion. The King, it must be said, did most of the listening. At his request, I stood next to him.

Boudicca was shorter than I expected, and older and plainer. She was soft-spoken, too, a peculiar trait in a leader of armed men. When we drew close, I sensed something else about her: she could not work magic. The mist had been mine after all.

Yet if Boudicca was no magic-worker, she nevertheless had real power. There was something commanding about her, and something enormously compelling, too. After only a few minutes in her presence, I could understand why so many had followed her. When our two sides met, she looked right into my eyes as she greeted me, and I had the uncanny feeling that she saw to the core of me. What exactly she perceived, however, she kept to herself.

We were the only two women there; the rest were all men. This, however, did not seem to disturb Boudicca in the least. She had extraordinary self-assurance, and in her broad country accent she told the King that she was glad he had summoned her. She was certain that he wanted to know how his subjects—her followers—were suffering. And she was certain, too, that once he fully understood their troubles, he would help them.

I think the King feared, at first, that she expected him to set everything to rights in a day. But she was wiser than that; she had a very practical turn of mind. She accepted at once his offer to suspend the fortification program. She agreed that it would help matters if he sold off some of the royal estates and jewels to help feed the hungry. And she grasped immediately the importance of Nat's contribution: the potatoes.

"They'll feed thrice as many as wheat?" she said. "You're sure of it?"

"That's right," Nat said. "In a given field, potatoes will make three times as much food as wheat. And the wheat blight won't harm them. You have my word on it."

She studied the lumpy, brown vegetables—part of the small store Nat had brought earlier to Greenwich to persuade the King and Council of the usefulness of the crop. And then she studied Nat, taking his measure, just as she'd taken mine. He met her gaze unflinchingly.

"I have some sacks you can take now," he said, "and I can arrange for shiploads more. Seed potatoes, ready for planting, and others to eat now."

"And what will you charge for them?"

"Nothing," the King interjected. "I will pay all costs myself."

Boudicca nodded, acknowledging this, and turned back to Nat. "But be they good eating?"

Nat grinned. "The best. But you needn't take my word for it: the King's own cook has baked and fried some for you."

I hadn't been with Nat when he'd negotiated this with the cook, but I'd heard that it had taken all his persuasive powers. At first, the cook hadn't wanted anything to do with the dirty lumps. He'd changed his mind, though, after they were done and he'd tasted them.

As I watched Boudicca and the King take forkfuls of hot, fried potatoes from the same dish, I wished that I could have a taste too. They smelled delicious, and I was reminded, forcibly, of how long it had been since I'd eaten a decent meal.

There were no leftover potatoes for me or for anyone else, however—and for the best possible reason: Boudicca had taken a fancy to them.

"So we have an agreement?" the King said over the empty dish.

"Aye," Boudicca said. "That we do." She motioned to her followers to bring Wrexham forward.

"You're certain your people will stand down? That they'll go home peacefully?"

Boudicca nodded with the certainty of a born queen. "That they will, now as we've settled things."

And thus the peace was kept.

† † †

On the way back from Greenwich Hill, Nat and the King began to work out the best way to arrange the purchase and distribution of potatoes. I followed behind them, keeping a close eye on Wrexham. He'd sprained a knee when he'd been captured and was being carried back on a litter. The humiliations of the day had silenced him, and he refused to meet anyone's eye.

Back at the palace, Nat and the King continued discussing potatoes, with Penebrygg and Sir Samuel offering helpful suggestions. Nearby, various Council members talked in low voices, and from the way their glances darted in my direction, I guessed they were speaking of me. I saw a respect bordering on awe in their eyes—and outright fear, in some.

Even Sybil was tentative when she first approached me, though her sheer exuberance soon won out. "Oh, Lucy, you *are* a wonder! I knew you were powerful, but this is something else altogether. I'm so proud—and so relieved you're safe. . . ."

She hugged me close, warming my heart. But when I saw Nat over her shoulder, talking with the King, the moment turned bittersweet. I was glad to see Nat given his due by King and Council, but it hurt that he had shown no desire to come near me. Indeed, we'd hardly spoken since we'd left Sir Isaac's room— though given all that had happened, perhaps that was not so surprising.

It's only been a few hours, I told myself. *Give it time.* Looking away from Nat, I turned my attention to the one other concern that still niggled at me. "Have you seen Margery?" I asked Sybil.

"No, I haven't. Not since last night, when we were all in your room. Is she all right?"

"Probably," I said. But I was worried. Where was she?

I finally found out when I went to my rooms. The guards were gone from my door, but Margery was waiting for me inside, seated on a small footstool by the fire.

"My lady." Her face paled when she saw me, and she gripped her hands tight in her lap. "I heard . . . they're saying the Stone didn't work. But you look so fine, my lady, and they say it was you who made that wave. . . ."

There was a question in her voice, which answered the question in my mind.

"So you *did* overhear what Sybil and I said." I came over to where she was sitting. "I thought you did, but I wasn't sure."

"Yes, my lady."

"You knew about the Stone. And how I'd lost my powers. And yet you said nothing to Wrexham?"

"No, my lady." She shook her head vigorously. "I couldn't. Not once I knew you wanted to help me. And not once I knew what was stopping you."

"Then I owe you a lot, Margery. And I won't forget, I promise. Now that my magic's back, I'll do everything I can for your family."

"Then it worked?" She clasped her hands even more tightly, but now there was hope in her face. "You did make the Stone?"

"No. Sir Isaac—" How could I explain it? "It turned out Sir

Isaac was trying to betray the King, trying to betray me. He wasn't intending to make the Stone at all. But I got my power back anyway."

"So what they're saying is true?" Margery spoke almost in a whisper. "The wave . . . that was you?"

"Yes." There was no point hiding it. Indeed, there was every reason not to. "I was the one who made the wave."

Margery looked at me, her eyes shining. "Oh, my lady."

Uncomfortable being the object of such hero worship, I smoothed my skirts and sat down on a chair beside her. There were still parts of the story I did not understand, and I was determined to get to the bottom of them. "Margery, why did you leave the room last night? And why did you bolt when I saw you up in the gallery?"

Fear came into her face again. "My lady, do you remember when you sent me after Miss Dashwood yesterday? And she said she saw me by Lord Wrexham's rooms?"

"Yes."

"It was true; I was there. I'd overheard him earlier, you see, speaking to someone in one of the rooms off the library. He said something terrible. Something truly evil."

"He threatened you?"

"Not me," she said ever so softly. "He didn't see me. Nor could I see him. But I could hear him, and he was talking about the King."

I straightened in my chair. "The King?"

"I know I was supposed to keep searching for Miss Dashwood," she said in a rush, "but I couldn't, not after that. It was so awful

I knew no one would believe me, except maybe you. And if you went to the King and I was wrong, then Wrexham would starve my family for certain. So I knew I had to search his rooms. I had to find proof."

"And did you?" I asked.

Margery's hands twisted open, revealing a tiny packet of paper. "I don't know." She handed the packet to me. "I finally got into his rooms just before dawn, and I found these under the felt at the back of his writing desk. They're in cipher."

I looked them over. The cipher meant nothing to me. "Margery, what was it he said?"

"He spoke of the King's death, my lady. And . . . and about being king himself."

We looked at each other over the papers.

"We had better go straight to King Henry," I said.

CHAPTER THIRTY-NINE

REALITIES AND DREAMS

"Treason," the King said to me six hours later. It was evening, and we were alone in the small study near his staterooms; he was seated at his desk, and I had taken a chair close by. After an exhaustive search of Wrexham's rooms, all had been laid bare. The cipher had been cracked, the plot unraveled, and Wrexham was in the Tower.

"It was treason, pure and simple," the King went on heavily, looking far older than his years. "Wrexham was planning to have me shot during a tour of new fortifications in the North this spring. It would be made to look like a rebel ambush. At which point he would use his armies and his connection to the Tudor line—and, most likely, his marriage to you—to put himself on the throne."

I nodded. The outlines of the plot had already been made clear to me, even if I didn't yet know all the details. "It seems we've all had a narrow escape."

"The worst of it is, Wrexham wasn't working alone," the King said. "He was the leader, but others are complicit: Roxburgh, Ffoulkes, and half a dozen others. They will all have a proper trial, of course, but the evidence is damning. Wrexham will go to the block, and probably others, too." He bent his head. "It seems I had far less to fear from Boudicca and her rebels than I did from some of my own sworn noblemen. Even my Chief Alchemist turned out to be a traitor."

The betrayals had clearly shaken him, and no wonder: After this, who could he bring himself to trust?

The answer ought to have been obvious, but I didn't see it until the King raised his head and turned to me.

"I need your help, Chantress." He tapped the documents before him, listing royal houses and treasures to be sold. "These plans we've made will be popular with the people, but not with the mighty. Nor will they be pleased with the other ideas I have to give ordinary people more say in affairs. At worst, there may be more plots against me. At best, it will be hard to make headway. But it would be easier if you were here, Chantress."

"Because a rebellious lord would think twice before crossing me?"

"Yes," he said. "That is one reason. But there is this, too: I sorely need advisers I can trust. I am certain you long to be back in Norfolk, and you may go there immediately if you desire. But I must ask you this: Will you instead stay at Court a while longer? Will you help me steer the kingdom through these difficult times?"

I did long to go back to Norfolk. The King was right about

that. And I had less faith than he did in my power, being all too aware of my weaknesses. But I understood now that there was a price to be paid for isolating myself—a price paid by me, a price paid by others. For I did have power, however imperfect it might be, and that power was needed now, not at some distant, more perfect point in the future. Like anyone else, I would have to do my best with what I had.

"I will stay," I said.

The King gave me his first real smile of the evening.

"That is," I added quickly, "if we can settle one more matter between us."

The King eyed me cautiously. "And that is?"

"My marriage."

The King grabbed another set of documents. "As to that, I should tell you that several Council members have already approached me to suggest themselves or their heirs. . . ."

"Your Majesty, I decline." I braced myself for a storm.

To my surprise, the King set the documents aside and said, "I rather thought you would. I take it you wish to decide for yourself who you will marry?"

"Yes."

He raised his chin; the bruises on his throat were still livid. "And the good of the kingdom?"

I met his eyes squarely. "The good of the kingdom isn't served by having the Council fight over me like a bone. We'll all be better off if I make the choice myself."

He was silent for a moment. "Possibly you are right. Of

course, it is customary for these matters to be decided by the Council—"

"For kings, perhaps, but not for Chantresses," I interrupted. "For Chantresses, there is no clear precedent."

He conceded the point. "I suppose not. Well, then, let us create a new precedent: you shall choose your own husband, Chantress—on one condition."

I tensed. "Which is?"

The King smiled. "That you tell me in advance who he is to be. Do you have someone in mind?"

"Oh." I felt myself turn pink. "No, Your Majesty."

"No?" He looked surprised. "Judging from the way Walbrook looked when he came flying down the steps to rescue you, I thought you and he might have an understanding."

An understanding? Of each other, perhaps. But of our future? Never, really, as far as I could tell. And we certainly had none at this point.

Yet now that I was free to make my own choice, I could hope that an understanding would come.

"Well," said the King when I remained silent, "I don't mean to pry. If you do make plans to marry, tell me."

"Thank you, Your Majesty."

The King turned away from me, looking preoccupied, as if other matters were already crowding in on him. I rose to go.

My hand was on the door when he said quietly and with great sadness, "Truth to tell, I rather envy you your freedom."

I wasn't sure he expected a reply, but what was the use of

being an adviser if you couldn't give advice? "Then perhaps it's time you created a new precedent for kings," I said.

Without waiting for an answer, I slipped out the door.

† † †

After I left the King, I went looking for Nat. It was nearly midnight, but I thought it likely he was still up and busy somewhere. To my dismay, I discovered that he had already left for London to handle urgent matters relating to the settlement with Boudicca. He was expected to be away from Court for the better part of a week.

Disappointment hit me hard. Since the meeting with Boudicca, I had only seen Nat across the table from me in meetings, or deep in discussion with other Council members. We hadn't had a moment to ourselves today, not even a chance to say good-bye.

It doesn't matter, I told myself. *Now that no one's trying to force a marriage on me, we have all the time in the world. And he'll only be away for a few days. I'll be so busy I'll hardly notice he's gone.*

I was halfway right, for the following days were indeed frantically busy. From early in the morning until late at night, I met with the King and what remained of his Council, and I had little time to think of anything but the difficult business of governing a kingdom. But when the meetings were done, I wondered what Nat was doing and whether he was thinking of me, and at night I dreamed of him: Nat turning away from me in the secret room, Nat running from the guards, Nat locked in a palace where I couldn't reach him . . .

Only dreams, I told myself. But they felt very real. I lay in the dark for a long time before falling back asleep.

†　　†　　†

On the fifth day, my work finished early, in midafternoon. The King had noticed how tired I looked, and he urged me to get some rest.

When I returned to my rooms, Margery leaped up to greet me, bubbling with excitement. She was a new person these days, not so much because of the reward she'd received for discovering Wrexham's plot, but because she knew her family was safe. Wrexham's son was now the King's ward, and Wrexham's lands and property—like that of all traitors from time immemorial—now belonged to the Crown. Although the King intended to sell some of the estate in order to raise funds to relieve the famine, he had promised Margery that her family would remain under royal protection.

All in all, it was becoming hard to remember the dour Margery I'd known at first. And today her smile was wider than ever.

"They're here, my lady!"

"Here?" I looked around the room, confused.

"Your new clothes. The seamstresses have finished the first set."

"Not the red silk," I said in dismay, remembering Wrexham's gift.

"No, no. I started them on something else, something that I think will suit you very well. Come and see." She walked over to the bed, where pale primrose skirts glimmered in the late-afternoon sunlight. "They've finished it off in time for the dancing tonight."

"The dancing?"

"For the King's birthday." Her eyes widened. "You haven't forgotten, my lady?"

"N-no. Not exactly." After all, I had been there when the King had scaled the whole affair down. Instead of an extravagant banquet, there was to be only a simple reception and dancing. But the details of the affair had slipped my mind. "I've paid my respects to him, of course, and wished him well. But I hadn't thought I'd go to the dance."

Margery looked distressed. "Why ever not, my lady?"

"Oh, I haven't been in a dancing mood."

I tried to speak lightly, as if it hardly mattered, but I couldn't quite carry it off, for my voice was as flat as I felt. That morning Penebrygg had mentioned that he'd had two letters from Nat. He'd assumed that Nat had been writing to me, too, but I'd received nothing from him at all.

This time, of course, there could be no question of the Council not allowing Nat to write to me, for the King had settled the matter: my attachments, friendships, and correspondence were now my own affair. If I'd had no letters from Nat, it was because he hadn't written any.

Was he still upset that I'd refused to run away with him? Had he cooled for other reasons? Or was he simply very busy, and determined to wait to speak until he could see me in person?

Margery looked crushed. "You mean you won't even try the dress on, my lady?"

In truth, I couldn't bring myself to care much about clothes. But Margery had done a great deal for me—and really, it wasn't much for her to ask. With her assistance, I slipped into the silk skirts and bodice, then stood still as she concentrated fiercely on arranging the sleeves just so.

"The length is quite good. And so is the fit." Margery sounded pleased. "We'll just need to make a few slight alterations to the sleeves."

"I'll take it off, then." I reached for the buttons.

Margery stopped me. "Not yet, my lady. Come see how you look in it."

She pulled me over to the looking glass, and my breath caught.

Every time Margery had brought up the subject of clothes, I'd told her that I didn't want anything extravagant: no cloth-of-gold, no jeweled bodices. There were other ways I could spend that money, on people who needed it more. Margery had always nodded, but with a glint in her eye that worried me. I feared she harbored designs to turn me into an ostentatious court lady, a figure of fashion to outdo all others.

It was a shock, instead, to see a dress that was made in every way for *me*. It was simply cut, yet fitted every curve precisely, and silvery threads shone like scattered stars on the pale yellow silk. When I turned, the skirts shimmered like moonlight.

"Lucy?" Sybil pushed open the door. "Thank goodness you're finally in! I've brought you a visitor."

She barreled into the room, towing a companion behind her: a stocky, wrinkled woman who meant the world to me.

"Norrie!" I cried. Forgetting the dress entirely, I flung myself at her.

Norrie did not seem to notice the dress either. "Oh, my lamb." Stroking my hair, she hugged me close. "What dangers you've faced! And me not here to help you."

"I'm just glad you're here now." Her embrace didn't take the pain of Nat's silence away, but it did make it easier to bear.

"For a few days there, I thought I'd never get on my feet," Norrie went on, as if she hadn't heard me. "And when I did finally start after you, I had every kind of delay imaginable—"

"As long as you're all right, nothing else matters," I said, trying to soothe her.

"But you were here all alone—"

"It's fine," I said. "Really and truly fine. You were right: I was stronger than I knew."

My words seemed to reach her then. She stepped back to survey me, and I saw a look in her eyes that reminded me, oddly, of the look I'd seen in Nat's: half regret, half pride. "So you are, child. So you are. My goodness, I've only been away from you for a fortnight, and you've gone and grown up on me. How splendid you look." She nodded at Sybil. "And this one too. To think I can remember the pair of you making mud pies in the garden. And now you're such fine young ladies."

"I can't have changed all that much," Sybil protested. "You still knew me the instant you saw me."

"Of course," Norrie said comfortably. "The image of your mother, you are. And those dimples—who could forget them?"

And there was my answer about Sybil, long past the point when I needed it. I started to laugh. "Oh, Norrie, what a comfort you are!"

Sybil grinned. "And what about me?"

"You too."

I reached over to hug her, but she waved me away. "No, no—you mustn't crumple that gorgeous dress of yours any more. Margery, is this your work? You're a genius. No one will have eyes for anyone but you tonight, Lucy."

"I'm not going to the dance—"

"But you must!" Sybil said. "It will be such fun. And you haven't had much of that lately, not with all those Council meetings on your plate." She made a wry face. "To say nothing of what came before."

"I'd rather stay in with Norrie," I said, putting my arm around her.

Norrie shook her head, smiling. "It's kind of you, child, but I'm all in from the journey, and I'll be wanting an early night. So you go and enjoy yourself with Sybil. I wouldn't dream of spoiling your evening."

She did look tired. Stricken that I had not noticed it before, I guided her to a chair. Norrie heaved a great sigh as she sat down.

"You won't be spoiling anything," I told her. "Truly, I don't mind staying here."

Norrie's eyes twinkled. "Perhaps you don't, but I'm sure young Nat would have something to say about it. I saw him as I was coming up—"

"Nat's *here*?" My heart shot up like a firework.

"Why, yes. Is that so strange?"

"He's been away." My voice sounded strange even to myself. "In London."

"Well, he's here now," Norrie said, chuckling. "He said he had some business to attend to, but he was hoping to see you later on. He meant this dance, I expect."

"Of course he did." Sybil linked her arm with mine. "So that settles it, Lucy."

Excitement rippled through me. "All right, then." I spread a hand over my silvery skirts. "I'll go."

CHAPTER FORTY
AN UNEQUAL MATCH

Before the dancing began, I stayed with Norrie, hearing more about her journey and answering her questions about what had happened at Greenwich. When I explained that the King had asked me to stay at Court, she took it well.

"Now that I've finally gotten here, I wouldn't mind staying put for a while," she said, sipping at the chamomile tea Margery had made for her. "Your rooms are lovely and warm, aren't they? And it's a great pleasure to see Sybil again. She says her maid Joan's here with her too."

"Do you know her?"

"No, but I'd like to meet her. I remember her sister well: she was Sybil's nursemaid, just as I was yours, and she was kind to me that summer at Dashwood Hall." She set down her cup, and I saw again how tired she was.

"Time for you to rest," I said. "You're to take my bed."

She started to protest.

"You must," I said. "Margery and I will make up a pallet for me later."

"But you won't be comfortable—"

"I'll be fine. Truth to tell, I was planning to dance all night anyway."

At that, she chuckled. "Very well, lamb. You do that. And I'll take your bed and be grateful for it." She laid her gnarled hand on mine. "Give that Nat a hug from me."

I smiled. "I will."

† † †

Later that evening, with Norrie safely tucked in bed, I went down to the birthday dance. Even on the stairs, I could hear the harmony of viol and flute and bass. My feet tapped in time to their beat; I was eager to dance.

When I finally reached the Great Hall, I found an enormous crowd had already gathered there. I could only just wedge my way in—and for once no one looked at me, even though I was the Chantress. Instead, people were craning their necks toward the center of the room. I obligingly craned mine too, hoping to glimpse whatever it was they were gazing at.

At first I saw nothing except the backs and heads of the people in front of me, but I caught the whisper of gossip here and there through the music.

". . . might break off the negotiations . . ."

". . . heard him say he won't marry a girl he's never seen . . ."

". . . the third time he's danced with her . . ."

"The fourth, old chap, and the night's hardly begun!"

". . . can't say I blame him. A beauty like that . . ."

The crowd shifted, and through a gap I saw what had attracted so much attention: King Henry, dancing a stately minuet with Sybil. She was laughing, and he was clearly entranced.

Watching them, I missed Nat so much I could hardly breathe.

As the crowd jostled forward again, I scanned the room for him.

"Chantress?" Gabriel was at my elbow, aglow with exuberance. "What a pleasure to find you here. I've only just returned."

That caught my attention. "Returned? From where?"

"Visiting my estate. Didn't you hear? The King has restored it all to me." Gabriel paused. "That is, not precisely to me, not yet—he'll hold it in trust until I'm twenty-one. But I have his word that it will all come to me then, and he'll make good the part that Wrexham lost.

"And, of course, it's you I must thank for Wrexham's fall," he went on, bowing to me. His eyes, as he rose, were merry and just the slightest bit teasing. "Perhaps it is you who should be called Chief Alchemist."

"No," was all I said.

Something about the way I said it, however, made him push back his tawny hair and look down at me, contrite. "I'm sorry, Chantress. I shouldn't be making jokes about it, not to you. Believe me, I had no idea Sir Isaac meant to harm you. If I had, I swear I would have put a stop to it. You know that, don't you?"

"I do." After all, Nat had made it clear that Gabriel hadn't understood what he'd been copying.

"Then all's well between us?"

His eyes would have melted a heart considerably more hardened than mine. "Yes," I said. "All's well."

Gabriel gave me a brilliant smile and bent his head close. "You really are the most extraordinary woman, you know," he whispered. "Come dance with me."

I almost let him take my hand. But then I spotted Nat on the wide steps by the door. He was scanning the packed room, his sober expression entirely at odds with the general joyous mood. Was he looking for me?

"Excuse me," I said to Gabriel, and plunged into the crowd. But I was only halfway across, still trapped in a sea of people, when I saw Nat turn and leave.

I caught up with him on the dim landing of a quiet staircase, just as he was about to disappear down it. "Nat, wait. It's me."

"Lucy!" His eyes widened as I stopped just short of him, below a small alcove filled with white hyacinths. "I couldn't find you. You look . . ." He shook his head as if words failed him.

It didn't matter. His eyes had said enough. Happiness flooded through me.

"It's good to see you too," I said softly. He'd dressed with unusual care, not in the showy fashions that Gabriel favored, but in fine black cloth that fit well over his shoulders, and snowy linen that set off his dark hair and the shadows and angles of his face. The only incongruous notes were his boots. Although they were carefully polished, most men wore something less sturdy for dancing. But what did I care? He was here.

"I'm afraid I can't stay," he said.

My happiness faded. "You can't? But Norrie said—"

"That I wanted to see you? Yes. I thought I should tell you in person . . ."

I held my breath.

His eyes flickered back toward the Great Hall. The players had struck up a new dance. "I was wrong about Sybil."

It wasn't what I'd expected him to say. "Sybil?"

"I misjudged her," he said. "She's been a good friend to you. I see that now."

"I'm glad." I wasn't sure where this conversation was going. "So you approve of the match? Between Sybil and the King?"

"If the King proposes, I wish them joy," he said, yet his eyes looked doubtful.

"But . . . ?" I prompted.

"I'm not sure he will."

"He might," I said, thinking of what I'd said to the King about precedents. "He just might."

Nat shrugged. "Even if he does, it's an unequal match."

"Unequal how?" I demanded.

"Because he's royal, and she's not."

"Only by accident. When they met, as children, they moved in the same circles; their fathers were friends."

"They knew each other as children?" He took this in. "Well, perhaps that will make things easier between them."

"Of course it will."

He shook his head. "You underestimate the obstacles. To be King is to be far removed from anyone, to have worries and cares and powers that cannot be shared. And there will be objections to the match, you can be sure of that. In the face of so much opposition, it's hard to make a marriage succeed."

I leaned back against the wall. "Are we talking about the King and Sybil?" I asked slowly. "Or are we talking about us?"

His cheeks darkened then, but he met the question head-on. "What is there to say about us, except that we face even more obstacles?"

"What obstacles?" I felt brazen speaking so plainly, but I had to make him see. "I've spoken to the King, Nat. I've told him I won't allow the Council to decide my future, and he's agreed."

"So I heard."

"You've heard?" I pushed away from the wall. "The King told you?"

"Yes. And so did Penebrygg."

"Oh." Hot humiliation washed over me. He'd known all this time that I was free, and he hadn't acted on it. I didn't feel brazen anymore.

"Lucy, don't look like that. Please." Nat started toward me, then stopped himself.

He was mere inches from me, but it might as well have been a hundred miles. The staircase was silent as a tomb, and the scent of hyacinths was overpowering.

"You've had a change of heart?" It was hard to speak, but I had to know.

"Lucy, my heart hasn't changed one whit."

My breath quickened. "Then why—?"

"Because it won't work." His hazel eyes were full of pain. "Surely you can see that as well as I can."

"I don't see any such thing. Who cares what other people think?"

"It's not that," he said. "It's the mismatch between us."

"What mismatch?"

"It's been a long time since I've seen you work magic," he said. "I'd forgotten just how powerful you are. And you're becoming more powerful all the time. And I—well, let's face it: I'm just an ordinary person."

I started to protest, but he put up his hand. "Don't misunderstand me. I'm glad that you could save yourself, gladder than you can imagine. Because even with my best efforts, I couldn't do it. I couldn't protect you. I can't give you what you need. That's the long and short of it."

"How do you define need?" I countered. "You keep me grounded, Nat. You listen to me. You're someone I can trust absolutely." I leaned toward him, so that our lips almost touched. "You're all that to me—and more."

He almost gave in; I saw it in his eyes. But there was something else there too: the same despair I'd seen when he'd given me the snowdrop. *A man who wants what he cannot have.*

He stepped back.

"Nat?" I said, suddenly afraid.

"I wish it were that simple," he said. "But it's not. That night when we quarreled—when you wouldn't run away—it's stayed with me."

"Because I said no? Nat—"

"Because you were *right* to say no. I had nothing to offer you. Nothing, at least, that you truly needed. I had no position, no standing, no wealth. I wanted to protect you, but I couldn't. And that has to change."

"I don't care about money or power." How could I make him understand? "You have yourself. That's enough for me."

"It wasn't enough that night," he said quietly. "And I learned something from it: If we're to have any hope of a future together, I need to prove myself. As things stand, I have no right to court any woman, let alone you. That's why I'm going away."

A cold draft blew down my spine. "Away?" I echoed faintly.

"I've accepted a commission as the King's envoy. I'll be traveling all over the kingdom and on the Continent as well— wherever I need to go to end this famine and reduce the odds of another one following it. I don't know if I can succeed. But I'm going to try."

I couldn't deny it was a worthy goal. All I could think, how-ever, was that he was leaving me. As steadily as I could, I said, "But you'll write, of course. We can write to each other. And surely you'll be at Court sometimes. We can see each other then."

"Lucy, no." He was gentle but unyielding. "I meant what I said: I have to do this on my own. Otherwise, whatever I achieve, people will say it came from you, from your power. I came here to say good-bye. I leave tonight for Holland."

Good-bye? I grabbed at my skirts—my beautiful, useless skirts. "You don't need to do this. You really don't."

"Lucy, I do. I need to stand on my own two feet. It's the only way forward."

That was all he said, but the desperate certainty in his voice silenced me. His mind was made up. I bit back the pleas and arguments that crowded onto my tongue. They wouldn't change anything, except to make the parting more bitter.

But I couldn't help asking one question. "Tell me this: If I didn't have magic, would you stay?"

He was silent for a long moment.

"That's not a fair question," he said at last. "You *do* have magic. It's part of who you are. To wish it away would be like wishing *you* away." He touched his hand to my face. "And whatever happens between us, I will never do that."

I closed my eyes. Willing myself not to cry, I pressed my hand over his and felt his strong, cool fingers against my hot cheek. When he kissed me, I held on even tighter.

"I love you," he said.

And I love you, I wanted to say, but my voice had deserted me. Instead, I did what only love could make me do: I let his hand go.

When I opened my eyes, he was walking away. I watched him stride down the stairs and swing out the door. And then I was alone, with only my music and my magic to comfort me.

HISTORICAL NOTE

Chantress Alchemy, like *Chantress* before it, is set in an alternate seventeenth-century England where magic is possible. Yet some of the most fantastical elements of the story are true.

Calendar houses, for instance, are rare but real. One of the best—Knole, home of the Sackville-Wests—inspired the Greenwich Palace that appears in this book. The real Greenwich Palace was a simpler affair and no longer exists, but you can still get a wonderful view of the site (now home to the Old Royal Naval College) from the top of Greenwich Hill.

Though alchemy had its detractors in the seventeenth century, it also had its disciples, including a number of eminent scientists (some of them members of the real-life Invisible College). Isaac Newton, for example, wrote more than a million words about alchemy, much of it in secret cipher. While alchemists disagreed about the exact nature and powers of the Philosopher's Stone, some did indeed describe the Stone as a red powder or liquid, as King Henry does in this book.

Although we tend to think of alchemists as male, legend has it that some key early practitioners were women, including Pernelle Flamel. In the sixteenth and seventeenth centuries, we have good evidence that women such as Sophie Brahe, Lady Margaret Clifford, and Anna Maria Zieglerin were practicing alchemy either on their own or alongside men.

While there was no leader named Boudicca in seventeenth-century England, that part of the story is inspired by Britain's long history of rebellion and civil protest. As the Inner Council notes in *Chantress Alchemy*, the Peasants' Revolt of 1381, led by Wat Tyler, is part of that history. Other events include the Pilgrimage of Grace, the unrest caused by the Holy Maid of Kent, and, of course, the revolt of the real Boudicca (also called Boudica and Boadicea) in Roman times.

Believe it or not, potatoes really were a miracle food in this period. In *Chantress Alchemy*, I credit Nat with seeing their potential, but in the real world the first ruler to fully grasp this was Frederick the Great, King of Prussia, in the eighteenth century. He pushed his country to plant the newfangled crop so that he would have a better-fed populace to power his army. It is in no small part due to potatoes that Prussia was able to turn itself from a motley backwater into a great military power.

ACKNOWLEDGMENTS

The first *Chantress* book took years to write, but this one came together in a whirlwind. I am so grateful to the wonderful writers who read the entire draft at short notice and offered comments: Jo Wyton, Nancy Werlin, Teri Terry, Paula Harrison, Kristina Cliff-Evans, and Kit Sturtevant. I was also lucky to have Nicki Thornton, Penny Schenk, Sally Poyton, and Nick Cross critique several early chapters. Warmest thanks to all the other people who encouraged me along the way, particularly the great crew at BIC-WriMo and the writers on retreat with me at KW-UK, SCBWI-BI, and the SAS's Winter Warmer at Folly Farm. I also send a huge thank-you to all the readers and bloggers who've supported *Chantress*, and to all the fans who've asked what happens next!

My editor, Karen Wojtyla, championed Lucy from the first, and I'm grateful to her for editing this book with skill and insight. I'm also fortunate to work with assistant editor Annie Nybo and a whole host of fine people at Simon & Schuster, including Justin Chanda, Paul Crichton, Siena Koncsol, Bridget Madsen, Clare McGlade, Ebony LaDelle, and Bernadette Cruz. My thanks also go out to Michael McCartney and Ali Smith for the beautiful covers, and to Alison Velea for terrific copyediting.

My agent Julie Just continues to amaze me with her kindness, tact, and savvy; I'm so glad to work with her. I am also deeply grateful to Michael

Steger at Janklow & Nesbit for handling negotiations with aplomb, and to the fabulous team who have welcomed me at Pippin Properties: Holly McGhee, Elena Giovinazzo, and Michael Steiner.

My parents, in-laws, and extended family have been a tremendous support, as always. Mom, Dad, Pat, Bert, Steve, Sabine, Jonathan, Valerie, Sofia, Carlo, Vivian, Stephen, Sarah, Ruth, and Grace—my heartfelt thanks to you!

Above all, I want to thank my daughter, who reminds me every day of what matters most, and my husband, who listens, reads, and loves me through everything. I am so lucky to be able to share my life—and my stories—with you.

CONTINUE LUCY'S STORY IN
CHANTRESS FURY.

I heard the mist before I saw it, a shimmering tune that crept in with the dawn. Rising, I wrapped my mud-stained cloak around me and went to the cracked window. Sure enough, the mid-September sunrise was veiled by wreaths of fog. From the sound of it, it would burn off within the hour—which was just as well, given what we needed to do today.

I turned back to the room. Though it was tiny and dilapidated, its roof hadn't leaked in last night's hard rain, and its mattress had been softer than most. I'd slept well—perhaps too well, for I'd been dreaming when the mist song had woken me, dreaming of Nat. Awake now in this shabby room, I suffered the loss of him all over again.

A gruff call came from the other side of the door. "Chantress?"

I was always called Chantress these days, never Lucy. But if the greeting was formal, the grizzled voice was nevertheless one I knew well. It belonged to Rowan Knollys, former leader of the King's guard, now the trustworthy captain of my own men. I shook my head free of troublesome dreams and lifted the latch.

As always, Knollys's ruddy face gave little away. Only his voice betrayed any sign of strain. "Time we were off."

"I'll meet you outside." I shoved my belongings into my bag, swallowed a quick breakfast of cheese and day-old bread, then made my way down the rickety inn staircase to the stable yard outside.

Most of my men were already there, checking their muskets and saddling their mounts. After more than a year in their company, I knew their moods almost as well as my own. As I strode over to my horse, I could feel tension in the air, as real and thick as the mist. Everyone was all too aware of what lay before us.

Our newest recruit, Barrington, waved at the mist, wide-eyed. "Did you sing that up, Chantress?"

"No," I said. "It came on its own."

Barrington nodded, but I could tell he was disappointed. This was his first journey with us. Unwilling to miss anything, he kept hopeful eyes on me always, even if I was only eating my dinner. Evidently he'd been expecting more magic than he'd gotten so far.

Knollys clapped him on the back. "Never mind, boy. If Lord Charlton doesn't surrender, I warrant you'll hear plenty of Chantress singing before the day's out. Now get on your horse."

That morning's ride pushed me to my limits. Constant practice had made me a skilled horsewoman, but today we were driving ourselves hard. As the mist rose and the footing became clearer, we raced through fields and woods alike.

I had just begun to worry that perhaps we'd lost our way, when Knollys swerved right, going uphill through the woods. Moments later we saw what had brought us here: the wall.

Higher than a man's head, it ran as far as the eye could see, a line of tight-packed gray stone imprisoning a forest of ash and oak. It had been built to intimidate, and even with us on horseback it was a daunting sight.

I sidled my mare next to it, listening for what I could get, which wasn't much. Stones never wanted to sing to me. But there had been heavy rains this week, so the wall was damp, and water was something I understood. I could hear it humming in the gaps and on the wet surface of the stones themselves.

"So this is Charlton's new park," one of the soldiers said behind me.

"Part of it, anyway," Knollys said. "He's taken the best pasture and meadowlands, too, and a long stretch of the river. The village is in a dire state."

It was an old story, repeated time and again in England: Powerful lords fenced in common lands and called them their own, depriving villagers of their time-honored rights. No longer able to graze a cow or catch eels or cull deadwood for fires, poor villagers starved and froze.

Determined to put an end to these landgrabs, King Henry had outlawed the practice of enclosure a year and a half ago. But Lord Charlton was a great power in this county. He'd continued to build his wall regardless—partly in stone, partly in timber— and he'd repeatedly refused to take it down.

Our assignment was to demolish the wall, by whatever means necessary. First, however, we were supposed to give Charlton one last chance to take it down himself. The King had no desire to appear a tyrant. He had impressed upon us that Charlton must be given every possible opportunity to set matters right.

In most cases, my arrival would have ensured compliance; usually the mere sight of me made rebellious lords crumble. Yet my men and I had doubts about Charlton. Hot-tempered and arrogant, he was reputed to have scoffed at my magic, saying the stories about me were exaggerated. He'd threatened to shoot the next royal messenger on sight.

"Let's approach the castle and see what kind of reception we get," Knollys said. "If you're ready, Chantress?"

I nodded, and we moved off.

Soon we reached the half-abandoned village of Upper Charlton, which lay within sight of the new wall. Nervous faces appeared at the windows as we marched, and a subdued cheer went up when they saw the royal colors, and again when they saw me at the center of a score of soldiers in tight formation. The cheers grew louder as we passed through the village and started up the hill that led to Charlton Castle.

I'd seen the maps and read the reports. Charlton was a redoubtable castle, well-positioned and well-fortified, with a particularly massive gatehouse. The walls of the enclosure led right up to this gatehouse, so that the gate controlled access not only to the castle but to all the land that Charlton had claimed. The front of the gatehouse was further guarded by a half-moat, fed by the local river. Inside, the castle was blessed again by water. A deep well in its keep had allowed it to withstand many a siege. Listening hard as we approached, I could hear both the moat's vigilant melody and the faint, sulky song of the well water.

"Halt!" Knollys cried out. We were only halfway up the hill, still out of musket range, but the gray walls of the gatehouse seemed to tower over us. The gates remained shut, the draw-bridge up. There was no sign of welcome.

Knollys picked one of the men to serve as emissary—young Barrington, eager for action—and sent him toward the castle on foot, bearing a white flag to show he was there to parley, not attack.

As soon as Barrington came into range, Lord Charlton's men fired from the gatehouse. A bullet caught the boy just below his helmet; he fell to the ground. Even back where we were, we could see the blood.

"Chantress?" Knollys said, but there was no need. Still in the saddle, I was already singing, honing my anger to a fine edge that worked for me and not against me.

Unrestrained emotion could make a song-spell veer in danger-ous ways, yet I needed to maintain a certain flexibility. I didn't command the elements so much as charm and persuade them, and I had to work with the melodies I could hear in the world around me. These changed with the day and the season and the weather and a hundred other factors, so my magic was always a matter of improvisation. I never sang the same song twice.

What suited my purposes now was the sulky tune I'd heard

coming from the bottom of the castle well. There was restlessness there, and resentment. I had only to play on these for a few moments before the water shot up, splintering the well cover and spouting into the sky. As it jetted upward, I felt a fierce pleasure— partly an echo of the water's own relief at being set free, and partly the intoxication of the singing itself, and the power in it.

Yet pleasure too could be a distraction. I needed to focus on the job at hand. Working quickly, I sang some of the fine spray into the castle weaponry and gunpowder, wetting them so they could not fire.

If Charlton's men had put up a flag of truce, that would have been the end of it. But when I finished my song, arrows flew from the windows, landing within a foot of Barrington and the men who had gone to his rescue.

"Get back," I shouted to them. "All of you, get as far back as you can!"

Clamping down on my anger, I turned my attention to the water in the moat. Vigilant it might have been, but it was frustrated as well—always on the edge of things, forever locked out. I harped on those notes in my own music, until the moat water rose up as vapor, drenching the walls of the gatehouse. Feeling again a fierce thrill in the singing, I worked the vapor deep into the mortar. Within moments, the mortar softened, and the gatehouse suddenly took on the appearance of a sandcastle in the rain. The foundations bulged. Walls sagged. The parapet collapsed.

I held on just long enough to give Charlton's men a decent chance to flee. Then, with another burst of song, I turned the mortar to liquid. The entire gatehouse peeled away from the castle and rumbled down the hill, a roaring landslide of slick stones and mud. When it stopped, all you could smell was earth, and all you could hear was silence. And then, in the silence, moaning.

Was that Barrington? Or had my landslide taken some of Charlton's men with it? My throat tightened, and the brief pleasure I'd found in the singing disappeared. Even after more than a year of this work, I found some of its consequences hard to handle.

They wanted to kill you, I reminded myself. *And your men*.

With the gatehouse fallen, the castle was wide open to the world. Moving closer to it, Knollys bellowed, "Surrender now, or the Chantress will sing again."

Men appeared at the wide gap in the castle wall, hands over their heads. They watched me as rabbits watch a snake. After divesting them of any remaining weapons, my men tied them up.

"It's treason to shoot at the King's forces," Knollys told them. "But if you cause no more trouble, and if you tell us where to find Lord Charlton, your lives may be spared."

This was our usual policy—if we were overly harsh, it might provoke more rebellion—but most of our current captives were too petrified to speak. A few, however, were eager to take Knollys up on his bargain and told us where we might find Charlton. As the hunt began, my men moved into the castle, leaving only a handful of us outside, including the guard by Barrington. At my request, Knollys set some of Charlton's men to checking for survivors in the landslide.

"I think you can take care of the rest of the wall now," Knollys said to me as we both dismounted. "We've waited long enough for it to come down. I'll go inside and take charge of the castle."

I nodded offhandedly, not wanting to let on what a challenge the rest of the wall presented. But a challenge it most certainly was. As we'd seen for ourselves, Charlton's enclosure went on for miles. It was by far the biggest wall I'd ever had to bring down.

At least there was no one shooting arrows now. I could take what time I needed. Listening to the world around me, I chose my songs carefully. First, a song to draw water up from the ground and into the wall, and then another to call a wind down from the chilly sky.

Wind was something I was still learning to work with. No matter how sweetly or imperiously I sang, it would not always do my bidding; sometimes it ignored me completely. But today my luck was in. If anything, the wind responded rather too strongly. I had to weave a tight net of song around it as I soaked the wall, then froze and melted it again and again. Only at the very end did I set the wind free. With a burst of explosive joy, it drove the stones and timbers apart, demolishing the wall all down the line.

A kindred spark of joy lit up in me. I'd done it. I'd taken the wall down.

"Chantress!" A call from my men.

As I turned, a wave of weariness hit me. Great magic was always draining. Yet if I'd learned anything as a Chantress, it was that I couldn't afford to show any weakness. Certainly I'd have been a fool to betray any vulnerability now, when my men were dragging Charlton out to me, his velvet-clad arms tied behind his back. Above his cravat, his face was apoplectic, and he was cursing the men with every step.

"Save your breath, Charlton!" I called out. "You're my prisoner now, and the King's, and you're bound for the Tower. And it will go better for you if you show some remorse."

If there was any remorse in Charlton, he hid it well. As the men shoved him forward, he spat at my feet. "You hellhound!"

I blinked. Was he too furious to care what I might do to him? Or was he deliberately trying to goad me into doing something rash?

"She-devil!" From the crazed look of his eyes, it was fury alone that drove him. "The King will rue the day he allied himself with you. You suck men dry, you harpy! Even the ones on your own side."

"Take him away," I said to four of my men.

Charlton kept spouting filth as they grabbed him. "But they're growing wise to you, aren't they? You're a witch, they say. You're a freak. No man will touch you. Even Nat Walbrook's abandoned you—"

"And shut him up," I ordered, more harshly this time.

Words, I told myself. *Just words. They can't hurt me.* But even after Charlton had been hauled off, I found myself shaking with anger. How dare he speak that way to me? How dare he mention Nat?

I looked up at my men. Not all of them met my eyes. Although I thought of us as a unit, the truth was that they always kept a certain distance from me. I was a woman and a Chantress; like it or not, that set me apart. When all was said and done, what did they think of me? Had Charlton's words struck some kind of chord in them?

You're a freak. No man will touch you. Even Nat Walbrook's abandoned you—

What could I say in my own defense? I couldn't tell anyone the truth about Nat. Indeed, after all this time, I was no longer sure what the truth really was. And to address any of the rest of Charlton's accusations was to give them more credence than they deserved.

Never mind, I told myself. *You are strong enough to handle this.* And I was. But as I stood looking at my men in the shadow of our victory, my loneliness went bone deep.

Six weeks later, cushioned on the red velvet seats of the royal barge, I watched London slip by in the late October twilight. Keeping the peace in the far reaches of the kingdom meant I rarely saw the city, and I was grateful for this chance to savor its sounds. Some were audible only to a Chantress—the gossamer-fine melody of the gathering haze, the rollicking music of the river itself. Yet as the sunset faded and the glowing sky turned a melancholy hue, it was the ordinary sounds I appreciated the most—the pipes and drums of street musicians, the last cries of the seagulls, the roar of a raucous theater crowd, the bass chime of the great bell at St. Paul's.

Across from me, King Henry watched the city, his blue eyes bright as ever under his copper hair.

Nodding at him, I pointed to a wall where people stood waving in the last of the light. "Listen! They're cheering for you."

His sober, freckled face broke into a smile. "They could equally well be cheering for you, you know."

"No." I could just hear the words drifting across the river. "They're cheering for you and the Queen."

It was almost six months since the King had married my friend Sybil Dashwood. I counted myself lucky that I'd been able to come to London—however briefly—for the ceremony. Their wedding had been an occasion to remember, the first time in centuries that a monarch had married a commoner. Although some at Court had objected to the marriage, many ordinary Londoners had been only too happy to celebrate the union.

The city's buoyant mood still had not dissipated. After many dark years, we'd finally reached a season of peace and plenty. The tyrannies of Scargrave were ended, and so was the year of famine and unrest that had followed his rule. We'd had a good harvest last summer, and a record one this year, thanks to Nat's brilliant work—

No, stop. I mustn't think about Nat.

Pushing back a wave of sadness, I said quickly, "Your Majesty, has Dr. Penebrygg told you about the fireworks he's designed for the opening of Parliament?"

"Not yet, but that reminds me . . ." The King reached for a box at his side. "I believe there are a few more items on today's docket. Shall we go over them now?"

I stifled a sigh. When the King had called me back to London to help with the opening, I'd been delighted. I couldn't wait to spend time with Sybil and Norrie, my childhood guardian. Both women were very dear to me. But ever since my arrival, the King had kept me so busy that I might as well have been in farthest Cornwall.

Of course the opening was important. I couldn't deny that.

This would be the first Parliament in a generation, and one elected on more democratic lines than ever before. It was critical that it be a success.

To that end, my days had been filled with endless worries about schedules, protocol, and security. This morning, with the help of Captain Knollys and my men, I had searched the Parliamentary rooms at Westminster Palace for potential threats. In the afternoon I'd gone up and down the river for a series of meetings with the King and some of his chief supporters. Now I was returning to Whitehall Palace, the main royal residence, after which the King would proceed to Greenwich for a supper engagement with the Lord High Admiral.

I knew there would be more matters for me to attend to once I was back at Whitehall. There always were. And we still had a week to go before Parliament opened. Was it really so much to ask, to have a brief moment of peace here on the Thames?

One look at the King's conscientious face, and I knew the answer. Henry never rested, so how could I? After all, this was what I had signed up for a year and a half ago, when he'd asked for my help in governing the kingdom.

"Let's see." Henry paged through the papers. "Here's a letter from the Earl of Staffordshire, who enthusiastically supports our Parliamentary reforms."

"Enthusiastically?" I reached for the letter in surprise. "Are you sure?"

The King grinned. "It seems your visit was most persuasive. He says quite complimentary things about you."

I raised my eyebrows as I scanned the florid words. "He did not say them at the time. Indeed, I had the distinct impression that he was horrified to see me." And no wonder, for I'd made that visit shortly after bringing down Charlton Castle.

The King flipped to the next document. "Viscount Hatton writes in a similar vein." He turned a few more pages. "Oh."

"Is something wrong, Your Majesty?"

"No, no. It's just a note from Sybil." He smiled as he pored over it, though there was a slightly worried look in his eyes. "Er . . . a private note."

I was surprised by the worry, but not by the smile. He and Sybil were a wonderful match—the King so steady, and Sybil so lighthearted, and each of them adoring the other. It made me happy to think of them together. Yet I felt wistful, too. Twenty months had passed—twenty months and two days—since I had last seen Nat. And what a painful parting it had been . . .

Don't think about it, I told myself for the ten thousandth time.

After all, there was no chance our paths would cross anytime soon. Although Nat was often at Court, he'd departed for the Continent two weeks ago, just before I'd arrived at Whitehall. Certain delicate negotiations were said to require his presence in Paris and Amsterdam, and he would have to miss the opening. I didn't know if this was true, but I had been relieved to hear it. For if Nat had planned to be at the opening, I would've had to find some excuse to miss it myself. Those were the rules. And I was grateful to be spared such difficulties. Nothing could take away the pain of our separation, but at least this way I didn't have to deal with the additional humiliation of rearranging my plans, while everyone at Court gossiped about my leaving and speculated as to why.

Don't think about it. . . .

"There." The King was rifling through the papers again. "I think that's everything of note."

We were nearing Whitehall Palace. Already the oarsmen were slowing, the better to maneuver themselves close to the ornate landing.

"There should be more dispatches waiting for us in the State Rooms," the King said. "And if there are any ambassadors waiting to see me, perhaps you could have a quick word with them in my absence?"

"Of course, Your Majesty."

With great precision and a little splashing, the oarsmen brought the barge toward the landing. It was tricky work, as they had to take care that the barge's gilded frieze of growling lions didn't scrape against the pilings. I heard an impish note in the river's music and made sure I had a good hold on my seat. If we bobbled about, I didn't want to go flying.

"And there are some more papers on my desk you may wish to see," the King said. "One is from Walbrook."

From Nat? My fingers tightened on the seat.

"He's found a way to get the seeds we need much sooner than he expected," the King went on. "He'll be back for the opening of Parliament after all."

Nat? Here? My heart slammed into my shoes.

It was an effort to speak. "When does he expect to arrive?"

"As soon as possible. If his luck has held, he'll be sailing over right now."

Worse and worse.

"He made quick work of those negotiations, I must say," the King mused. "But it's possible there's more to the story, something he needs to tell me in person." The barge swayed and rocked. The King looked round. "Ah! We've docked."

The master of the barge rapped on the glass door. "Lady Chantress, if you wish to disembark?"

Numbly I rose and bowed to the King. Nat could be at Whitehall any day now.

He must not find me here. That was one of the cardinal rules of the game, and so far I had never broken it. *But what possible excuse can I find to leave just before the opening?*

I went up the gangplank and stood between the great torches on the dock as the barge pulled away. As I waved good-bye to the King, it took all my self-control to present a cheery face.

"We'll meet when I return?" he called out as the oarsmen sculled.

"Yes, Your Majesty." He might not be back till midnight, but it was not unusual for us to work into the small hours as we prepared for the opening. "I'll be waiting." *Unless I find some perfect way to vanish before then.*

Once the barge was out of sight, I turned toward the looming bulk of Whitehall Palace. Built in a motley mixture of brick and timber and stone, it was almost a city within a city, boasting more than fifteen hundred rooms, all of them encircled by a high embankment that had been put up in Scargrave's reign and never taken down. It was the King's favorite of all the royal residences in London, a place that I usually returned to with pleasure.

But not now.

What on earth am I going to do?

The palace doors opened. I couldn't ask for time to think; I was about to be swept up in my duties again.

As I went up to the door, however, I heard a flurry of female voices above and to the left of me. Caught by the note of fear in them, I looked up. The disturbance was coming from one of the Queen's windows. As I listened, the babble of voices grew louder, and a terrible cry rent the air.

Was it Sybil? Was she in danger?

Forgetting my own problems, I broke into a run.

GRAPPLING WITH GRIEF IS HARD ENOUGH

WITHOUT REPEAT VISITS FROM

THE RECENTLY DECEASED.

PEARL DEALS WITH DEATH, LIFE, AND FAMILY

IN THIS HAUNTING, HUMOROUS,

AND POIGNANT DEBUT.

the year of the rat

clare furniss

IN A WORLD WHERE DUKES PLOT THEIR
WAY TO THE THRONE, A PERFORMER'S
LIFE CAN GET TRICKY. AND IN JOHANNA
VON ARLO'S CASE, IT CAN BE FATAL.

"THIS TALE OF MURDER, KIDNAPPING,
AND MAGIC HELD ME FROM START TO FINISH!"
—TAMORA PIERCE,
AUTHOR OF THE SONG OF THE LIONESS QUARTET

BECKY WALLACE

THE STORYSPINNER

THE KEEPERS' CHRONICLES

PRINT AND EBOOK EDITIONS AVAILABLE
FROM MARGARET K. MCELDERRY BOOKS
TEEN.SIMONANDSCHUSTER.COM